STRONG

A NOVEL

CHRIS VITARELLI

God bless !
Enjoy

ISBN: 978-1-7346203-0-6

Fiction, Christian, General

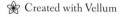 Created with Vellum

STRONG

DEDICATION

*To my wife, who on the night of our eighth anniversary spoke
words of encouragement and inspiration that started this
book.*
*To my parents, who encouraged my imagination all along.
And to Gabriel, Angelina, Landon and Sofia, whose
imaginations inspire me daily.*

ACKNOWLEDGMENTS

My Lord and Savior, Jesus Christ
Jody, Gabriel, Angelina, Landon and Sofia
George and Lillian Vitarelli
Ken and Loretta Hovis
Rich and Debbie Lambert
Misty Sack
Natalie Sowa
Matt Schiavone
Busti Public Library
Wegman's
Tim Horton's
Lakewood Baptist Church

STRONG

"And the Spirit of the Lord came upon him in power..."

Judges 14:19

As his patient awoke, Dr. Kelso observed that the man did not like being restrained. He was strapped in by wide metal bands looped over his wrists and ankles. One band spanned his hips, and another pressed against his chest. In the dimly lit room he watched his patient strain against the metal bands to take in his surroundings. Kelso had purposely tilted the man at an angle that would limit his view. All he would be able to see was the one-way glass and the small tray next to the exam table.

Kelso caught his patient's attention when he slammed the door and walked purposefully across the room. He could see the confusion in his patient's eyes.

"Good evening. This won't take long." Kelso picked up a small rectangle of plastic from the tray.

The patient tried to respond to the curt and European-accented greeting but was unable to speak. Kelso observed his patient pleading with his eyes, asking questions, asking for help. This didn't bother him. He wore a protective white plastic suit that covered everything but his eyes, and to this

1

patient he was anonymous. It was strictly business, and the test subject would soon be dead.

Dr. Kelso used forceps to pick up the piece of plastic. He held it against the patient's cheek and from under the table pulled a small gray box. There was a black button on its side, and as he pressed it, a red laser appeared and swept the reverse of the plastic. He promptly put the instruments down, turned, and walked from the room.

From behind the one-way glass another man watched, fascinated. He turned to Kelso, who had just entered the observation room, and asked, "How long will it take?"

"We estimate less than twenty-four hours," the doctor said as he watched through the glass.

"How will we know the effects as the virus progresses?"

"We will do that test in forty-eight hours. First we want to test for speed," the doctor replied as he continued to watch his patient.

"Tell me again, Doctor Kelso, how this works."

There was something perverse in the pleasure Kelso's boss took in hearing this over and over again. But he had to admit that it was fascinating—and certainly miraculous. Nanotechnology was a breakthrough that had changed everything. It had certainly changed Kelso's profession. Funding for Kelso's research had decreased, so his work had lost some of its inspiration. Now it was new and exciting again. And deadly.

"The nanobytes imbedded in the plastic are released into the bloodstream and immediately rob the entire body of its white blood cells and the capacity to produce more. The body cannot recover from this complete takeover. As it tries to catch up, it becomes vulnerable to every other virus or bacteria operating in the body. As these illnesses come crashing down on the system, it is unable to carry the load, and the body simply collapses. There is no cure, and the nanobytes never stop."

"You say it so beautifully, Kelso." He nodded toward the glass. "Our patient is already beginning to feel some discomfort."

It was so. The men watched as their patient began to squirm and strain against his restraints. His face twitched, and his eyes rolled back, showing only the whites. These unseeing eyes stared directly into the one-way glass as the rest of his body convulsed and perspired. In another moment his body slumped, and the head rolled forward.

"Dr. Kelso, I want a full report on this new development and its effects as soon as possible. We have a timetable."

"Yes, Mr. Gallinger." Kelso turned to leave.

"Ah, Dr. Kelso?"

"Yes?"

Rolf Gallinger continued to stare through the glass at the weakening test subject. A faint smile crept over his lips. "Excellent work."

[1]

Second chances are like eclipses—rare and stunning. Some people are willing to give a second chance. Most would accept if it was offered but never have the opportunity. For Ethan, "second chance" was not even in his vocabulary. He had rarely been given one and was not prone to handing them out either. Today was different.

He had been given a second chance, but he wasn't sure who to thank. He hoped he would find out soon. The buzzer sounded and the steel gate swung open just as it had every morning for the last seven years.

"Step out!" the prison guard shouted once the door had swung out completely. Ethan stepped into the walkway outside his cell. His black hair was in a tight ponytail, and he wore a thick-soled pair of black shoes. His 170 pounds hung on a five-foot-nine-inch frame. He didn't look like the type who could cause trouble for the guards at the Attica Correctional Facility, though he could have. He had purposely given no reason for them to worry during his stay. The last thing he wanted was extra security around him or a loss of what little freedom he did have. Now, it looked like he'd be getting even more freedom than he'd hoped for. He walked to the gate leading out of his cellblock.

"Lucky man." It was the guard at the gate. "Gettin' let out like this, eh?"

"Ethan, what's up, man? You leavin'?" This was the inmate next to the gate. "Hey, come visit me, all right? Bring somethin' nice from New York City. My girl still lives there. Let me give you her address!"

"Shut up," the guard shot back. "Like you don't know he's leavin'. He's not takin' any messages to anyone for you. C'mon, Ethan, let's get you checked out of here." He led Ethan through the next two checkpoints, and finally they were standing at the window where Ethan received the few possessions he had in this world. "You got someone pickin' you up, Ethan?"

"I think so. I hope so." The letter hadn't been clear. It was very official looking but somewhat mysterious. Ethan was being summoned by the United States government to Fort Bragg, North Carolina. He picked up the bag that held a change of clothes and the money that accompanied every departing inmate. He had to be checked through two more locked doors, and then he was standing outside the prison. It was the first time in seven years he had stood outside as a free man. His time outside was normally spent behind razor wire and high fences and was never before ten in the morning. He had always enjoyed mornings. They were peaceful and held such promise.

His eye caught movement in the parking lot. It was the door of a black sport utility vehicle opening. A man stepped from the passenger door and looked in Ethan's direction. Ethan stared back, not sure if this was his ride or a challenge. He had often wondered if anyone would reach out from his past, someone just waiting for him to be released so they could take revenge. Of course, they had had their revenge in more ways than one.

The man who had exited the SUV was walking toward Ethan. "Are you Ethan Zabad?" The man asking was about Ethan's age with an athletic build. He was wearing khakis, a polo shirt, and casual shoes.

"Who's asking?" Ethan responded.

"John Smith," he answered, extending a hand.

Ethan eyed the hand, shook it half-heartedly and then replied, "You might as well say, 'Here's my alias for the day.'"

"It is what it is." He paused a few seconds as he sized Ethan up. "We're on a schedule. Would you come with me please?"

Ethan followed "John" to the vehicle and was directed to sit in the passenger side back seat. He was not alone.

"Hello, Ethan. I'm Colonel Wade Murrow. Pleasure to meet you." He extended his hand across the back seat.

Ethan quickly assessed Colonel Murrow. From what he could see sitting down Murrow was stocky and strongly built. His white-flecked brown hair was closely cropped, and his eyes were close together, looked narrowed. The whole of his face suggested that he was not one to tangle with, verbally or physically. Ethan shook his hand and remarked, "Better alias than John Smith here."

"Not an alias, son. Let me see the letter we sent you."

Ethan pulled the letter from the small bundle of personal belongings and handed it to Murrow. "You know why we sent you this?" Murrow asked, holding up the letter.

Ethan gave a shrug in response. "You're gonna tell me."

"First of all, this isn't army, navy, air force, or marines.

This is counter-terrorism." Murrow paused and spoke to the driver. "Tom, let's get rollin' here. Clock is tickin'."

"Yes, sir," Tom replied.

Good riddance, Ethan thought as they put distance between them and the razor wire–covered fences.

Murrow continued. "You are joining an elite group of soldiers who risk their lives every day to prevent and resolve terrorist issues all over the world. What we are doing with you is unprecedented. You are a civilian. The men you will serve with have been through the most difficult and extensive training administered in the armed forces. Our last class to come out of selection started with one hundred and forty-two men. We took *nine* of them into our unit. Nine. Do you understand what I'm telling you?"

Ethan was stunned. He heard what Murrow said but had no frame of reference for what he was hearing. It was a lot to take in. The look on Ethan's face must have alerted Murrow to the fact that he'd perhaps gone too far too fast because he stopped and asked, "Do you need something to drink? Are you hungry? We can stop up here," Murrow said, gesturing to the gas station on the corner. "We have a short drive to the airport in Buffalo. The air force will fly us to Wright Patterson in Ohio and from there to Fort Bragg. You all right? You gonna make it that far?"

Murrow had given Ethan the itinerary hoping to ease his mind. He wanted him to know that there was a plan in place and it wasn't all going to feel like a crazy rush.

"I'm fine," Ethan finally answered. "I just didn't know what to expect."

"That's good 'cause if you can't handle a day of travel, we'll just turn around and drop you off at that funhouse again. I'll admit you have a lot to learn. You'll be tested beyond what you think you can handle. But if your file is any indication, I think you'll make a fine soldier."

"What if I don't want to do this? What if I say no?"

"You were released into my care. You're under my watch. You want to go, you tell me. We'll send you back. But"—Murrow leaned toward Ethan to emphasize his point—"you leave without my say-so or screw around like some college freshman havin' his first beer, you are done. Do I make myself clear?"

Ethan felt like he should shout, "Yes sir!" He settled for a simple and quiet "yes."

"Now, it's not going to be easy. Some of the men are already talking about the fact that you haven't been through any of our training. They are not going to cut you any slack."

"I've never been given any. Nothin' new."

"Even so, we are going to give you an abbreviated version of our selection process. I won't tell you anything about it because that's part of it. You'll also be living in the barracks with the newest class to start selection. We want you acclimated quickly. We are on a very demanding schedule." Murrow had started slowly but now every time he talked it was in a quick, clipped fashion. He was directly to the point and intense. Ethan liked him.

"Colonel, what is the name of this unit?"

"For now, that's classified, but I'm sure you've heard rumors about units like this. And trust me, it's nothing like what you've heard. It's harder, more dangerous, and more demanding than anything you'll do in your life. But it's also more rewarding."

"You've got good men serving already. What do you need a guy from prison for? I've never done anything but get thrown in jail."

9

"When you made headlines almost a decade ago, we noticed. We also did some more digging. Trust me when I say you're exactly what we need."

Murrow seemed to think the matter was resolved and pressed on in telling Ethan about the unit. "We do quick ins and quicker outs. We are designed to stop terrorist acts before they happen and in some cases resolve them. When we started this unit back in the late seventies, it seemed that anyone with a gun and taking crazy pills was hijacking an airplane. The world has changed, but our mission hasn't. We operate in teams. Each team consists of four or five men. They rotate duty depending on the situation. Sometimes they all deploy together, sometimes in twos or threes. You'll be working with a larger team. We're putting an A and B team together for this mission. I'll introduce you after we arrive and you've settled in."

Ethan began to think about how he was going to handle this. At first he was glad just to get out of prison. Now he potentially had something much more difficult to do than deal with captivity. He was going to be a soldier. He had to admit that there was nothing about him that would inspire anyone to lead him into combat. He was as average as they come. He was relatively thin and had never worked out in his life. There had been a six-week period in high school where he thought he'd add some bulk to his physique, but it had only resulted in a suspension. He smiled at the memory. A simple dispute over who was next on the leg press ended with five members of the football team draped unceremoniously over various weightlifting apparatuses. He was saved from expulsion only because the fight itself had been witnessed, and self-defense was accepted as a rightful cause. His attempts to bulk up had always failed. He was not destined to have the makeup of a bodybuilder.

"Ethan?"

Ethan jerked himself out of his daydream memory. "Sorry, I was...just thinking."

Murrow actually seemed to understand. "It's a lot to process. The guys in this unit have devoted their lives to the armed forces and the protection of this country. You made no such choice, and let's not pretend you came with us because you saw the latest ad for the army and were carried away by a wave of patriotism. You're here because it got you out of prison. That's okay. But do your thinking now because when you are committed to this there's no turning back."

"I wouldn't turn back. But here at the start I can't help feeling like an intruder. An outsider. I wouldn't blame these men if they didn't want a guy like me along." Ethan reached back and pulled out the small rubber band holding his hair in a tight ponytail. His black, wavy, shoulder-length hair fell forward and framed his face. Pointing to his hair, he said, "This alone sets me apart from guys in the military."

Murrow gave Ethan a tight-lipped smile and raised his eyebrows as if he had a secret. "You'll be glad to know that in the unit we don't require uniformity in appearance. It's hard to work undercover or in other countries if we look like we just stepped off an army base. Wear what you want unless specifically ordered otherwise."

"What about my record? Do the men in the unit know about that?"

"Son, are you looking for reasons to not do this? I already told you we can take you back. Somehow I don't think that's what you really want."

Ethan glanced out the window. They were on Interstate 90 now heading west and getting closer to Buffalo, to the airport. What did he really want? Joining up with this unit could be a great thing for him. But it could be another opportunity to experience the same kind of pain he'd felt his whole life. The pain of being different, of being rejected. The pain of not living up to expectations or his potential.

"I want to do this, Colonel. I think this could be a good thing for me. You seem to think it will be a good thing for you. As long as we both know what I'm really like and who I really am—"

"What does that mean? 'What you're really like'?"

"Well, we both know I'm a freak," Ethan interjected. "I know it, you know it—the guys I'll be serving with know it. You don't think they know me?"

Murrow sighed and then spoke with authority. "This is going to work. I know it will. And you're not a freak. You're exceptional. The army has need of a man like you." He looked at Ethan for a few seconds before continuing. "I know what your past is, but you have what we need."

"What, an administrative headache?" Ethan quipped.

Murrow ignored the comment. "A man who possesses your strength has the ability to make a difference. You don't understand, Ethan. The current state of affairs has robbed us of some of the best and the brightest. We need you."

The current state of affairs was not good. With the complete and sudden withdrawal from Iraq in the last year, the nation was technically no longer at war, but terrorism had spiked in that country along with heightened threats to Israel, United States military installations around the globe, and greater threats at home. Several domestic bomb threats had been thwarted through sound intelligence, but the threats never stopped. There was no rest for any of the national security organizations.

"It's a good thing I got your attention with my life of crime," Ethan said sarcastically.

"Speaking of your life of crime, after we reach the base I've arranged for you to talk to the base psychologist, Dr. Remont."

"You did what?" Ethan asked.

Murrow calmly responded, "I want you to talk to the base psychologist. You've got issues, Ethan. You're exceptional in many ways, but I think the doctor can help you sort some things out. I can't have you part of a team on the other side of the world if you're frustrated."

"I'm not frustrated!" Ethan seemed not to see the contradiction between his earlier thoughts and this statement.

"Ethan, every man in this unit undergoes a thorough psychological examination. It's standard operating procedure, and it's painless. In the early days, we had a really sick individual who tried to get the men undergoing selection to crack under the pressure of severe psychological torture. We got rid of him in a hurry. We want to know the pressure points of our men. Not scar them for life. That's what your exam is for."

Ethan was satisfied and replied, "I understand, Colonel." Ethan turned and looked out his window, watching the hills of western New York roll by. The scenery was nice. Ethan was a city boy, and of course being in prison didn't allow him to see much of the surrounding countryside. Seeing it now he wondered what it would be like to just slip off into the mountains somewhere and live a life of solitude. Deep down he knew he was called to something greater. Time would tell him what it was.

The plane touched down at the airfield at Fort Bragg, North Carolina. Fort Bragg was a training ground for many new recruits, but it was also home to the Special Forces units. Their selection course, training, and deployment all took place at Fort Bragg.

Upon landing at Pope Air Force Base, which is adjacent to Fort Bragg, Murrow gave Ethan a tour of the Special Forces training facilities on the west end of the base. He dismissed Tom and John and personally drove Ethan around in a plain-looking Ford Taurus.

"I had no idea this place was so big," Ethan commented as they drove toward Murrow's office after their brief drive through.

"We need to be able recreate combat situations here and make them as realistic as possible. This area has many types of terrain that we can use to our advantage. The only thing it doesn't have a lot of is snow. Thank God Almighty for that."

Ethan smiled at the expression of gratitude. His parents probably wouldn't appreciate a comment like that. Murrow stopped the car in front of a plain building. Ethan didn't see a sign that designated it as anything at all. His furrowed brow caught Murrow's attention.

"This building contains our offices and the command center. People know we're here. We just don't advertise."

Ethan nodded slowly in acknowledgement. "So what now?" he asked.

"My new staff sergeant, Andrea Kaplan, will escort you back to your barracks." Murrow gestured toward the building, and that was when Ethan noticed the woman standing to the right of the main door.

"Go on," Murrow urged as he reached across Ethan to

open his door. "You'll be notified when it's time to meet again."

Ethan got out of the car and walked up the sidewalk. As he got closer, he realized that Staff Sergeant Kaplan was not at all what he expected. He studied her for a moment. She was probably five years younger than Ethan. About five two, she had shoulder-length blonde hair and green eyes that looked at him with some interest but not too much. It was a careful woman that stared back at him. She was standing straight with her chin slightly lifted. He wasn't sure how he knew, but he had an overwhelming sense of this woman's strength.

"Are you ready?"

Her question made Ethan realize he had been a little bit lost in those green eyes. "Yes, I'm ready." Ethan could feel his face getting warm. He realized that Andrea Kaplan was the first woman he had spoken to since he entered prison and the first that he'd actually noticed since he left prison early this morning.

Murrow, still sitting at the curb, spoke from his car window. "Hey, Private! That's a sergeant you're talkin' to. I didn't see a salute."

Ethan could tell from the way he said it that he was teasing. He hadn't even saluted Murrow. In fact, he'd been told very little about military protocols. Ethan wasn't yet sure about Murrow. He hadn't had many allies in life, and Murrow had at least tried to give him a chance to do something better than sit in jail. But the fact that it would probably get him killed wasn't a real bonus. He turned back toward the road and began walking, assuming they were headed to a vehicle nearby.

"Do you always try to take the lead?" Kaplan asked.

"No, I just thought we were—I mean aren't we?"

"Having a little trouble forming sentences today?" Kaplan fired another volley.

Ethan went from feeling a little attraction for Kaplan to being ready to launch a verbal assault on her. He hated someone having an advantage over him and reminding him of it regularly. Ethan spoke deliberately with exaggerated diction. "I can form sentences. I'm sorry I went the wrong direction. I'd be happy to follow you since you know where we're going."

"Fine. Follow me." Kaplan turned quickly and sped back into the building. Ethan had to step swiftly to keep up with her. He soon discovered that walking behind Kaplan did have its advantages. But he also realized that if he didn't pay attention or keep up he would be hopelessly lost in the maze of halls and offices they were walking through.

"Why are you walking so fast? Maybe you could give me an idea where we're going?" Ethan ventured. Kaplan did not respond. "Hey! Sarge! Where are we going?" Again, no response. Ethan was starting to get upset. Just as he was forming some choice words to unload on Kaplan, they arrived at another door. It simply read, "Exit."

Kaplan put her hand on the knob and turned to Ethan, catching the angry look on his face. "Ethan Zabad, I've heard of you. I read about you." Ethan said nothing, so Kaplan continued. "You ever consider working on self-control?"

"That's an interesting way to start a conversation with a total stranger. You ever consider working on tact?"

"Don't have time for tact in the military," she said as she pushed open the door and exited into the steamy heat of North Carolina. In the parking lot a Humvee was waiting. Kaplan got inside and motioned for Ethan to ride in the passenger seat.

As he got in, Ethan decided to try a more sensitive approach. "Did I do something wrong? I feel like I must have offended you."

"No."

"I'm a pretty decent guy once you get to know me. If you can get past the whole ex-convict thing, that is. Well, actually I'm still a convict because . . ." Ethan glanced at Andrea and realized she was trying not to smile. "Hey, are you laughing at me? Because I'm just trying to get along here."

"I'm not laughing at you. I'm . . . I'm glad."

"You're glad?"

"I'm glad you're normal."

Ethan had never heard that word applied to him. "Normal? You said you'd read about me so you would know I'm not, you know, normal."

"Murrow asked me to do the research on you. He wanted me to compile all of our information so he could determine your fitness for this assignment. I know you on paper pretty well."

"But?"

"But—you're different than the person I expected."

"Different good or different—"

"I'm not sure yet. Just different."

Ethan looked for clues on her face as she steered the Humvee around a corner.

She noticed. "What are you looking at?"

Ethan shrugged.

"All right, fine. I'm sorry I was a jerk to you. Like I said, I expected you to have a chip on your shoulder."

"You never said that. You said you were glad I was normal."

"Right, I just meant that—I mean I was trying to—"

"Having a little trouble forming sentences today?" Ethan laughed.

"Okay, I may have deserved that. What I was trying to say is that I found your case, your history, intriguing. I was hoping I could . . . you know . . . learn more." Andrea pulled into a parking spot and stopped the Humvee. "Here we are. You'll be sleeping here."

Ethan slowly opened his door and started to exit, not wanting the conversation to end. "Oh, by the way, apology accepted. And thanks for the ride."

"It's my job."

Ethan jumped out, waved at Kaplan, and gave her a quick nod. It seemed to Ethan that there was a barely concealed smile. She was the best part of this day so far. According to Murrow's briefing during the drive from Attica and the following plane ride, he would not have time to think about Kaplan, but thinking about her was something he really wanted to do.

The barracks he had been assigned to were nothing special. He had been given a bunk in the middle of the room. He could only assume this was so that many eyes could be kept on him. The military was giving him a chance, but they were not stupid. He was still an ex-con.

He walked into the barracks, which added ten degrees to the temperature. He glanced around, looking for a clock. It had to be after lunch time. He had eaten on such a regular schedule for the last seven years that he really felt it when he missed a meal. He began to unbutton the shirt he had been wearing since he walked out of the prison. If there was a way to get comfortable in this ridiculous heat, he was going to find it. He was just contemplating a cool shower when he felt a sudden sharp pain in his side. The movement of pulling his shirt over his head had stretched a part of his ribs that was still tender. He had been full of anticipation and adrenalin while waiting to be released and had all but forgotten the injuries he had sustained the day before. His other injuries had healed quickly, but the pain in his ribs had lingered.

In his mind he reviewed the events that took place just twenty-four hours before he was supposed to be released from Attica. Somehow word had gotten around that he would be leaving. He didn't know how, and it didn't matter. Information traveled quickly in prison.

The inmates were supposed to be eating. Ethan had just sat down when he realized that many of the men around him had fallen silent. He glanced at the guards nearby, but none of them seemed alarmed. He turned and saw John Farrar, a beefy, broad, yellow-haired inmate and notorious troublemaker, standing behind him. He'd had a few minor run-ins with Farrar. He was over six feet tall and muscular. He had a smile that employed only his top lip. Looking at his teeth made Ethan think that at a young age, a third tooth had been knocked out, leaving a gap in his two front teeth big enough to hold a pencil.

"Heard you're leavin' us. I'm real disappointed. The freakin' Jew gets to go back to New York, don't ya?"

"That's really none of your business," Ethan responded. He was cautious as the burly inmate took a step closer. Ethan noticed two other inmates approaching the table and standing ready. For what, Ethan could guess.

"It doesn't matter if it's my business or not. I want to give you a little going-away present," Farrar said.

"I don't need anything from you. Why don't you just go sit down and eat." Ethan waved him away.

"You've always had a smart mouth. I'm gonna shut it."

Farrar stepped closer and balled his hand into a fist.

The other two inmates stepped closer. A scenario was forming in Ethan's mind. This type of thing had happened so many times before. It was as if he could predict the outcome blow by blow. Being baited into a fight was nothing new. He turned his back to Farrar and prepared to eat. Ethan knew what was coming next, and he only hoped the guards would act before Farrar took things too far. Farrar lunged at him, words forming on his lips.

"Don't turn your back on me," Farrar snarled. Then the big man's hand struck Ethan on the back of the head, snapping his upper body forward. Immediately the guards sprang into action, but Farrar must have anticipated this and had several friends keep them occupied so he could work Ethan over. Farrar grabbed Ethan by the back of his shirt and jerked him to his feet. His fists started swinging, and Ethan did his best to block the blows and stay on his feet. Farrar connected with one in Ethan's side and then another on his head. Ethan fell back onto the table, knocking trays of food onto the floor. Farrar took advantage of the fall and was on him, swinging away again with his powerful fists. Ethan took a blow to the face and then another to the ribs. He rolled off the table away from Farrar. When Ethan landed on the floor, he looked up to see Farrar's booted foot coming straight down on him. Ethan jerked his head away just in time to make Farrar miss. He did miss, and it gave Ethan a split second to plan his next move.

Ethan knew he had to end this without doing major bodily harm to Farrar. It could delay his release by months if not longer. He pushed himself off the floor; and as Farrar lunged toward him, Ethan sidestepped, leaving Farrar's back exposed for a moment. It was all Ethan needed. He quickly grabbed Farrar by the shirt at the back of his neck and his pants at the waist. All Ethan had to do was pick Farrar up off the floor and hold him at arm's length. Farrar could neither turn his body to hit Ethan or reach back with his legs to kick him with any force. It was a comical sight, seeing a man as big as Farrar reduced to a kicking, screaming, helpless opponent. The other inmates laughed at the sight, but later the talk turned to how a man Ethan's size could hold over two hundred pounds straight out from his body without straining.

Ethan woke with a start. He had dozed off after taking a quick shower. A glance at the window above his bed told him it was late afternoon. His stomach was telling him the same thing. He rolled out of the bed, stood, and stretched. That's when he saw John Smith standing in the doorway. It startled Ethan, and he felt his heart skip a beat.

"You sneak up pretty quiet," Ethan remarked.

"Murrow wants you outside," John Smith replied and then turned to leave.

Ethan was going to ask if he needed to bring anything, but John was a man on a mission—always. Ethan left the building and saw a Hummer sitting at the curb. John Smith was in the passenger seat and waved to Ethan, motioning for him to get in.

Ethan thought they were going to Murrow's office again, but instead they headed for what turned out to be a training area. The brief drive was silent except for the occasional throat-clearing grunt by the driver. They pulled up next to a hut near a path that led through a thick stand of trees. Ethan could see very little down the path. He glanced around outside the Hummer, taking in the surroundings. Nothing unusual. He leaned his head back onto the headrest and realized how hungry he was. His door opened, and he was escorted to the hut at the start of the path. Murrow was there, waiting.

"Have a nice nap?"

"Yes, I did. Your military beds are great. Almost as comfortable as my prison mattress," Ethan shot back.

"Excellent," replied Murrow, either not recognizing or purposely ignoring Ethan's joke. "I wanted you to meet me here because I need to brief you before you meet the team tomorrow."

"Sounds like I have a busy day tomorrow."

"You have a busy month ahead of you, son. Tomorrow's just the start. You will be tested. The day someone says getting into this unit is easy is the day we'll see pigs flying through a frozen section of hell announcing there are no more taxes." Murrow paused and smiled at Ethan. "Did I overstate that?" he asked.

"Just a bit, sir," Ethan answered.

"Ethan, the men you will meet tomorrow are all you will have to help you complete this mission."

"Which is?"

"Come with me, Ethan," Murrow said as he walked down the path that led them into a clearing. At the center of this clearing was a brick house. The brick house looked suburban except in the windows there was no glass. It lacked other home-like qualities, but there was no doubt that it was a model of a house in the middle of the field.

Ethan's ribs tensed slightly with each step. His breathing was becoming shallow. Murrow glanced over at him as they walked.

"You're not hurt, are you?" Murrow asked with some surprise.

"Yeah, I got into it yesterday at the prison. They tagged me pretty good in there."

"I thought a few shots like that wouldn't bother a guy like you."

"Murrow...sir, I'm still human in spite of my...abnormalities."

"Right. I'll have one of the base doctors check you over when we get back. All right, here we are." Murrow was looking ahead twenty yards or so at the brick house. "This is your objective, Ethan."

"A house in the middle of a field?"

"Not just any house. Home to something more powerful than you can possibly imagine. The actual house is located in Afghanistan."

"Is this an exact replica?"

"From all of our intelligence, yes. There may be slight differences. Come with me." They walked inside the brick house and descended a flight of stairs to a concrete floor. One light bulb hung from a wire in the center of the room. Murrow walked purposefully under it, across the open basement toward the corner of the room. He stopped at the corner and, using his fingertips, felt along the top of the wall. He found what he was looking for, and Ethan heard three soft musical tones. The corner of the basement surprised him by swinging away toward what should have been nothing but dirt. Murrow stepped through the new opening and down a short spiral staircase. At the bottom, embedded in the floor, in a room no more than eight feet by eight feet, was a steel door. In the faint light it looked as if the locking mechanism was in the shape of a wheel, much like what Ethan imagined the hatch of a submarine to be.

"In there," said Murrow, pointing to the hatch, "is what we're after. Try opening it."

Ethan tried to see the expression on Murrow's face in the dimness. "Are you serious?" Murrow nodded at him, so Ethan bent down and tried to pull up on the mechanism. It was heavy, but it moved slightly. He hadn't encountered many things he couldn't move, so the resistance he was meeting irritated him. He pulled harder, and this time the door came up four or five inches. He set the door back down and looked at Murrow. "Is this some kind of joke?"

"Ethan. You'd better be able to open that hatch."

Murrow's tone spurred him on. He bent over and grasped the door tightly. Almost without thinking, he lifted the door, and it swung back and slammed against the wall. It was then Ethan realized that Murrow was back against the wall. It dawned on him that this was a one-man job. There was no way more than one man would be able to stand at this door and exert any force on it.

"Ethan, I need to know if men are willing to go with you. To protect you. Maybe die so you can accomplish this mission. You need the protection of a team, but the mission won't matter without you. You're the only man who can complete the task. In a sense you need to lead and get out of the way at the same time. I will brief you on more of the details after you meet the team. I know you have a lot of questions. They'll all be answered soon."

To say that Ethan had a lot of questions was an understatement. He followed Murrow out of the house and into the waning heat of twilight.

Back at the base Ethan did as Murrow suggested. He saw one of the doctors on base. Dr. Siegers was an older man with more than a little gray at his temples. "Hi, Ethan. Have a seat." He motioned to the table in the center of the examination room. Ethan moved slowly and scooted his way onto it.

"I understand you had a little fight yesterday," Dr. Siegers began.

"I'd say it was a bit more than a little fight. I gave them what they deserved."

"Looking at you, I'd say you gave a lot more than you got."

"I guess that means I won. Isn't that the whole point?"

"The point is that it's my job to make sure every soldier on this base stays healthy. I hope we don't have any fights here. That would make my job a lot harder," Dr. Siegers said without a smile.

They stared at one another for a moment. Ethan broke it off, venturing, "I guess next time I'll just take a beating so I don't make work difficult for you."

"Whatever you want." His mood then seemed to change. "Now let's take a look at you."

Ethan lifted his shirt and showed Dr. Siegers the ribs that were still in pain. He had taken at least two heavy shots to them. Siegers probed Ethan's rib cage, making him wince a few times.

"Nothing's broken. But you will have some deep bruising. How about your face?"

"I got hit. Rang my bell, but it didn't break the skin."

"You're fortunate. I understand prison fights can be quite nasty."

Ethan failed to suppress a laugh. "What would you know about prison fights?"

Dr. Siegers cleared his throat. "Hardened criminals will resort to any means. What do they have to lose?"

"Hardened criminals? Like me?" Ethan was amused.

"You know what I mean," Siegers said correctively.

"Yeah, I got your meaning loud and clear, Doc. Can I go?"

"In just a moment. I wanted to ask you about something." Siegers leaned in, making it seem as if the question would be profound, or at least secret.

"Is it true? I mean about your strength? I've been told about things you've done, but looking at you...I just don't see it. I don't mean to be rude, but you're not built like a weightlifter."

"It's true," Ethan said simply. He had an idea where this was going.

"When I learned you were coming here, I have to say I was a bit surprised. But I did some research." Siegers paused, seemed ready to get to the point. "Would it be all right if I examined you?"

Big surprise, Ethan thought. He'd had his share of doctors wanting to figure him out.

"Blood tests, DNA, brain scan," Siegers was saying. "I had hoped I could, just to see if we could..." He must have been searching for a word that sounded better than exploit. "Discover, together, the source of your strength. I'm sure you would want to know why you are...the way you are."

"I know exactly why I'm this way, and I'm okay with it," Ethan bluffed.

"Then for me, the medical community?"

"You have permission to do tests on me..."

"Oh thank you, Ethan. I—"

"...when I'm dead. Then you may do all the tests you want."

Siegers's mouth went into a thin-lipped line, and he simply said, "I see." Siegers's mood shifted again. "We're done here. I want to see those ribs in a couple days just to make sure nothing develops. I can give you some pain pills."

Ethan took the medication with him and walked back to his new home for the rest of his stay. Food was what he needed now.

2

Ethan awoke at first light. He turned over in bed and felt sharp pains shoot through both sides of his rib cage. Yesterday came flooding back to him. His release, the flight, the mysterious brick house. His watch said it was just after 6:00 a.m. He let out a long sigh. *What am I doing here?* he thought. He knew military life was not for him. But at this point in his life, it was better than sitting in a jail cell. Prison was constant torture for a guy with a severe case of claustrophobia. Every evening for the last seven years it was all he could do to relax in his cell so he could sleep. And every morning he had to keep himself together until the cell opened for breakfast.

"I'll get the team together. Just see the doc today and then stop by my office. Nothing strenuous...except the briefing on your mission."

That was Murrow's final encouragement before he let Ethan off at the barracks. He pulled himself from the bed and walked gingerly to the bathroom. He felt the start of a headache, and there was still some tenderness in his ribs. He threw down a few of the pills Siegers had given him and jumped in the shower. The other men who were part of this Special Forces selection class had been roused at four in the morning for a run. Ethan had started to rise until an officer identified himself and simply said, "At ease, Zabad." That was all Ethan needed to hear. He rolled over and slept for two more hours. He had not slept that late since going to prison.

Today was his first and hopefully only meeting with Dr. Remont, the base psychologist. He wasn't sure why, but he had very little respect for Erik Remont's profession. What could a psychologist really do anyway? Didn't they just sit there and listen? Perhaps it was the fact that most of his life he had been forced to just deal with things as they came. His parents never made him go talk to someone. Of course they had their own explanation for his condition. It never occurred to him to go talk to someone about it. Women talked. Men suppressed most of what they were feeling. If he could just get through today, answer the questions the way he thought Remont wanted them answered, he might get away without having to "share" his feelings.

He looked at the slip of paper he held in his hand; it said 225. "Well, here goes," Ethan whispered to himself. He pushed open the door and was looking at a modest office. There were two pieces of art on the walls, each above a couch. A stack of magazines sat on a table in front of one couch. He walked over to it and scanned the titles. Skateboarding magazines, video game tips and reviews, and rock music news dominated the stack. Not one *Newsweek*, *Time*, or *People* in the whole pile. Not even a *National*

Geographic. Not a typical military office and certainly not what Ethan imagined a psychologist's office to look like. What did he expect? Doctors in white coats leading around people in straightjackets?

"Ethan Zabad?"

Ethan heard the voice to his left. He glanced up from the table and saw his first hint as to the magazine selection. Remont was about Ethan's height. His hair was brown, but it was gelled and spiky across the front. He was wearing ripped blue jeans and a brown T-shirt with a skateboarding logo emblazoned across the chest.

"I'm Ethan," he replied casually to Remont's inquiry.

"Come on in," Erik invited with a wave of his hand.

Ethan followed Erik Remont into his office and was directed to sit on a wide and very comfortable couch. The couch was parallel to Remont's desk and to one side was a matching chair, which Ethan could only assume was for the doctor during "analysis." When Remont sat down at the desk Ethan had a better chance to assess what he was dealing with. Erik Remont looked younger than Ethan. He had piercing blue eyes that made him look wiser than his age. He seemed very relaxed. Ethan glanced over his shoulder toward the now closed office door. Hanging just inside was what he had to assume was Remont's required dress for work. A uniform. Caught looking, he heard Remont say, "I change when I come in and when I leave. I can't work dressed like that. But it reminds me that even though I do this for a living I could still be deployed. I *am* in the armed forces."

Ethan must have had an inquisitive look on his face when he turned back. Remont spoke again.

"Not what you expected? I hear that a lot. Everyone thinks only an old fart would take a job like this. But I love it." He leaned back in his chair and clasped his hands behind his head. "So what's your story?"

"That's it? That's your first question?"

"Were you expecting a long introduction? I don't have all day. Tell me what you need to tell me so we can move on."

Ethan wasn't sure what to say. Did he have anything *to* say? About what? "I really don't *need* to tell you anything. I was just told to come here. I guess you have to figure out what to do for the next hour."

"Why don't we just sit and stare into space? Better yet we could empty our pockets and compare lint."

If Dr. Remont was a professional, he had a strange way of showing it. "That sounds like a total waste of time."

"Then you got my point. C'mon, just tell me something. Anything. Tell me a story from childhood. Talk about where you grew up. Just tell me something. You know the last guy who came in here, all he wanted to talk about was these dreams he kept having about not being able to load his gun properly. Talk about a painful hour."

"So I tell you something from my childhood, and I get to leave?"

"Does it smell bad in here? Are you afraid of me?"

"I just don't want to be analyzed."

Remont seemed offended. "Analyzed? I just want you to talk to me. I don't know you. I don't know your story. I can't even write a sentence about you based on what you've said so far."

"You could say I'm paranoid," said Ethan, trying to be helpful. The moment the words left his mouth, he realized he had played into Remont's skilled hands. Then again he wasn't sure. He couldn't tell if Remont was playing games with him or was really as relaxed and unconcerned as he seemed.

"Mmm, paranoid," Remont said as he mockingly wrote on a notepad. "Just talk to me, man. Where do you come from?"

"Where do you come from?" The question was so simple. But Ethan couldn't just say "New York," could he? There was so much more to it than that. Ethan decided to start with something that, while obvious, was a defining factor in his life. Perhaps it alone would answer Remont's other questions. "I'm Jewish."

"What else?" Remont quickly responded.

"What do you mean what else? That ought to explain a lot."

"It doesn't to me. I'm French. Ooh la la. Tell *you* anything?"

Ethan tried hard not to crack a smile. He had to admit, Remont reminded him of himself. Tough, not taking garbage from anyone. He decided he liked him, for now. "All right. I grew up in a Jewish family. Both my parents were devout. They always tell"—Ethan corrected himself —"*told* this story to people about how they prayed for me before I was even born. I'm supposed to be some kind of gift from God." Ethan said it with a wave of his hand as if to brush it off.

"Are your parents deceased?"

"No. It's just—well—let's just save that for later."

Remont gave a slow nod and simply said, "Okay."

After an awkward moment, Ethan sighed. "Keep talking, right?"

Remont shrugged. "Sure."

Ethan thought about seeing how long Remont would last in complete silence but had a feeling it wouldn't faze him at all. He decided to continue. "My parents were thrilled when I was born. You know, 'gift from God' and all that. I never really understood it. One thing they made sure I knew was that God had made me special. I never wanted to be special. I just wanted to be normal."

Remont interjected. "That may be because you've never been normal. No offense intended. It's just that normal people want to be special."

"They can have it. My mother told me how seven years before I was born she'd had a miscarriage. It was the most painful thing of her life..." Ethan hesitated. He was on the verge of saying things he'd never told anyone. Why would he tell them to Remont? Something about him made Ethan feel he was trustworthy. He had met very few people in life who struck him that way. People he knew tried to use him. People who knew of his uniqueness tried to pick fights, manipulate his ability into a side show. Remont seemed not to care about any of that.

"Are you okay, Ethan?"

"Yeah, I-I'm okay. I-I just, I'm trying to collect my thoughts. Where was I?"

"You'd just shared about your mother's miscarriage."

Right. The miscarriage. The memories that had been stirred just moments ago now swirled in Ethan's head. He forgot about Remont, about the military, about being afraid to talk, being afraid of pain. Images flashed past his consciousness—an accident on a busy street, a school play-ground, kids laughing, blood. His mind grabbed onto the image of the accident. It was just an image to him. The details were from his mother. He was half-aware that he had started talking, but it felt more like he was reliving the story than retelling it.

Ethan, just eighteen months old, was buckled into the

car seat, and his mother got into the front seat. It was a cold December day. Tara Zabad only needed to go a few blocks from her home on 187th Street to get some groceries. The market that used to be nearby had closed and now a shopping trip was more than a stroll down the block. As Tara turned onto 75th Avenue, she was confronted with a long line of cars. Her two-minute drive looked like it would take around fifteen. They crawled along in the traffic. Finally at 180th the pace quickened, and she was able to see the parkway ahead. Her glance up the street to check traffic took her eyes from the car in front of her for a split second. When she looked down, she realized she'd had her foot on the brake and the car in front of her had gotten across the intersection. She gave the car a little gas to catch up.

The car behind them saw it before she did and honked the horn. A car coming down the cross street had seen an opening in the traffic from about a half a block away and was speeding up to make the gap. When Tara suddenly appeared in the intersection, the other driver locked his brakes. His car slammed into the Zabad's and pushed them across the divided highway into the opposing lane of traffic, where a car promptly hit them head on. It caused the Zabads' car to flip toward the driver's side. With the two different points of impact and the fact that Tara had not buckled for the short drive, she was ejected from the car only to be pinned beneath part of it. Ethan was in the backseat still hanging upside down in his car seat, dazed but unhurt. At eighteen months, he knew how to walk and even knew some words. One of those was "help," and he heard it now, spoken by his mother. But he couldn't see her.

As she continued to cry out, the voices of people outside the car became audible. Ethan began to grow frantic. Where was his mom? Why was she calling for help? He began to cry and struggle with the straps of the car seat. As his frustration grew he pulled harder and harder until he snapped one of the straps. He wormed his way out of the other strap and began to fall toward the ceiling of the car. His foot snagged on the remnant of the strap, and he hung there, one foot in the car seat and his tiny hands touching the ceiling of the car. Ethan was bawling now and started calling, "Mama! Mama!"

"I'm here, baby! Mama's here." Tara struggled with the words. She was having trouble breathing and was just as distraught as her son. She heard a thump from the car and saw Ethan crawl out of the window onto cold pavement and broken glass. She saw a crowd gathering nearby. A man ran from the group and knelt beside her. "We're going to help you out, ma'am. An ambulance is on the way."

"Thank you. Get my son. Get my son, please."

A woman from the crowd came forward and picked up Ethan from the glass and debris. He kicked at her and continued to cry. "Mama!"

The woman put him back down and tried to lead him away by the hand but he wouldn't go. He pulled away and tottered toward his mother. "It's okay, Ethan. Mommy's going to be okay." Tara fought to speak, trying to reassure her son.

A man from the crowd organized almost a dozen men, and they gathered around the vehicle to lift it so Tara could be pulled from beneath. The men lifting marveled at how easily they were able to move the car. Only Tara, lying on the pavement, was able to see her eighteen-month-old, who had crawled between the legs of the men, pushing up on the car, desperate to help his mother. She could not believe what she was seeing. It defied logic and explanation.

Tara was moved minutes before the paramedics arrived.

She had sustained severe injuries to her hips and legs and struggled to walk again throughout a long recovery. Aside from the ease with which the car was moved, the only mystery of the whole accident was how baby Ethan had removed himself from the wreck. No one seemed to remember cutting the strap of his car seat, and yet there it was, ripped, not along a seam, not where they hooked into the seat, just torn in two at the middle.

Ethan's mind locked onto another image. A school playground. It was fifth grade.

"Another beautiful spring day, class!" Mrs. Mason was saying. "I think we'll spend some time outside."

Ethan's heart sank. He hated the playground. He was never asked to play anything. And it wasn't his Jewish heritage. There were other kids in the class with last names like Benjamin and Rosenberg. *They* always played. It was him. His mother always told him he was special, and she was right. So special that no one wanted to play with him. Usually the things that happened weren't his fault. And, he had to admit, sometimes they were; not to mention the fact that these incidents could also be funny. In one recess, Ethan had been told he was too weird to play on the seesaw. He walked up behind one the students and pulled down on the seesaw—hard. It launched the boy on the other end head over heels, tumbling down the board into his friend.

When he was denied a seat on the merry-go-round, Ethan offered to spin a group of classmates. He was not motivated by kindness. He spun them to the point where some of the kids started asking to get off. Then they started to beg. Ethan spun them faster and faster. Their dads had never given them a ride like this. Some of the kids started to cry. And then one by one they gave up and started to let go. They flew off in several directions, each one crash-landing in the nearby grass. Ethan spun until the last kid had let go. He stepped back triumphantly and looked at the destruction he'd caused. Then he felt the teacher's hands on his shoulders and was marched to the office, again.

These incidents and the students inherent dislike for and rejection of Ethan led him to make a game out of hiding behind the bushes lining the playground looking for opportunities to hit kids on the head with kickballs. His aim was good, and he threw hard. More than one child had his playtime ruined by Ethan's hitting his mark. Although this behavior was Ethan's response to cruel and constant teasing, he never seemed to be excused from a trip to the office. It became a game of sorts for the rest of the class to get him sent to the office. And they were good at it.

With that kind of track record, Ethan knew recess was not for him. And so, on this day, it was unfortunate that Mrs. Mason really wanted to go outside. The class lined up in the hall and marched to the back doors of the school. Mrs. Mason opened the doors, and all the kids bolted for the playground equipment. Except for Ethan. He moped down the steps to the patch of dirt worn in the grass by countless students and sat down. It was better to just sit here than get into trouble again.

But on this day, trouble seemed to find him. A kickball rolled up to his feet. He just looked at it wondering if he should bother to throw it back. Then he heard, "Hey, stupid! Throw the ball!"

He picked it up and tossed it lightly across the playground. It didn't roll very far.

"I said throw it! Or are you retarded?"

Ethan glanced over and saw Mrs. Mason talking to another teacher. They didn't hear what was being said, but he knew that as soon as he responded they'd be on him. He stood and walked over to the ball, tossing it farther this time. The ball rolled up to the group of boys. One of them, Greg Holcomb, picked the ball up as he spoke. "Hey, I've got an idea. Let's play fetch."

Ethan was in no mood. "You can throw that ball all over the playground. I won't go get it."

Greg drew back his arm as if to throw the ball across the yard but instead turned and flung it at Ethan's forehead where it hit hard and careened away toward the swings. "Oops! You can still go fetch it though." He turned away with a nasty laugh, and the other boys joined in.

Ethan tried to block out the laughter. He turned back toward the teachers. Oblivious. "Just sit down and ignore it. It doesn't matter," he told himself. He sat back down only to receive another ball in the side of the head.

Anger welled up within him. He stood and walked to the two teachers talking. It wouldn't do any good to tell. Somehow it would become his fault. The only other choice was escape. "Mrs. Mason. I need to go inside."

"Ethan, recess will be over in ten minutes." She seemed irritated he was speaking.

"I really need to go in. I-I have to go to the bathroom."

"I think it can wait."

"Mrs. Mason—"

"Ethan. I've given you an answer. Please stop asking. You will be first in line when we go inside."

He turned away and walked a few yards from the teachers as he surveyed the playground. There was a set of seesaws, six swings on a steel-poled A-frame, two slides, the merry-go-round, a set of monkey bars, and a circular climbing toy with lots of places to sit and dangle by the legs. At each place his classmates played. Many of them were looking in his direction. He thought an animal in the zoo must feel the same way. Stared at, pitied, even admired in some way, but not befriended. Sadness overwhelmed him.

Greg had retrieved the ball and from a distance launched another attack. The ball made a long, slow arc across the yard. Greg watched with great anticipation as it made its way nearer to its target. When it hit the mark, Greg punched his fist in the air and high-fived his pals. The ball had hit Ethan square in the nose and made his eyes well up immediately. Everyone knows getting hit in the nose will make your eyes water, but to the kids near Ethan, it was more fun to accuse him of crying. It hadn't really hurt. The embarrassment was worse than the pain. He had the fleeting thought that maybe he deserved it for all the times he'd done it to other kids.

"Hey, everybody, Ethan's crying!"

"I'm not crying."

"That's what everyone says—when they're crying. You're such a baby." Greg had walked over to where Ethan was standing.

"I'm not a baby. And you'd better stop calling me that."

"What are you gonna do? Cry on me?" Balled fists went up to their eyes, and they pretended to wail like babies. More students gathered to join in.

Ethan bowed his head. His black hair fell forward and covered the sides of his face. While it may have looked as if he was bowing in shame, he was really just trying to control his furious thoughts. *They had no right.* Maybe it was his mom and dad's fault. Maybe it was God's fault. Whoever was to blame, he felt they should accept some responsibility for what he was about to do now.

"Shut up! All of you, shut up!" He glared at the class-mates that had surrounded him. "I hate every one of you!"

There were some wide eyes among the students but

mainly smirks and nudges as they realized they had pushed him past the brink. It was show time.

"I'm sick of being teased. I'm sick of being left out. If I can't play, then no one can." He pushed through a few students grouped in front of him and headed toward the seesaw.

"What are you gonna do? Seesaw by yourself?" Some kids laughed. Ethan turned and saw it was Greg speaking again.

"No. I'm not," he answered simply. And then he punched Greg in the nose. He hadn't even punched him hard, but it caused his nose to bleed, and to Ethan's enormous satisfaction, tears formed in Greg's eyes.

One of the girls called out, "Mrs. Mason! Ethan just punched Greg!"

"Ethan, you're dead. You'll get expelled," Greg said through blood-covered lips.

"For punching you? I don't think so. But I will get expelled for this!" He pulled at the seesaw and ripped it from the bolts holding it to the center bar. He threw it aside and marched over to the swings. He grabbed three of the chains holding the swings and pulled down with a hard, jerking motion. All three snapped and landed in a heap. He grabbed the center A-frame of the swing set and pushed with all his might. The swing set folded down like a collapsible lawn chair.

Mrs. Mason was there now. "Ethan! Stop it! What are you... How are you...?"

Ethan ignored her and walked to the merry-go-round. He grabbed the outer edge and lifted. There was a screech of metal, and in a moment the merry-go-round was sitting upside down on the grass.

His teachers had their hands on him trying to restrain

him. He shook them off. He was far too angry to stop now. He would go anywhere, a special school, home school, boarding school, anywhere to get away from these kids and these ignorant teachers. He made his way to the climbing toy and grabbed hold of it. He shook it as hard as he could and kept shaking until the concrete blobs holding it in the ground emerged and were sitting atop the ground. He turned and addressed his stunned and frightened teachers. "I'm done. We can go to the office now."

Expulsion had been inevitable. Not only were school administrators angry about the damage, but they were afraid for their safety with a "monster" like Ethan. For now, the best solution was home schooling. His mother, Tara, was working with his father, Abe, all day, every day, so they asked a friend of theirs, a woman they worshipped with each week, to come and tutor Ethan.

This new arrangement was fine with him. But it helped that his dad announced that they would have a talk about all that had happened. They sat together in their living room. Ethan knew part of what his father would say, but something in Abe Zabad's voice told him this would be different.

"Ethan. You are special."

"Dad. You have told me that so many times. I don't get it. If being special means getting teased and left out, I don't want to be special."

"Don't you realize you've been given a great gift? God told us—"

"It's not a great gift. Having no friends is not a gift." Ethan put his head down on his chest, breathing hard as he tried not to cry.

"Ethan. Look at me. Look at me, Son. There are things you don't know. Things you must now hear." Ethan looked up, questions all over his face.

"You remember your mother telling you once that she had a miscarriage, right?" Ethan only nodded in response. His dad continued. "That was the most painful experience of her life. Losing that baby was...was the beginning of a time of darkness for us. We doubted God. We doubted everything good in life. We believed there would never be another happy day. But in time we began to pray. We begged God to restore our faith, our happiness. To do as our Holy Scriptures say and restore to us what the locusts had eaten."

"And then I was born 'special,' and everybody was happy."

"No, Ethan. We have not told you everything. You are special for many reasons. Not just because you made us happy." Abe Zabad closed his eyes and seemed to be concentrating. Ethan watched as his father drew from his memories the words and events that changed his life and Tara's life forever.

"Ethan. You were a healer to us. You healed a wound in our hearts that only a child could mend. But before you were born, I had a dream. I was told about you before you were conceived."

"Told by who?"

"There is no other one who speaks in dreams. I heard from God, Ethan." He said it again slowly so there would be no mistaking. "I heard from God."

"God told you about my birth?"

"He said you would be a healer. A restorer. One who would be a healer and restorer of many hearts. So I knew you would not just be a joy to us."

"What else did the dream say? What am I supposed to do?"

"We were simply told to prepare you for your mission."

"But what is it?"

"We don't know. We only know that one day you will heal the hearts of many and bring restoration."

"To *what*, Dad? Why are you telling me this if I can't do anything about it?"

"So you will be ready! So you will be ready when the time comes! Follow God, Ethan. Ask Him to show you your path. His path."

"Why didn't God just tell you what it was?"

"We had lost one child already. He knew that if He told us we would do all we could to protect you and we wouldn't allow you to really live."

It took Ethan a few seconds to try and digest this statement. Finally he spoke. "So how were you supposed to prepare me for my...mission?"

"Several things. Strictly obey God's laws about food. All of them! Master self-control. Learn to give generously."

"There's nothing unusual about those. Every person in synagogue is trying to do that."

"I have learned not to question God when he speaks. Just know that your mother and I love you very much and we want you to succeed in life. Your gift is from God. I am sure that one day it will be used to accomplish your mission for Him. Don't turn your back on Him in anger. He has made you special for a reason."

"He has made you special for a reason." Ethan finished his story with this sentence. Even as he repeated it to Remont, he thought it over again. It was such an exciting prospect at the time he first heard it. Now it was a fantasy, a charming little folk tale.

"You've had it rough. No doubt about that." Remont hadn't written anything down. He hadn't even interrupted to ask a question. He had simply listened.

"So are we done?" Ethan started to lift himself out of the couch.

"I just want to know one thing. Have you been preparing for this 'mission' of yours? Or do you consider the whole story just that—a story?"

Of course. The question Ethan had never been able to answer. His parents swore over and over that it was true. The only thing Ethan had to back it up was his freakish strength. "I can't answer that. I haven't been preparing, no, but as for their story—I just don't know. My mom tried to get me to follow the food rules in the Law, but I was always sneaking snacks from the store a few blocks away. The other stuff?" Ethan just shrugged.

"Let's talk again. I'll make an appointment for two days from now. Same time?"

"Sure." Ethan stood and walked out through the waiting area into the hall. It hadn't been as bad as he'd thought it would be. But digging up painful memories was like raking dry leaves into the wind. He walked out of the building and back into the heat. His next stop was Murrow's office. The team was assembled and he was scheduled to begin training today, starting with the briefing.

[3]

The limousine, followed by a black SUV, pulled up in front of the slate gray building, and a black-clad security detail emerged. They scanned the sidewalk in front of Hyperteq's headquarters and then spread out to form a perimeter. Rolf Gallinger stepped out of the limo and walked briskly to the revolving door leading to the main lobby.

This building, the company, and the money he now controlled appeared to have come to him almost overnight. In reality it had taken years of preparation. Always driven, he had befriended the CEO of Hyperteq when it was still small. Rolf knew its potential even then. He pushed his "friend" all along, helping him to make choices that would position Gallinger to oust him when the time came. In the meantime, Gallinger had a few powerful friends whom he leveraged in order to place himself in an even better position to take over Hyperteq. Gallinger had been buying Hyperteq stock for several years. He had used two separate corporations, each purchasing interest in Hyperteq. Two of Gallinger's friends had a seat on the board at Hyperteq and were willing to invest in some of Gallinger's new nanotechnologies. The advances made by Gallinger were so compelling that rather than simply funding more research, Gallinger was able to gain a percentage of his friend's share in Hyperteq. His production profits went right back into purchasing Hyperteq stock.

The biggest break came when the market made its downward turn throughout 2007 and 2008. As investors left the market, they also left Hyperteq, and Gallinger was able to purchase almost all of the public offerings of Hyperteq stock. That and several board members stepping down due to their personal financial losses contributed toward Gallinger gaining his own seat on Hyperteq's board. When Gallinger's friends learned it was he and his corporations that had purchased such a large percentage of Hyperteq stock, they prepared to take the information to the chief financial officer and the CEO. Before they were able to let Hyperteq leadership know that Gallinger was preparing a takeover both men died. One was killed in a car accident while the other was stabbed leaving his office. The latter death was investigated extensively, but the conclusion was that a robbery had resulted in murder. There were no other leads.

When Gallinger finally stepped into the role of CEO, it appeared clean and smooth with no one the wiser to the years of preparation that had culminated in that moment.

Gallinger had always done honest, upfront business in order to fund and carry on his "other interests" behind the scenes. His takeover of Hyperteq was no different. It was like running two different corporations, the one the world saw and the one Gallinger saw. Today he was meeting with a group of investors who were paying for their stake in a new world financial order.

He exploded through the door of the conference room and made his way to the head of the twenty-four-foot oak table. He took his time, looking each man in the eye, nodding at some, letting the anticipation build. He wanted them to believe they were essential to the success of his plans. Of course to Gallinger they were expendable, but he wanted their complete trust...and their money.

Gallinger spoke with authority. "Gentlemen, there is a language common to all of us at this table—the language of money. Whoever controls that controls the world. For too long, weak politicians have made decisions about world finance without truly understanding the power they wield. The World Bank is controlled by people who cater to individual nations. They are weak and fickle. We now have the opportunity to seize control of the world's money and our means are fear and intimidation. Terror. Since most of you are here because of your proficiency in this very area, I have no doubt you will be comfortable with what I am about to tell you."

At 10:30 a.m. Ethan walked to the building he had been in yesterday with Kaplan. He had never been *briefed* before. If not for the special trip with Murrow to the brick house yesterday, he wouldn't even know what he was training for. Much of what he had seen made no sense to him. *Why a house like that? And what was under the door in the basement?*

Clearly he was once again being singled out for his unique abilities. He decided that at this point in his life that wasn't a concern, as long as things didn't turn nasty.

Ethan was escorted to a small room with twelve school-style desks all facing a larger desk. Murrow stood behind it. Kaplan was also there standing by. From across the room he nodded to her and mouthed "hello." She smiled back but before she had a chance to say anything else Murrow started the meeting.

"Hello, Ethan. I trust you're feeling all right this morning. We're about to start going over some details of your assignment. Let me introduce you to the team." He gestured to the men sitting in the desks.

"This is Theodore Willis. He's the team leader."

"Theodore?"

"Just call me Theo. Good to meet you." The young black officer extended a hand. He was probably a little older than Ethan and bore several scars around his neck providing evidence of his combat experience.

Murrow continued to Theo's right. "This is Robert Charles."

"Yo, Ethan. Everyone's called me Robbie all along startin' with my grandma. You can do the same."

"Sure, Robbie." Robbie was the largest of any of the men in the room. Ethan guessed he was at least six feet six inches when he stood up. He was even larger than the goon, Farrar. Robbie didn't look like anyone to mess with, and Ethan hoped he'd never have to. Next to Robbie was Casey Linz. Linz struck Ethan as a sort of "good ol' boy."

"How you doin', Ethan? Ain't got no nicknames. Whatever suits you." He leaned toward Ethan and asked, "Ya like guns?"

Ethan shrugged and answered, "I've never shot one."

Linz raised his eyebrows and looked at Murrow. "I'll help him out."

"You'll all help him," Murrow corrected.

Linz looked back at Ethan and smiled. "Automatic rifles, rocket-propelled grenades, mortars, fifty calibers. We'll have fun." His eyes were alight, and he finished this sentence with a big smile. It was clear he relished his work.

"Ethan, this is Cameron Mongezi." Murrow gestured to an extremely dark-skinned black man seated at a table near the door. He couldn't have been much more than twenty-two or twenty-three.

"Pleasure to meet you, Ethan. I look forward to working with you." Ethan was taken aback by his manner and bearing and suspected that as he got to know Cameron he would be impressed by his intellect.

"Barrett Barton." Murrow pointed to Barrett though he was not hard to spot. Barrett was another of the big boys. Ethan was beginning to feel very small in this room. Every soldier sitting before him had at least twenty pounds on him, all of it muscle.

"These are Anthony Pitner and Vic Dombrow. They're both top snipers." Murrow gestured to the two men in the back row. They both extended a hand.

"Pleasure. Call me 'Pits.' Not my disposition; it's just shorter than Anthony."

"Hi, Ethan. Just call me Vic."

"Ethan, every man here is highly trained and has experience in special operations units before coming to this unit. We are assigned and designed to deal with terrorism. Delta Force is not the oldest unit in the armed forces, but it has an excellent reputation and many good men have served and died while a part of it. You are the first person, ever, to join operators on a mission without having gone through selection. Each of these men has a specialty, but all have been trained in every area of combat. You're in good hands. One of the finest teams we've ever put together." Murrow concluded the introductions with this statement and then turned his attention to his desktop.

Ethan sat at a table near the desk and looked to Murrow, who was holding a small gray remote control. He pointed it at the wall behind his desk and something he hadn't noticed yesterday dropped down about three feet. It was a screen. Simultaneously, a projector lowered from the ceiling and clicked on. Murrow spoke.

"Gentlemen, we'll start today with a great deal of background. You need to understand the seriousness of what we're about to undertake. Tomorrow we'll start at 0200 with some prep work, mostly for the benefit of Mr. Zabad. Once we're all friends, we'll do some walkthroughs of the objective itself."

Ethan was still getting used to military time. It sounded like Murrow said two o'clock in the morning. *Prep work? For me?*

Murrow clicked the remote again and a logo appeared. "This is a symbol associated with the religion Cultus. A member of this organization provided us with our initial information about this mission. Before I get to that, let me tell you about them." Murrow turned and nodded to Kaplan, and she began handing out manila file folders to each team member.

"Cultus is a religion started by Rolf Gallinger." Murrow clicked the remote again, and a picture of a man filled the screen. He looked very distinguished and could pass for a law professor at an Ivy League school. He was brown haired with a square jaw and high cheekbones. His eyes were a steely gray, and wherever the picture had been taken, Ethan was sure the photographer had been intimidated. At the temples and across his forehead, his hair was turning gray.

"We have been working for months to gain some background on him. We haven't conclusively connected him to the information I'm about to share, but we have not counted him out as a possible suspect. As far as Cultus is concerned, we have discovered that they have their tentacles in several prominent governments in Eastern Europe and are starting to show up in the Middle East. Until now we have mainly observed them working in drugs, electronics, and weapons. But in the last few months, we've discovered they've also done some human trafficking and experiments with cloning and genetic mutation."

The looks on the faces of several unit members prompted Murrow to respond. "Strange activities for a 'religious' organization, I know. While Gallinger is certainly the head of Cultus and we have evidence he is even worshipped as god, we don't know yet if Cultus members are operating alone or under his direction."

"He's not much of a god if he doesn't know what all his people are up to," Pits threw in.

"God didn't stop *you* last weekend when you—" Vic was cut off by Murrow's aggressive throat clearing. He continued.

"We learned from this Cultus member that there was a weapon that had been developed and designed to deeply affect the world's economy and also put the health and safety of the world population at risk."

"Nukes could do that," Pits interjected. "Just the *threat* of nukes..."

"From our intel, it's not as materially destructive as a nuclear weapon. But the long-term effects are catastrophic," Murrow added. "This weapon appears to be an integration of computer and biological technology."

"Computer virus?" Casey asked.

"We wish it were that simple. This is a biological weapon delivered via computer technology."

"That doesn't make any sense, sir," Robbie said. "Computer viruses aren't biological. You can't send bacteria to a hard drive. Sir."

"I know that. But it doesn't mean someone hasn't figured out a way to combine the two technologies. Let me try to explain from what limited information we have." A company logo appeared on the screen, and Murrow began. "This is Qualtech. They have been a leading manufacturer of credit cards for over three decades now. Their parent company is Hyperteq. Hyperteq's controlling interest is a group of investors led by Rolf Gallinger."

"Sir, why isn't he the target?" Vic asked.

"As I said, we don't have any evidence that this new threat is coming from him. If there are some rogue elements within his organization, we'll need his help to root them out. And we need to focus on the weapon for now." Murrow cast a glance in Ethan's direction.

Ethan caught it, and it enhanced his feeling that he was very out of his league. He didn't even know what questions to ask. If there was an explanation for why he was here and what the house was all about, he hoped it was forthcoming.

"Gallinger will come into play later. Right now I'd like to try and explain what we know about this weapon. In traditional credit cards, you all know there is an electromagnetic strip across the back. In most of the newer versions, there is simply a microchip so that it doesn't have to be swiped. It is a contactless or touchless card. Some even have a built-in processor. With the current developments in nanotechnology, things are possible now that seem like miracles. Our informant told us that a method has been found to store live bacteria on the back of a credit card.

When it is swiped or scanned and the right computer code is transmitted, the bacteria are released into the skin of the cardholder. It kills within twenty-four hours. Again, we don't know if this is something Cultus has done or if it is technology Hyperteq has engineered without his involvement."

Ethan leaned forward and gestured to the screen. "Sir, that's the craziest thing I've ever heard. Where is the virus? How does it live on plastic?"

Murrow shrugged with his hands in the air. "I don't understand all the technology that makes it possible. But we have documentation on some of the victims." He clicked again on the remote, and gruesome pictures of people, unrecognizable in death, appeared. Their faces were grotesquely colored, and their mouths open in a death grimace.

"Victims? You mean they're already using the weapon?" Ethan exclaimed as he took in the images.

"They've tested it on humans. We know that for a fact."

"Why would anyone want to kill off every credit card holder in the world?" Casey asked.

"That's not the point. But the threat, the possibility, is the real power this weapon holds. Besides, the longer people use their credit and debit cards, the richer he gets. The accounts are tracked and funds are funneled—somewhere."

"Somewhere? Money is just disappearing?" Casey wondered aloud.

Something in Ethan's mind clicked, and he realized he already knew the answer. He had been there yesterday.

"That's not all. We believe that Cultus, or one of its rogue elements, is already using this technology, not to kill or bankrupt, but simply to see if it works. Our informant told us of a master computer that records credit card transactions from all over the world and redirects a percentage of each exchange to separate accounts."

"What percentage?" Cameron asked.

"We don't know. The occurrences seem random, in amount and frequency."

"But if there are one billion dollars worth of credit transactions, Cultus rakes in a cool million every day. And we all know there are well over a billion dollars worth of transactions every single day. It's small enough to go unde-tected but large enough to add up quickly. Especially if Cultus's reach is worldwide. Again, in one day, billions of dollars are exchanged via credit and debit cards."

"I can't believe no one would notice this," Cameron argued.

"It's possible that it's happened to you and didn't realize it. If they can do this—and we know they can—they're not going to add a line to your bill announcing what they've stolen." Murrow responded. "With the tech-nology Cultus has developed and is using, anything is possible."

"Not for long," Casey added with a smirk.

"Another factor is that there may be random percent-ages, transactions where no percentage is taken at all. The logarithms necessary to program such a computer are extremely complex and require thousands of man hours to decipher."

"And there's no way anyone can hack this computer? We have access to every high level computer network in the world, and you're saying we can't find a way in?"

"The firewalls and security protections they have on this supercomputer and Cultus's own computer network are of a sophistication beyond anything we've seen. We have our folks at Langley and at the Pentagon working day and night on this thing. They're getting blocked at every turn. The only way is direct access."

"You mentioned Gallinger twice already. Cultus *and* Hyperteq. I still don't understand why he's not a suspect." Cameron finally spoke up.

"Our informant had nothing relating directly to Gallinger. From everything we know this could be someone on the inside of these groups using what's available for their own gain."

"But isn't Gallinger responsible?" Cameron questioned again.

"You don't arrest the bank's CEO when one of his branch managers is caught embezzling," Murrow answered.

"Unless the CEO knew all about it and was getting a cut," Cameron persisted. It was quiet in the room for a moment until Murrow finally spoke.

"We respond to the intelligence we have right now. You boys know we do what we're ordered to do. We're not detectives. If anything else comes up, we certainly factor that into the equation. For now, this is what we know. We work from there first." He took a deep breath. "All right, men. No more questions. I want to finish briefing you on this part of the mission. There will be time for more questions later."

He resumed his briefing. "This computer not only stores the data collected from financial transactions, it also contains the coding that unleashes the bacteria. It's only released if Cultus starts the program that controls it. Just the threat of this kind of weapon would be enough to stop commerce all over the world. If people stopped using their cards, we would not have the cash to sustain the kinds of transactions that take place each day. It would effectively destroy the world economy."

A computer-generated image was projected onto the

screen, and Ethan recognized it as the house he'd been in yesterday. It was a 3D layout showing the secret basement room.

"This is the location of the primary computer. We believe this location was chosen because it's so remote. It's more easily monitored and defended. The set up leads us to believe there may be more than one of these supercomputers. We haven't yet confirmed that. Information is downloaded and stored here." Murrow pointed to the circular hatch housing the computer. "There are ports where the information can be downloaded, but it is stored in the basement of the house. Whoever has masterminded this has chosen security over portability. The computer can only be raised from the enclosure by a hydraulic lift, but the lift controls are accessed from a point thirty miles away. You all know that one team has gone in unsuccessfully."

It seemed this was news only to Ethan. "Define 'unsuccessfully,'" he demanded.

"What do you think it means, Ethan?" Murrow fired, instantly angry. "And from now on you will address me as 'sir' along with the rest of the team." Murrow tried to downplay his flare-up as he scanned the team. "The last attempt failed because we tried to be in both places at once. A mistake we will not repeat." His eyes landed on Ethan. "One team was destroyed by a security system they didn't know about. The security measures at the site of the lift controls were hidden and lethal. The other half of the team made it out of the house and gained some important information. They learned that the computer, if not raised by the lift, could not be touched at all by anything other than human flesh. The door enclosing it is estimated to weigh over a thousand pounds. When that team tried to use its own hydraulics, the vault and the computer emitted a charge of some kind, destroying the device. The team also tried to lift the door together, but because of space, only one person was able to exert any pressure at all on the door. It's a one-man job. To get in requires sheer strength. To get out requires the same. We need to get in, download the key components of the computer program that makes Cultus's theft work, destroy the computer, and get out."

Ethan felt the eyes of the team on him. This was it then. The reason he was here. He zoned out several times during Murrow's briefing. He wasn't tired. He wasn't even bored. But in his mind, he thought he now knew his task and nothing else seemed to matter. He was very wrong about that.

Ethan had never heard of anyone doing anything at 0200 hours. So when the lights came on and selection instructors started shouting, he rolled over and tried to sleep through it. He got about thirty seconds of extra sleep before one of the instructors stood over him and shouted, "There is no sleeping in when you're in the United States armed forces! You are now a soldier whether you like it or not, and you will get out of bed!" Ethan wasn't sure if he should laugh or move at the speed of light. Seeing a grown man screaming like that was somewhat comical, but at the same time, Ethan believed he was completely serious. Either way he was annoying enough to wake Ethan up. He staggered from the bed and began to put on the clothes and gear he'd been given. For selection and training, the men were given green and tan camouflage. There was also a vest with small black squares attached. A belt contained more black squares, as did the helmet he was issued. A small patch over his breast pocket said "Zabad." Slightly better than prison issue. At least there was a name and not just a number. And the best part—he got to go outside instead of into a tiny cell. He followed the stream of men from the barracks, all while being shouted at to move faster. Once outside the men were being directed to the left. Ethan felt a hand on his arm and was jerked to the right. An instruction was shouted into his ear. "You will get into the second vehicle!"

In the dark of the night, Ethan could make out three Humvees. He made his way toward the middle one. It was a cloudy night, dark; faces were just a blur, so he was unsure who had yelled at him. He got into the vehicle.

"Mornin', soldier!" said a voice next to him. Ethan guessed it was Casey. That twang was the giveaway. "How'd you sleep?"

"Like I had to get up at two a.m. Woke up every few minutes to check the clock."

"Gosh, I hate that. Find you a boring book and read it. Works every time."

"I tend to sleep best in the half hour before the alarm. One of life's little gifts to me," Ethan said with sarcasm.

Murrow was in the lead Humvee. They drove for at least a half hour. The night seemed to get darker as they drove. They were definitely not heading toward civilization. Ethan could see trees whipping by and an occasional critter along the side of the dirt road in the glow of the headlights. When they stopped, Murrow stepped to the driver's side of the line of Humvees, which had carried the eight team members. He carried a spotlight. "This is the first of several exercises designed to prepare you for what you might encounter when this mission is finally 'go.' This field is approximately two hundred yards across. You'll need to cross it." Murrow motioned to his left, in the directions the Humvees were facing. "Your objective is simple. Across that field is a small box. Retrieve it for me. You have half an hour. You are being watched."

Ethan then knew beyond a doubt that he was out of his element. He watched as Murrow moved back to his Humvee with the light and opened a wooden box that Ethan soon saw contained guns. They looked like automatic machine guns, but there was something different about them that Ethan couldn't place.

"These guns are designed to work with the MILES system. You'll each be given a gun. You know how it works."

Ethan did not. He was about to ask what it was when he heard a few groans from the rest of the team. Barrett spoke up. "Sir, we haven't used MILES since basic training. I thought this would be a live fire exercise."

"Not this time. You boys'll do some training in the room, but not tonight." The room Murrow referred to was just that – a training room versatile enough to simulate hostage rescue situations. The set up was always different and live rounds were used to shoot at wooden targets.

"Sir, our timetable is short. If we're going to be ready we should be using live rounds," Barrett insisted.

"In case you haven't noticed I've added a man to your team who has never fired a gun, in or out of battle. Do you think it would be wise to enter combat training with someone so inexperienced?"

"No sir."

"Do you think he knows where to stand when entering an enemy-occupied building?"

"No sir!"

"Do you think he knows where to shoot first when clearing a room with three or more teammates?"

"No sir."

"You will use the MILES system tonight and for every training exercise I feel it necessary. Do I make myself clear?"

"Yes sir," Barrett shouted back.

Now that his complete ineptitude had been firmly established, Ethan finally had his opportunity. "Sir, what's the MILES system?"

"It is the Multiple Integrated Laser Engagement System."

If the blank look didn't convince Murrow that Ethan was confused, the silence helped.

"Look, did you notice the black squares on your vest and belt?"

"Yes, sir, and I was—"

"Good. Each rifle and machine-gun is equipped with a laser light device. When you pull the trigger, the gun still goes 'bang,' but we're using blanks. A coded laser light fires as well. If another soldier is in the way, his laser light detectors will sense your laser, and he will hear a buzzer go off. This means he's hit. It's the same for you."

"This sounds like a kids' game."

"This isn't your little brother's video game. A shot from one of these will take you out of this exercise. There's no extra lives. You don't get to come back from the dead. Each of you is connected to a computer via GPS, so we can track your movements and know when you have been - eliminated. The computer also tells us the extent of your 'injury.' You have ten minutes to plan for this mission. Your radios as well as any gear you feel you may need are here in the Humvee." Murrow motioned for them to come and take a gun and then trotted off into the field carrying the spotlight. It bounced across the open space Ethan could now see just a few yards away and then faded back to black. *No more instructions? Just go get the box?*

"All right men. You know the drill." Theo, the team leader, pointed to a different team member as he said, "Left, center, right. Stay in pairs or threes. Keep an eye on our time. We have no idea what's out there or what the box looks like. Stay within sight distance. We go silent as soon as we get on our bellies. Ethan, you come with me."

Ethan didn't know how often these men had worked together but they all seemed to know what to do. A gun was thrust into his hands, and Theo pushed him toward the field, which was just blackness. He looked up hoping for some ray of moonlight. Nothing. Then Theo thrust what felt like a heavy set of binoculars into his hands. Night vision goggles.

Theo whispered to him as they reached tall grass. "Get those on your face. Get on your belly and crawl behind me. Don't stand up for any reason unless I tell you to. Don't talk unless I tell you to. And don't fire that weapon unless I tell you to."

"So basically just do whatever you say."

"Shut up. On your belly." Theo spoke with confidence, not aggression. It made Ethan want to obey even though he remembered a time when someone told him to shut up, and he had broken the man's jaw. They began to crawl. *I'm looking for a box in a field near a military installation with guys I met less than twelve hours ago. I'm carrying a gun loaded with blanks and a laser that I'm not supposed to use. This is not right.*

Ethan was crawling and repeating these thoughts to himself when he heard a shout from his right, immediately followed by gunshots. He brought his head up off the ground. Just then the clouds broke and in the faint moonlight he could see Pits and Barton crouched, firing into a line of trees Ethan could just make out in the distance. He heard a dull buzz and saw Barton grab his shoulder and roll slowly to the ground. Pits dropped to the ground, and he heard him crackle over the radio.

"Barton's been hit," Pits whispered over the radio.

"Keep your position. We'll adjust." Theo radioed back, still calm, in control.

There was no cover in the field that Ethan could make out. Just tall grasses. He didn't know much about their location except that it was somewhere in North Carolina. That meant ticks and chiggers. If anything would attract them, it was being sweaty on the dew-soaked ground in the middle of the night. He crawled behind Theo for what seemed like five minutes. His pants and shirt were soaked at the knees and elbows, and he was having trouble keeping his hair out of his face in spite of the helmet. They stopped to rest for a moment while Theo raised his head just above the grass for a look around. "We're about fifty yards from the trees. We still have twenty minutes. Let's go easy."

Ethan strained to see to the tree line. His eyes were having trouble adjusting to everything being in green. He couldn't make anything out, and it was only fifty yards. They began to crawl again, this time slower. After what seemed like another ten minutes, they stopped and checked their distance. Only thirty feet from the tree line. A popping sound that was becoming familiar rang out, and over the radio Ethan heard Casey groan.

"We're both hit. Cameron is down. I still can't see anything in the tree line. They are under heavy cover."

"Switch off, Casey," Theo ordered. "I'm sure your equipment is like mine. It's been disabled. I can't get a heat signature."

"Murrow's idea of a good joke," Casey responded before leaving the exercise.

"They're about a hundred yards to our left," he whispered now to Ethan. "Whoever is opposing us is higher than we are. That means in the trees and they have night vision too."

"What were you saying about heat signatures?" Ethan wondered.

"These goggles are supposed to be equipped with hardware that scans for heat. Kind of like firemen use to look for fires in the walls of houses. I may not be able to see anyone in the dark, but I can see the outline of their body since they are warmer than the air. Someone disabled our goggles." Theo sighed. "We can't come in right under their noses. It's suicide." Ethan saw perfect logic in this.

"The longer we stay here, the easier targets we become. Let's get to the tree line, Ethan. Team, on my command we break for the tree line. Stay low and get cover at the trees. No one goes in. Now!"

They rose up, the five who were left. Pits, Theo, Vic, Robbie, and Ethan all stood and ran for the cover of the trees. After three steps, shots began to ring out. Ethan felt something whip by his face. He dropped immediately and crawled for the trees. He clawed at the long grass until the base of a large oak tree came into view. Safety.

"Theo?" The radio buzzed back in Ethan's ears. "Theo, where are you?"

"I'm here, but I'm finished," Theo radioed back.

Ethan spoke into the radio again. "Is anyone still out there?"

"Sure, Ethan. Just you and me."

"Robbie?" Ethan guessed.

"The one and only. What's your position?"

"Uh, next to a really big tree." Ethan replied.

"That's good, but there are a lot of big trees. There's a beacon on your headset. It's a switch behind your ear. Activates a GPS tracking signal."

"Robbie, I'm probably only fifty yards away," Ethan said with sarcasm.

"This is more fun. Besides, we've got a little time, and you need to learn this."

Ethan switched on the beacon, and within minutes Robbie was just a few feet away. "We can still do this, rookie. We have to penetrate this tree line a little farther. There's no telling where our enemies are, but they know we're coming."

"Any ideas? You've done this before."

"If you ask me, Murrow set us up to fail on this one. Trying to teach us a lesson or something. Ten minutes to plan an assault across open ground with an uncertain objective, and no knowledge of the enemy? He's messin' with us," Robbie surmised.

"Why didn't you guys say anything?"

"Didn't anyone tell you you're in the army now? You don't question the commander," Robbie said.

"Well, I've got a question. If we're using blanks, why did I feel something go past my face?"

"You almost caught the plug!" Robbie exclaimed.

"The plug?"

"Yeah, you know the plastic that holds the powder in the case. We get the noise but not the bullet. That means whoever fired at you was close." He paused. "You came right to this tree?"

"Yeah, why?"

Robbie nodded upward indicating someone was in the tree. He wrapped his arm around the tree and fired a few rounds straight up the side facing away from the field and heard the satisfying buzz of another soldier's training "death."

"So now what?"

"We go tree to tree," Robbie suggested. Just then the soldier who had been in the tree dropped down a few feet from Robbie and started walking across the field.

"That's worthless, Robbie. Whoever is firing on us has a height advantage and can see us! We're dead as we sit here. And we can't shoot at what we can't see. Does this MILES stuff work in close quarters—I mean without a gun?"

"Yeah. You get close enough to someone without their seeing you, and you can make that thing buzz. It's right here."

Robbie showed him how it was done. "But don't worry. You won't get close enough to do anything like that. I prefer a big gun in my hands. Now, whoever was above us couldn't get an angle on you or me. Without giving away his position, that is. You work with what you've got. And by the way, I think I have a little more experience than you."

"I agree." Ethan paused. "What have you got?"

"What?"

"What do you have that we can use?"

"Two signal flares. My rifle, pistol, goggles, radio. Everything you got."

"I wish we had some explosives."

"You couldn't use those anyway, Ethan. This is a training exercise. We're not trying to kill anyone."

"Whoever the enemy is, they have the upper hand because they've got a better vantage point *and* they can see us. What if we took away one of those?"

Ethan was making an assumption that if correct would be immensely helpful. With about five minutes left, they made their simple plans. They removed their night goggles. Robbie pulled two signal flares from his belt, and Ethan did the same.

"Robbie, are you sure this is okay to do?"

"It'll hurt. An explosion could blind someone, but all this will do is make them say a few choice words."

They lit one flare and threw it into the field. Then they ran into the trees, shots popping off as they ran. They lit a second flare and threw it close to the tree line. They continued to run at an angle into the trees and away from the flares. Their hope was that with each flare, they were making it impossible to see beyond the flares with any clarity and giving Robbie and Ethan time to get in a better position. After they used their last flare, they ran another twenty yards into the woods and away from the field and huddled next to a large, mossy tree.

"Now what?"

"We find the box."

"Done."

Ethan nodded at a small opening in the trees. There on a smooth, flat rock was a metal box.

Ethan ran forward as Robbie said, "I'll cover you."

Ethan snatched the box off its perch and ran back to Robbie. Wherever their opponents were, he hoped they could not see him.

They quickly ran back to the tree line and along its border for about forty yards. Then they cut into the field, and Ethan sprinted back to the Humvees while Robbie backed away and covered their retreat.

The rest of the team was waiting.

"Nicely done, guys." Theo stepped toward them. "That was a simple solution. We've been high-tech for so long it's easy to overlook the obvious."

Just then Murrow stepped out of the tall grass. "You completed the objective. But there were only two of you left to enjoy it. We'll pick this one apart later this morning. Let's move on."

They jumped back into the Humvees, and another monotonous ride through the dark began. Ethan got into the backseat of the nearest Humvee and didn't even notice who got in with him. In the dark, with only the glow of headlights before them he heard the other men griping about leaving the exercise. From the griping going on, it was obvious that the pain inflicted to their ego by the buzzer was an injury they would feel for some time.

"That wasn't even a legitimate training exercise. That was suicide and stupidity." He could just make out Vic speaking in the passenger seat in front of him. Vic had said very little up to now, and Ethan was surprised to hear him say something.

"Just chalk it up to Murrow trying to teach us a lesson." He recognized Casey's voice.

"Thanks, Casey. I'll make sure I increase my self-awareness tomorrow as I think about this one," Vic responded.

Casey glanced over at Vic from the driver's seat and continued, "He's trying to humble us. Show us how little we know. The old 'break 'em down, build 'em back up' routine."

"You have to admit, though, Theo telling us to 'break for the trees' was like elementary school maneuvers."

Casey laughed. "Maybe he's not taking this real serious yet. We're way better than what we did out there. Even Murrow said this is one of the best teams in this unit's history."

Vic answered, "Yeah, except the ex-con from New York. By the way what is he? On parole? Or does he go back when this is done?"

Casey shrugged. "If he comes back. Murrow hasn't had him training with a rifle, with any of our gear. Nothing! He's just supposed to tag along with us until he serves his purpose, I guess."

"And then what?" Vic asked.

"Murrow probably hasn't thought that far ahead. I guess it depends on how things go."

Vic was not satisfied. "So for now we've got dead weight on the team. Great."

"He's not dead weight, Vic. He hasn't been through the training. Give him a chance," Casey said.

Ethan had heard enough. He leaned forward. "Talk about me all you want. But if—"

"What the—! Geez, Zabad. Are you tryin' to give us heart attacks? You were so quiet, we didn't even know you were back there." Casey glanced over his shoulder. "Hey, Ethan, sorry for talkin' about you like that."

Vic jumped in. "Yeah, Ethan, I was out of line."

Ethan was surprised by the apologies but still felt defensive. "It's okay, guys. But I have done my share of fighting."

Vic was first to respond. "This is different. You don't know how to handle a gun. You don't know how to ghost your way through a forest or infiltrate a building with hostages inside. You've never done a HALO jump into enemy territory. You've—"

Ethan cut him off. "I get it. But you forget that I didn't pick this. Murrow found me." Ethan was beginning to feel his old insecurities coming back.

Vic was still not fully convinced. "Just pull your weight, okay? I shouldn't have called you dead weight, but we're talking about my brothers. These guys are my family. Everyone on this team needs to do their part."

"I can pull more than my weight. Much more. Just give

me a chance." Ethan sat back and was quiet for the remainder of their ride.

When they stopped, Ethan could see light emanating from a tent that looked to be at least fifteen feet square. He rolled and groaned out of the vehicles. The ride had stiffened him up. The sky had started to lighten a little to the east. Ethan guessed it must be close to four in the morning. Murrow stepped to the tent, held back the canvas flap, and motioned everyone in. After they had assembled around the heavy wooden table they found inside Murrow spoke.

"Your performance this morning has not been up to the standards we've set for this unit. Theo, your final decision before leaving the exercise was indefensible."

Theo snapped to attention. "Sir, whoever opposed us had—"

Murrow held up a hand. "Do I need to define 'indefensible'?"

"No, sir!"

"Good. The rest of you know what you did wrong. You were sloppy, careless, and acted like you'd been awakened at 0200. Your enthusiasm for this job had better increase. Your lives depend on it."

Cameron spoke. "With respect, sir, we had no intel, no info about our objective, no knowledge of our enemy, and no way to locate them. It was a worst-case scenario for operating in the field."

"You win the prize, Mongezi. We just performed a worst case scenario which means it can only get better from here. Havin' fun yet, Zabad?"

"Yes, sir."

"We have to be prepared for every possibility. What you just experienced was one of those possibilities. I wish I could promise perfect information on this and assure you that all will go as planned. But you and I both know that's impossible. We have a limited time, and it's unrealistic to prepare for every possibility. But I want that first exercise to serve as a reminder to you that things can and will go wrong. You all have excellent records, fine performances in the field. But it's too easy to get sloppy." He scanned the faces of the men, each of them taking it in. "Let's see what we're dealing with now."

He spread a map before them, and they all leaned in to look.

4

Ethan leaned in with the rest of the team as they scanned the map. He felt better about knowing there was more to this training exercise than a vague command about crossing a field. That whole exercise had felt more like a game than military training. He had a hard time believing that six top soldiers were taken out of the exercise within twenty minutes, leaving only himself and Robbie. Could it have been just a test for him? The conversation Vic and Casey had in the Humvee was troubling to him.

"This map shows your objectives," Murrow was saying. "Your goal is to enter this building on the northeast corner of the clearing. It is heavily guarded with at least four guards on each floor. The building has two power sources. One is this power station about two and a half kilometers from the building. The power station has two guards at the gate and another two that patrol the perimeter. The other power station is a set of generators that surround the building itself. You'll need to eliminate both sources of power before you attempt to enter the building."

"What's inside?" Theo wanted to know.

"On the bottom floor, there is a vault. You will remove its contents." Murrow pointed to another schematic, which showed an exploded view of the building's interior. "Your rendezvous point is three point two kilometers from the building in this clearing. Whether or not you are successful, there *will* be opposition to your departure."

"What is our time frame?"

Murrow looked at his watch. "It is now 0430. You need to be at the extraction point by 0800. Any other questions?"

Cameron spoke up. "What is the terrain between the power station and the building and from the building to the extraction point?"

Murrow pulled a large topographical map from under the pile that was spread out on the table and began pointing out the contours of the land and the areas that were most heavily wooded. "If you follow this path here, you'll be able to stay under cover and on low ground." His finger traced across the page. "You will have to cross this ridge here, but by that time the sun should be up strong and at your back, making it difficult for your opponents to see you." Murrow looked up at the men standing around the table. "Time's a wastin', boys. Giddy up."

Ethan was glad to see that they had some clear objectives. They exited the tent and spent the next few minutes planning their approach, and then Theo gave orders to Casey and Pits to head west. Barrett and Vic followed them into the tree line bordering the clearing. Cameron and Robbie flanked Theo and Ethan and the four of them started in the same direction as the other four. They were quiet and serious. There was a much different attitude among them than a few hours ago. Earlier they had seemed too relaxed, at ease rather than geared up for battle.

Ethan had been given a gun again along with a pistol also equipped with the MILES gear. They were also outfitted with the equipment they'd had before with the exception of the night goggles, which would have become dead weight very soon, as the sun was on its way up. As they walked, the only sound Ethan could hear was his own footsteps. His teammates walked soundlessly and cautiously. They didn't so much walk through the woods as glide through. And even in their caution, Ethan found himself breathless trying to keep up with them.

It was not as dark as before, a little gray light creeping through the trees. Theo put a hand up, telling the others to stop. Ethan assumed they were close to the first power station. Theo had taken all the headings and seemed to know exactly where he was going. Ethan crept up behind Theo and strained to see through the still-dark morning.

He could just make out the images of Casey and Pits crawling toward the two small enclosures where he assumed guards would be stationed. The power station was situated in a clearing with a good field of fire all around. The underbrush had been cleared, and there really wasn't anything in the way of cover. He could also make out the two perimeter guards.

Suddenly one of them crouched and raised his rifle toward the trees. He moved along the fence toward the guard houses, keeping his gun trained on whatever had alerted him. As he neared the part of the fence closest to Ethan and Theo, they heard a faint buzz telling the guard he'd just been shot. He knelt on the ground, out of the exercise. Ethan realized that Barrett and Vic must have circled the clearing to get a near silent approach with their silenced weapon.

As the first guard knelt on the ground, Casey and Pits

sprang up and sprinted toward the two enclosures. Shots rang sharply in the early morning, and Ethan saw fire bursts from within the enclosure. The guards were firing only to be cut short as Casey fired a few shots into the small building. Pits was crouched outside the second enclosure, and Ethan saw his blurry image leap through one of the windows just before the bursts of fire from that enclosure were silenced.

The second perimeter guard came sprinting from the far side of the clearing and began firing at the small buildings, knowing there were enemies inside. His bravery quickly turned to foolishness as Cameron and Theo opened fire on him from the tree line.

Robbie ran forward from the trees and laid an explosive charge at the gate enclosing the transformers. Though the training explosives went off with a minor bang they had little real-life impact, but they provided the noise and the valuable timing information the team needed to plan each step of a mission.

Next he went inside laying charges at the transformers which led to another small blast indicating they had been destroyed, like a distant crack of thunder during a storm. And then the woods were silent again.

Theo gave a command over the com link. "We have just over two kilometers to the building. Same formation. No one moves until we're all in place. Let's go." Theo led Ethan, Robbie, and Cameron away from the clearing. Mere minutes had passed since they first arrived. The ghostlike movement through the woods resumed, and Ethan again was hard pressed to keep up.

How far is a kilometer? Ethan asked himself. He was never good at math, and metrics perplexed him.

"Ethan, keep up."

The quiet voice in his radio was Theo. Ethan realized he was falling behind. He quickened his pace but couldn't seem to move as quietly as his teammates. There was more gray than black now, and a morning mist was rising. The air was humid, and he could feel beads of sweat forming on the back of his neck. They maintained their pace for a few more minutes. Finally, Theo held up his hand and pointed Robbie and Cameron to positions about ten yards to the left and right.

"All positions—report."

"Casey and Pits in position."

"Barrett and Vic in position."

"All right. Let's move."

They were again at the edge of a clearing with a large brick building in the center. This was the building Murrow had shown him not long ago.

Ethan had not noticed the four generators positioned at the corners of the building about thirty feet away. Each one was on a slab of concrete, and over it was a steel box to protect it from gunfire, the elements, and saboteurs. The only way to destroy it was by announcing their presence to everyone in the vicinity with a very large explosion.

Robbie crawled to the base of the first generator. In the growing light, Ethan could make out a steel box about three feet square. The cover for the generator. Robbie placed one of his charges at the base of the box, but when he touched the box itself, his MILES gear buzzed telling him he'd just been killed.

"What the..." The radio in Ethan's ear came to life as four or five voices fought to be heard.

"What just happened?"

"Did you hear a gun shot?"

"Robbie, do you read me? What happened?" Theo's

questions went unanswered. Ten seconds of silence passed. Then quietly Theo spoke, "All right, we have a man down. Vic, I want you to go to him and assess his condition. Barrett, maintain your position. Casey, I—"

Whatever Theo was going to say was forgotten as gunfire erupted from two of the upper windows of the brick building. Had the shots been real, they would have torn through the leaves above Ethan, Theo, and Cameron.

"Get down, Ethan!" Theo screamed.

Ethan didn't realize he hadn't ducked at the first clatter of gunfire. He was too busy thinking. He shouted, "Theo, when Robbie touched that generator, he must have set off an alarm of some kind."

Theo agreed. "Yeah, that would mean the system registered the contact he made with the box. That's the only way our opponents would know to open fire on it and the tree line."

"It's a simulation. If Robbie's MILES gear was triggered, it's telling us these boxes have an electrical charge," Cameron suggested.

Theo spoke over the radio. "Vic, are you on your way?"

"I'm just past the edge of the clearing, probably twenty feet from him now."

"Well, get there. Now's our chance. We're losing the cover of darkness. When that sun comes up, whoever is shooting is going to have a much better chance at us." Theo turned to Ethan and smiled. "Is today your first time being shot at?"

"Would it surprise you if I said no?"

"Yeah, it would. You got a target on your back or something?"

"Most of my life."

"I have yet to see why."

"Be patient."

Vic checked in. "Theo, I'm with Robbie. His MILES readout says he would have sustained a high voltage shock and wouldn't be conscious if this were the real deal. That must have been a huge amount of electricity."

The MILES gear enabled teammates to assess the type of injury sustained and the medical condition so on field medics would be able to simulate treatment.

"Do we still have voltage?" Theo pressed.

"There's no way to tell." Vic reported back. He took his hand off the box. "My guess is that we have a piggy back circuit, each generator providing power for the security of the one next to it."

"Can you get him clear and blow the charge?" Theo wanted to know.

"You're talking to Vic here."

"Clock is ticking," Theo said. "Get it done. There are three more of these things around the building. Casey, you and Pits get to work on the other side. We want to blow these simultaneously."

Ethan saw Vic get his arms under Robbie, who was half again his size. After thirty tense seconds, Vic came through breathlessly on the headset.

"Robbie is clear. I need to set the timer on that charge."

"Good. Off you go. All right, Ethan, let's you and me and Cameron take a walk to the far side of this place."

They crouched low and made their way around.

"Cameron, the last generator is yours," Theo reminded him.

"Yes, sir." Cameron slid his way to the box covering the last generator. He removed the charge from his pack and placed it at the base of the box. Suddenly gunfire again exploded from the upper and lower windows, forcing Ethan and Theo to duck. They must have caught a glimpse of Cameron from the upper windows. They heard Cameron's MILES gear register several hits.

"We have another man down. Vic, where are you?" Theo demanded.

"Getting clear. We're about to have fireworks!" Vic informed him.

True to his word, Ethan's ears filled with the now familiar sound of the charges being detonated. That told him that three of the four generators had been disabled.

Theo was immediately on the radio. "Do not advance! Hold your positions! We have one generator still active."

The minor explosions had rattled Ethan, shaking something deep inside him, a feeling he'd known all his life. It was a call to action, not verbal, unmistakable. He'd never defined it. 'It' was as specific a name as he could give it. It rushed through him, and he felt energized, alert, as if his senses were taking in everything all at once. Yet he could separate everything, the important from the unimportant. And right now, this mission was important.

Ethan couldn't stop himself. He turned to Theo and said, "I have to do this." He sprinted to Cameron, pulled him back from the generator box about two feet and grabbed the charge. He tossed it away.

The gunfire intensified, and Ethan knew sooner or later he would hear the buzz telling him he was dead. The steel box offered some protection from this threat. It was that box he grabbed; he lifted it off with one hand and laid it on its side as a shield of sorts. He had exposed the generator underneath.

Without a moment's hesitation, he lifted the entire generator unit from the ground. The wires leading to the house snapped as the generator tore away from its concrete slab. He raised it over his head and threw it at the house. It connected with the corner of the house and created a large opening in the brick wall. He had just ducked back down behind his shield and drew Cameron inside next to him when he heard, "Let's go! Let's go!" The guns temporarily quiet, Ethan left Cameron behind the steel box. There was a hole in the corner of the house and brick strewn everywhere. Barrett, Casey, Pits, Vic, Theo, and Ethan ran into the house.

"Casey, Pits, upstairs. Barrett, Vic, clear the main floor. Ethan, with me! Let's move!" Gunshots rang out again. Theo pushed Ethan to the basement door, and Ethan kicked it open. As the doorjamb splintered with the force of the kick, gunfire came rattling up the stairs at them then stopped. The Herculean effort of throwing the generator at the house hadn't slowed him in any way. He looked down, and his pistol was in his hand. He didn't remember pulling it out of its holster. He looked across the doorway at Theo.

"Give me your pistol." He said it so plainly and so calmly, yet with a look in his eyes that made Theo pull it out and toss it the three feet across the doorway to Ethan in full view of the shooters in the basement, who began firing again. When the guns from the basement went silent, Ethan spun into the doorway, began firing into the basement, and followed his shots down the stairs. When he reached the bottom, he knew the MILES gear had put the buzz of death in someone's ears telling them the hard truth.

Ethan could hear gunfire above him and hoped the rest of the team was making progress. He holstered his gun and handed Theo's pistol back to him. "Thanks."

"Anytime," Theo said grimly. "Alright Ethan. Over here." Theo pointed to the corner Murrow had led him toward not too long ago. "We need what's in there."

"Do we have the combination?" Ethan asked, remembering the musical tones he had heard.

Theo reached up, and Ethan heard the same musical tones as before. A second later, the corner swung open for Ethan to slip through. He was glad he didn't have to break through a wall. Not that he had ever tried.

"You can open that vault, right?" Theo asked.

"I'll try."

"We don't have time for *try*. We need to get it and get out of here."

Ethan slipped down the small stairway to the location of the vault. He remembered the strength of the door and summoned his strength for one great pull. There was only one way into this safe. He thought about the things his strength had done. He had torn metal, lifted cars, moved huge stones. Just minutes ago, he had hoisted over a hundred pounds and thrown it with enough power to demolish a brick wall. But opening a vault with his bare hands? He wasn't sure. He took a deep breath and reached for the handle. He pulled hard, and to his amazement, it began to give. The door lifted from the floor. He swung it up out of the way and reached down into the vault for whatever he was supposed to retrieve as proof of his accomplishment. His hand closed around a handle. He lifted out an incredibly heavy steel briefcase. He hefted it as if to assess its weight and contents and then made his way up the stairs and out.

"Did you get it?" Theo asked.

Ethan waved the case in front of him.

"I guess you did. All right, let's go."

Ethan did not know exactly how heavy the case was, but he was sure that by the time he'd walked a few miles he'd want to put it down. He followed Theo out of the basement and onto the main floor.

Around the perimeter of the building, he could see the rest of the team minus Cameron and Robbie spread out and scanning the wooded clearing.

"Ethan, go get Robbie and Cameron. You'll carry them out of this mess."

"And what about this?" Ethan asked, gesturing to the case.

"Barrett will handle it."

As Ethan made his way through the hole in the wall of the house, he saw Barrett try to heft the steel briefcase. He wasn't sure which task would be harder. Hauling two men out of a combat zone or carrying that case. He ran to the steel box where he'd left Cameron.

Although the MILES gear was all electronic and similar to a high tech game of laser tag, the soldiers were obligated to act out the extent of their injury for the benefit of the remaining team members. As Ethan leaned over to pick Cameron up, he discerned a stifled smile on the face of the young soldier. He put him over his left shoulder and walked briskly to the point on the clearing where Vic had put Robbie. Ethan laughed at the thought of picking him up, imagining the much bigger soldier draped over his shoulder with his hands and feet still dragging along the ground.

He reached Robbie and managed to get him up and over his right shoulder. He thought about the 3.2 kilometers they needed to cover to get to the end of this mission. It seemed a long way with two men on his shoulders.

Theo came in on the radio. "Ethan, do you have Cameron and Robbie?"

Ethan tilted his head slightly and pressed his ear into

Robbie's side to engage his headset radio. "Yeah, I've got 'em. Where do I go?"

"Meet back at the generator you trashed, and we'll head west," Theo instructed.

The team cautiously gathered near the remains of the steel box, and Theo instructed them about their return trip.

"We need to stay under cover as much as possible. All we know is that our extraction may be opposed. We don't know how or by how many. Casey, you need to stay on Ethan at all times. He needs to make it back with those two. Let's move."

They left the clearing by the house at a good clip and entered the woods. The ground sloped away and led them to a shallow ravine whose bottom held a small stream of water. They splashed in and out of the skinny creek all the while watching for movement along the top of the ravine. Coming up out of the ravine, they followed a low wooded ridge. The trees gradually thinned, and they found themselves in a clearing about three hundred yards across.

"Well," Theo said, "we've got the sun to our backs. It may be low enough to blind anyone watching from the west. Let's move a little to the south and see if we can get some cover. Between that and the sun, we may be okay.

Ethan glanced to the south and saw that there was some low brush in the field. They moved along the end of the ridge and down into the clearing. The brush, four feet tall in places, provided Ethan and his two-man burden with a small measure of security. He was the only member of the team that couldn't effectively crouch down. As they neared the other side of the clearing Theo turned and asked, "Are you okay carrying them?"

"I'm fine. How much farther?"

"About a mile and a quarter. Let's keep moving."

Theo turned and took one step before gunfire burst from the trees in front of them. The team dropped as one man, including Ethan, who managed to get Cameron and Robbie to the ground without treating them like sacks of potatoes.

"Anybody hit?" Theo inquired over the sound of gun bursts.

"Not yet," Vic replied, clearly not pleased with this new development.

Theo spoke with determination. "It's only a matter of time before they circle around us. We need to move. Now!" He continued, "Back about thirty yards there was a long slope leading south. We could back away down that slope and get into the woods on the south side of this clearing. It will add time to our trip, but we might be able to either avoid this engagement altogether or at least get into a better defensive position."

Pits spoke up. "Theo, I can get into this tree line. I can mess those guys up."

Calmly, Theo replied, "I'm sure you could, Pits, but we don't know how many there are. Or where they are."

Vic pushed back. "I'll go with him. I don't think we have time to back away anyway. We're pushing it as it is."

That was the last thing Ethan heard as he slowly backed into the brush away from the team. He had decided to take the decision out of their hands.

This was new for Ethan. Always in the past, his overwhelming desire to act, to move something or someone, came from anger. The last few hours had brought him a new motivation. Neither fear nor discomfort, nor his parents' sentimental references to something abstract and obscure, it seemed more like a sense of purpose. He had a reason to use his strength. This was something he could understand. Eliminate the enemy. Complete the objective.

He hadn't intended to desert the team, but he knew if he said anything about going it alone, they would object that he should leave it to professionals. So Ethan formed a plan of his own.

He worked his way through the tall grass and brush in a northwest trajectory. He realized that to the north there was less cover, but that was the very reason he'd chosen this direction. Whoever was opposing them in the tree line was not likely to waste time on such an obvious approach.

Ethan sensed a change taking place in his body, his psyche. He had started the day uncomfortable, nervous, out of breath. Since the moment he lifted that generator from its moorings he was a different man. He felt it now as he snaked his way through the grass. There was something instinctual about what he was doing now. He knew what he would do when he reached the trees. He could see himself doing it in his mind's eye. The problem was that somewhere underneath it all he wondered if it were humanly possible.

He crawled to the shelter of a wide elm tree. Looking back, he guessed that the rest of the team was under cover. They were nowhere to be seen. He counted slowly to three, perhaps for his own benefit, and then turned and ran into the trees. As soon as he started running he began hearing the pops of gunfire as the blanks and their lasers tried to find a bead somewhere on his body.

So far so good. He ran until the gunfire was well behind him and then he turned hard left, deeper into the trees. He thought that if he had calculated correctly he was now directly behind the men opposing them in the trees.

He made his way slowly through the mist still hanging in the thickest parts of the forest. He was trying desperately to be quiet. He stepped around a cluster of underbrush and saw his first target, a soldier in camouflage with some brush tucked in his helmet and clothes to conceal his location. His back was to Ethan, and he was peering in the direction Ethan had been just moments ago. Four or five big steps and he would be upon him. He tried to remember the conversation he'd had with Robbie a few hours ago about how to eliminate an enemy in close quarters with the MILES gear. He quickly reviewed what Robbie had told him and planned his approach.

Ethan sprang out from behind his sparse cover and crossed the distance to his opponent quickly, before he could react, and punched the man's buzzer mechanism. It worked. So this would be it. Tree to tree. Ethan made his way closer to Theo and the others. His radio sparked to life.

"Ethan. What do you think you're doing in there?"

"Making life easier for you," Ethan whispered. "One down, and I'd say two or three to go."

"You will rejoin us now." Theo's order sounded final.

Ethan had no words. Apparently he was wanted for the grunt work, but when it came to actual combat, he was supposed to take a back seat. But he was doing something that felt so natural right now that there was no way he could stop. He ignored the radio and hurtled along.

Five minutes later Theo, Barrett, Vic, Pits, and Casey watched Ethan stroll casually out of the trees toward them.

"Sorry it took me a little longer. I had some business."

Theo glared at Ethan. "I thought you and I were going to get along."

"That's still up to you, Theo. Now if you'll excuse me I have over four hundred pounds to carry for the next mile."

Theo turned away abruptly without a word. The next mile was through the very same trees Ethan had walked just minutes ago, now clear of gun-wielding opponents. They encountered no other resistance and arrived at the extraction point with very little time to spare. Murrow was waiting for them.

"Well done, gentlemen. You not only made it with the team intact, aside from some injuries, but you also completed all of your objectives. You have until 1600 to rest and then we will meet to debrief this exercise." The men who had driven the team's Humvees to the site joined Murrow as he strode to his waiting vehicle and drove down a wooded two-track road.

As Murrow was leaving Ethan finally set Robbie and Cameron down. "How much do you weigh anyhow?"

"I'm only one eighty-five."

"Not you, Cameron. Him." Ethan gestured to Robbie.

"Hey, you could have dragged me," Robbie protested.

"I wouldn't want to dirty your uniform."

Robbie laughed. "You've got a lot of nerve, Zabad."

Ethan just smiled back.

Theo stepped up behind Ethan and spoke angrily. "A little too much. You were out of line, Ethan. Way out of line."

Ethan turned to face Theo. "I thought this was a team. Do you want my help?"

"I want compliance. Not some renegade who endangers others."

Ethan bristled. "I did everything you asked me to do out there. Everything."

"Except stay with the team," Theo countered.

Ethan was not finished. "I saved your butt out there. You were pinned down, and you know it."

"We were forming a plan! And you bailed out. Playing the hero!"

"We just made it here in time. If I hadn't done what I did, we would never have made it back in time," Ethan reasoned.

Theo straightened and looked down at Ethan. "You will back off, or I will be forced to take action."

Quietly and with an even tone, Ethan replied, "Take action, Theo. Go ahead."

Several seconds of silence followed as Ethan and Theo stared at one another. Casey broke the silence. "C'mon, guys. We just need a good breakfast. That's all. A little bacon and eggs, some cornbread, maybe some fried potatoes."

Theo continued to stare at Ethan. "Yeah. That sounds good, Casey. Let's eat. And maybe next time you'll keep a closer eye on him." He broke his gaze and walked toward the other Humvees waiting to be driven back to base.

Robbie slapped Ethan on the back. "Ethan, c'mon. Let's go. We can't be doin' this. You have to find a way to get along with him. He's the team leader, and that's not going to change."

"I understand why you have to say that, Robbie. But there are things about me you don't understand."

"Like what?"

"Like the fact I can count the people I've gotten along with in life on one hand."

"And whose fault is that?"

Ethan swallowed hard and set his jaw.

"Let's get back to base. You need a shower anyway."

Ethan shook his head and as strange as it seemed, reminded himself to add Robbie to the very short list of people he considered friends.

5

Any reasonable person would understand that after half the night spent trekking through the woods, no one wants to do more than just relax. Wade Murrow was not a reasonable person.

"Sixteen hundred. That's this afternoon right?"

"Yeah, Ethan." Robbie was finishing his third helping of pancakes. Most of them had been pilfered from his teammates plates.

"That means I've only got six hours to sleep, max."

"Are you an old man or something? You need your eight hours every night?"

"No. I'm just not used being up at two in the morning."

"How old are you anyway?"

"Twenty-eight. Why?"

"Twenty-eight? Hm. Just wondering." Robbie answered, a little too casually.

"Just wondering what?"

"Nothin' man. Nothin'."

"No, what?" Ethan insisted.

"I thought you were younger," Robbie admitted.

"I don't have a baby face, so what made you think I was younger?"

"You just don't seem settled. Like you're not comfortable. Or maybe confident is a better word."

"Robbie, I already visited the base psychologist. He's doing a fine job."

"C'mon man, I'm just saying you got a lotta anger or somethin'. You don't just sit back and let people do their thing."

"Because people have been 'doing their thing' all my life, and it usually ends with a fight."

"That's what I'm sayin'. Just let it go. You don't have to let people do that to you anymore. When you let 'em rile you up, they're in control. See I'm a big boy, so a lot a guys think they've got to prove somethin' to me. To themselves more like. I don't pay any attention to 'em. By now they've learned they're wasting their time."

"I can't do that. Something inside me won't let me." Ethan lowered his head and shook it slowly. "I'm going to get a few hours of sleep. Later, Robbie." He pushed back from the table and walked back to his temporary home.

That "something inside" was so hard to explain. When he got angry or was motivated by some great cause, he would feel something deep inside and something pressing on him from the outside at the same time. The inside felt like a rush of adrenaline. Ethan had never done drugs, but he imagined it must be a similar feeling—actually feeling something powerful running through your veins. The feeling on the outside was hard to describe. It was almost as if some invisible force had clapped armor on his limbs and chest. With both the feelings on the outside of his body and the inside, Ethan felt indestructible.

He slept hard, and 1600 came quickly. Several things became clear to him at the debriefing. First, Theo would not be the friend Ethan thought he would be. A leader yes. But not a friend. Second, he realized that the first exercise had been merely a set up. Deep down, Ethan had known, but now he felt stupid for any satisfaction he'd felt at the time. Third, in spite of Theo's protests, Murrow was pleased with Ethan's flanking maneuver in the woods. He also learned that other members of the team were impressed as well. They gathered in Murrow's office.

"Ethan. I don't know how else to say this. After watching the video footage and viewing the MILES read-outs, I see you as a natural soldier."

Video footage? That was news to Ethan. "Half the time, I didn't even know what I was doing," he admitted.

"How many men did you eliminate in the brick house?"

"Maybe one?" Ethan ventured.

"Six."

"Six? I remember one guy in the basement but..."

"You shot three when you entered the house. Three more in the basement."

Ethan vaguely remembered reaching the basement door and finding his pistol already in his hand. But firing it at three people? And the basement? He remembered thinking about someone taking a hit but couldn't recall seeing anyone after he went down the stairs.

"Ethan, we have this entire exercise recorded on computer. The laser shots tell us who fired and when and where the target was hit. All six of your shots were to the head. Instant kills."

"I've never really shot a gun before."

"We gave you one for the exercise but didn't expect you to use it so effectively. We'll spend some time on the firing range. Get you using some other weapons." He paused as if unsure about continuing. "About the generator."

Ethan began to protest. "I know I wasn't supposed to do that. I just reacted."

Murrow ignored the comment. "Are you aware of how much that generator weighed? Close to three hundred pounds. You threw it a good distance with enough velocity to demolish a brick wall. Is there anything you can't move?"

"I'll only know if I try everything."

Ethan was amazed as he left the debriefing in Murrow's office. His skill with a weapon was a new development in his abilities. But then, he'd been discovering things all along.

It was with less trepidation that he approached the office of Dr. Remont the day after the briefing. He had been put enough at ease in his first session to know that Remont was not out to evaluate and probe Ethan's brain. He was just there to listen.

"Ethan, good to see you. Have a seat." While Ethan sat down, Remont flipped open a manila folder and scanned its contents for no more than five seconds then flipped it onto his desk. "Had a busy few days?"

"Training. Until yesterday I had never really handled a gun."

"And?"

"And I guess I handle one pretty well, but I can't figure out how."

"Based on our last conversation, there are quite a few things you can do well. You had a theory as to how they were possible."

Ethan was trying to remember how much he'd told Remont. "I told you about my parents. Their crazy ideas about hearing from God."

"You never really told me whether you believed them or not. Are they still living?"

Emotion swelled in Ethan's chest. "Yes. But I haven't talked to them in years."

"Why not?"

"You have my file. You can read."

"Ethan, I—"

"When I went to prison, I knew they wouldn't want to see me again. I—I destroyed their precious dream of doing something great, something special with my life."

"How do you know they feel this way?"

Ethan stared at his feet. He remembered the day of the sentencing, the look in his parents' eyes. It had ruined them. They left with brokenness etched on their faces and carved in the slump of their shoulders. Even their tears as he was led away spoke more to the death of their dream than the loss of his freedom. "They never said it. I just know."

"Did they attempt to visit you?"

"I don't know. Maybe. I was told when people wanted to visit, but I had the option to refuse it. I refused a lot of visits."

"Why would you do that, Ethan? What if it was your parents trying to talk to you? To let you know it was okay?"

"It wasn't okay. I knew that, and they knew that."

"How long has it been since you've talked to them?"

"I haven't seen them or talked to them since the day I was led out of the courtroom. That was seven years ago."

"I sensed last time we talked that you once had a good relationship with your parents. Where did that break down?"

Ethan glared back at Remont. It was not a friendly look, and it communicated that Remont had pushed a little too much. Ethan was pleased when it appeared Remont was changing his approach. "Last time we talked you shared some experiences from your childhood. What happened after you were taken out of the elementary school?"

There was a long pause as Ethan tried to decide if he really wanted to continue. "I told you I was schooled at home for a while. By the time I reached high school, I felt like I was ready to be with other kids again. I was sure they had forgotten me."

He remembered swinging open the high school's front door and walking purposefully toward the main office. It was his first day back. He was anticipating smooth sailing. No one would remember him. After all, he had changed in the last few years. His hair had grown to his shoulders, and he had gained a little height. Working at home had relaxed him a little, and the chip on his shoulder had decreased somewhat.

Ethan would find that his regular classes would not present much of a problem. It was time outside of class that offered the most opportunity for trouble. As a new sophomore, his locker was placed in the hall that had the most room. Senior hall. He never did anything to offer himself as a target. In fact, it would have happened to any sophomore who had their locker in that hall. Tradition is hard to break, so when a group of seniors were looking for their first target of the new year, Ethan seemed like a logical and easy choice. It was the first and last time anyone ever put Ethan Zabad into a locker. No one actually saw it happen, but everyone assumed that the locker, which had its door peeled away from every part of the frame except around the padlock, was the one he'd been in. By fifth period some students were venturing into the senior hall just to see it. The school custodians were furious and were trying to remove the padlock so they could replace the door.

Ethan had played it safe and allowed himself to be put into the locker knowing he could emerge at any time. He thought it best not to show his whole hand on the first day of school. The seniors who had done it knew what had happened, but they were not about to admit to abusing a sophomore. There were rumors about him, but nothing that could be confirmed. Ethan made it through his first day.

He managed to fly under everyone's radar until late in November. The dreaded gym class preceded by the locker room experience was Ethan's worst nightmare. If he played it safe in every sport, he came off as a wimp. Come on too strong and everyone would be afraid of him.

There was one in every locker room. "Hey, kid. What's with the hair?"

Ethan had learned not to respond to "kid."

"I'm talking to you! Are you deaf? I said what's with the hair?" Ethan felt the finger poked into his back as he crouched to tie a shoelace.

He stood and spun around. "None of your business." Ethan glared back at him in defiance.

"Ooo. Look, guys. He's giving me the evil eye. I'm *so* scared."

Interactions like this were a waste of Ethan's time. He began to leave the locker room to go to the gym. He only heard a snatch of the conversation behind him, and it wasn't good.

That day was basketball. The class was divided into

groups of five, and teams played three on three, rotating teammates in and out. As luck would have it, Ethan's team was up against his locker room antagonists first. Though Ethan didn't hear their plans in the locker room he soon discovered what they were. He was slapped, pushed, knocked down, and in general abused as he tried to play the game. If they were looking for a fight they were dealing with an unwilling participant. Ethan had determined he would not react the way he had in grade school. Instead, he played harder. He began to channel his energy to the ball and the game. He ran faster, jumped higher, and shot more accurately. This had the effect of enraging his opponents, who stepped up their efforts to stop him. Finally, Ethan's armor cracked just a little. He had possession of the ball, and so he leapt up over the heads of his antagonists and slammed the ball through the hoop. In the process he tore the rim from the back board and brought it crashing to the floor.

The whole gym fell silent as they stared at the aftermath of Ethan's slam-dunk. Dust hung in the air where the bolts holding the rim had torn through the thick plywood backboard. For all intents and purposes, class was over. This was one affair that couldn't be brushed off. Word got around that Ethan Zabad, the sophomore, could play ball and dunk like Michael Jordan. There were a few kids who connected the locker incident and the basketball hoop to form an opinion of Ethan. But most were just in awe over the strength it must have taken to tear the rim down, let alone the fact that he had jumped that high.

For a couple more months, Ethan was able to go to school without being teased. In fact, his tearing down of the rim had earned him some respect. His personality had some catching up to do with his new reputation. He was not very personable and home schooling for several years enhanced the gap between the two. Some people read him as cold or aloof. In reality it was introversion and fear of rejection. But he watched people. He wasn't blind, and he certainly wasn't afraid. He learned much by watching. That's how he started a high-school-long rivalry with several gang members.

The kid had been approached by a gang. He was a good kid, working hard, trying to stay out of trouble. He wanted nothing to do with a gang. Still, a few gang members attended school, not to learn but for the sake of their drug business, and they decided to make life hard for him until he gave in. When the few gang members who still attended school started harassing him they made it look like practical jokes—typical lunchroom pranks. Trip the freshman and make him spill his lunch. The mistake the pranksters made was doing it to the freshman walking in front of Ethan. Ethan typically tried to turn away from others being teased and contented himself with the fact that it wasn't him. As long as someone else was taking abuse, he didn't have to. But today was different. After the freshman hit the floor, he turned over and looked up at Ethan. His lunch was scattered on the floor and the front of his shirt. It wasn't the mess though. It was the look in the other student's eyes. It pled with Ethan to do something.

Ethan had thought of his strength as a curse for so long that he never considered using it for something noble. But if there was a time to use it that way, it was now. He turned to the student who had caused the freshman to fall. He spoke slowly and with a low voice.

"You owe him an apology. And you should help him clean up the mess."

The student to whom Ethan spoke stood from the table

and looked down from about six feet. "I don't think you should be telling anyone what to do."

"You owe him an apology. Right now."

"You gonna make me?"

"If I have to."

"You mess wit me, you have to mess wit all of us."

Around the lunchroom four more guys stood up and started walking toward Ethan.

"What's going on here?" A teacher finally saw a problem developing and attempted to defuse it. In a city school, it was easier to just ignore it.

"Nothing, Mr. Dodd. This kid just tripped," the ring-leader said while eyeing the freshman nearby. "Right?"

Ethan was ready. "Liar. You tripped him."

"You calling me a liar?"

"Are you deaf?" Ethan had no tolerance for stupidity. A shoddy intellect angered him. [This sentence is repetitive after the one before it.] Clearly this guy didn't know how to respond to such a blatant challenge.

"Guys, I'm sure this is just a misunderstanding. Let it go," Mr. Dodd encouraged.

"Mr. Dodd. You have no idea what happened," Ethan pleaded.

"I know I don't want a problem in this lunchroom. Now finish eating. And you...what's your name?"

"Ethan."

"Ethan, you can help this student clean up this mess." Mr. Dodd took the cowardly route of asking Ethan, the new kid, instead of the known troublemakers to help out.

"I hope you're a fast runner, kid," the gang leader warned, "'cause if not, there's gonna be a beatin' after school."

Yeah, for you, Ethan thought.

As he left school that day, sure enough, about twelve gang members had gathered to see him home. It was the first of many "escorts" he received in high school. They all ended the same as that first one. For some reason, all twelve of those guys were limping either at school or in the neighborhood. There was not one visible mark on them. They just couldn't seem to walk without heavily favoring one leg or the other. It was easier to blame it on clumsiness than on a skinny Jewish kid. But this never stopped them from trying to catch Ethan off guard. Throughout the next couple years various members of that gang ended up draped over weightlifting equipment, piled in dumpsters, or laid out on the school steps and in the bleachers at the athletic field.

At different times, they would bring along a ringer. Someone who boxed or some kid who fancied himself to be a karate expert. There wasn't a punch Ethan couldn't take or a submission hold he couldn't break. It didn't mean it didn't hurt and he didn't limp a little himself, but he was able to bounce back quickly and absorb a lot more punishment than other boys. The only time he considered ending the feud was when gunshots were fired and bullets struck a wall near where Ethan was walking. He ran, truly frightened for the first time.

Even while being harassed by the gang, Ethan was able to garner some respect among the downtrodden at school. They began to see him as a leader, someone who could stand up to the bullying they had received for years. It was not a mantle Ethan was entirely comfortable with. While there was a moment of nobility when he defended that kid in the cafeteria, he wasn't sure he wanted to be crowned king of the nerds, though they were certainly willing. Ethan's plan for survival was to lay low and avoid getting to know people too much, people who would ask questions.

But a day came when respect turned to fear and Ethan never had to worry about people asking questions. It was the only time he'd really lost his temper in high school. It closely mirrored his experience in grade school, and it frightened him to know the kind of power he possessed when he was angry, especially when the anger was over injustice. When Simon, a weak, underdeveloped freshman was thrown out of the locker room and into the hallway, naked, Ethan, now a senior, couldn't contain himself. He felt power coursing through him and knew he had to act.

His first move was to tear off the inside handle of the locker room door so no one could escape—unless he wanted them to. He stormed through the locker room to find the offenders. They slipped around the end of one row of lockers and ran for the door.

Without a handle they were reduced to pounding and yelling. Ethan heard them and smiled when he realized a crowd would be gathering. The poor freshman by now had likely been rescued by a compassionate teacher. He marched to the door and grabbed them both. He didn't hurt them. He just ripped their clothes from them and grabbed them by the hair on the crown of their heads. Their clothes were torn beyond use. He leaned back and used his foot to kick *out* the steel locker room door, which was normally a door that swung *in*. Two blows from his foot broke the door loose, sending it to the hallway floor. He deposited the two naked bullies onto the hallway floor and stood guard in the now empty doorway. Sure enough a crowd had gathered, but rather than use the opportunity provided by Ethan to mock the persecutors, they looked at the door and at Ethan in shock until administrators came and shooed them away. Not exactly what Ethan had anticipated.

Ethan, Simon the freshman, and the two bullies, now

dressed in lost-and-found rejects, were summoned to the principal's office. A familiar scenario played out. The bullies were given an in-school suspension for their cruel joke. Ethan was expelled. With only two more months of school, there couldn't have been a more unjust response.

After dismissing the other students, the principal had pulled a manila folder from his file cabinet. He flipped it open to what Ethan could only assume was a report from his former grade school. "Ethan, you've been a good student. But I fear for the safety of our other students. I suggest you finish your schooling some other way. There have been other incidents I've overlooked, but I'm afraid I can't overlook this one."

"So high school wasn't a great experience for me," Ethan concluded.

"But for a time you had the respect and admiration of your classmates."

"Dr. Remont. Respect and admiration gained by fear are worthless. I want the respect of others because of who I am, not just what I can do."

"Ethan. You've been given a great gift. Something you can use for the betterment of others." He paused. "Have you ever considered using your gifts in a public way?"

"What like as a cop or something?"

"Perhaps. Or maybe just as someone who helps others when it's needed."

"I can't fly. I don't have super hearing or spidey-sense if that's what you're suggesting. And I'm pretty sure vigilante justice is frowned on these days."

"I think there are people who could put your gifts to work in very practical ways."

"Like who? And what?"

"We'll talk about that later. I just can't believe you've been given this ability so you can join the army."

"Maybe there's more going on here than either of us can see. But until I know that for sure, this is where I am, and this is what I'm doing.

"Fair enough. But will you consider what I've said?"

"Yeah. But I still don't know what you have in mind."

"Let me work on that. You leave for assignment early next week. Come and see me as soon as you get back. I may have something for you."

"If I come back at all."

The next few days went quickly. Ethan proved easy to train with all the weapons the army could provide him with. The mission became more and more clear in Ethan's mind. What they were doing was essential to the safety and stability of the world. They needed to succeed.

[6]

He sat on the plane staring out the window. One thing he was grateful for was he didn't have to jump out of the airplane he was riding on. With a US presence in Afghanistan for some time now, there was no need to proceed with stealth. Though the war in Iraq was over, there were still terrorist elements in Afghanistan that needed to be dealt with. What Ethan didn't understand was how something like this Cultus organization could have sprung up under the noses of US and coalition forces. If it was operating in Afghanistan, why could the military forces already there not handle it? Most of the questions Ethan had during his brief training about the mission never got answered, just as most of the questions he had about himself and his own life's mission never got answered either. If it was something the marines on the ground could handle, they wouldn't have recruited him out of prison. As far as Ethan could see, there was only one reason he was along—a vault in the sub-basement of a brick house somewhere in the northeast corner of Afghanistan.

They touched down early on a Saturday morning in Kabul. They still had a long drive ahead of them. They were supposed to meet an Afghan in the city of Kunduz who would lead them to a building where they could prepare. It was from that location they would make final preparations to assault the brick house that had begun to invade Ethan's dreams. It was located near a river about thirty-five miles northeast of the city. From the house they would hike to the river for a pickup as they would most likely be under fire by that time. The original plan to make for the mountains was abandoned in favor of the quick getaway afforded by the body of water so close by. The most difficult part of the mission would be getting through the mountainous region that started near Kunduz and extended east into the narrow tongue of land that was surrounded by neighboring countries. To pass over almost thirty miles of rugged terrain would be a challenge, especially if Cultus had any kind of security, which they were sure to have.

The building they were prepping in was perfect. While Kunduz was only a city of about fifty thousand there were plenty of good, out-of-the-way buildings where no one would get suspicious. Within one such building, unless a person walked to the center and explored the abandoned office area, he would never see the interior room that was home to the team now readying their assault.

"Hey, Ethan. Look alive." Casey tossed something Ethan's way.

Ethan grunted as the weapon Casey had tossed landed squarely on his stomach.

"Let me see you break that down," Casey suggested.

"I've only done this fifty times, Casey," Ethan groaned.

"Do it fifty-one. I just want to make sure we cover all our bases."

Ethan had been grilled all the way over. It was understandable since he was the only one, technically, who could fully complete the mission. He had to know what he was doing.

Theo spoke up. "All right, gentlemen. It's time to sleep. We leave at sundown." Theo's attitude had been a bit cool toward Ethan since their confrontation during training. At least it was kept on a professional level. Theo was smart enough not to disrupt whatever chemistry this team had developed on short notice.

Ethan knew before he ever lay down that he would not be able to sleep today. Being in an interior room allowed him to forget what time of day it actually was. Along with his internal clock being messed up from the flight, he should have been exhausted. Instead he was kept awake by a gnawing in his soul. It had started in prison and been growing ever since. He was told to expect that he could die during this mission. That was obvious considering the danger, but something other than common sense and Wade Murrow was telling him to be prepared. It was something Ethan couldn't define. And the more he thought about possible death, the more he thought about his life. What had he accomplished in twenty-eight years? Had he done anything of value? He thought of his failures since high school, the fights, the pain he'd caused, the wasted years in prison. But this was his chance to redeem himself. Maybe he could go back to his parents with something that would make them proud. A medal. A commendation. Of course they weren't allowed to know what he was doing right now. But maybe someday they would know and they would be proud.

It seemed just minutes later Theo was quietly speaking to the team. "Rise and shine, boys. We have work to do." In a short while, the team was ready to board the nondescript van that would take them to their starting point. They would cover most of the distance between Kunduz and the house by van and then walk the rest under cover of darkness. The goal was to complete the mission before daybreak, allowing them to withdraw unseen. As they rode in the van they briefly reviewed the steps of their mission.

The simple version was, get inside the house and get out in a hurry. The complicated version involved technical terms and gadgets that Ethan had no idea how to use. The one that intrigued him the most was the one Pitts used to detect body heat inside the building. It would allow them to know where people were before they went inside. Once they had gotten inside, they needed to get into the basement, download the program components of Cultus's theft program, and then destroy the computer. In less than an hour, it would be Ethan's chance to save the world.

"What are you doing, Robbie?" Ethan noticed Robbie with his head down.

"Praying."

Ethan shook his head. "Waste of time."

"Don't believe in prayer?"

"Don't believe in who you're praying to."

"Aren't you—"

"Jewish? Yeah. But I haven't seen much of God in my life."

"What happens if you meet Him today?"

"I don't plan on ever meeting Him. And if He's actually there, He probably wouldn't want to meet me."

Robbie looked at Ethan for a few seconds as if trying to read his mind. "I'll pray for you, Ethan."

Ethan glanced up at Robbie and saw that he was sincere. Prayer or no prayer, he felt they would need something extra if they were to survive the morning.

Their first stop was the power station. They crept toward the clearing where the power plant was located. They had made the last few miles in under an hour after leaving the van on the side of the mountainous road behind some large boulders. It was quiet. A gentle breeze cooled them after their run from the van, and the moon shone intermittently through slow moving clouds. So far so good. Actually being in the remote location helped Ethan to understand why there was a need for a mini power plant like this one and the generators. There was nothing of consequence—not for miles. Cultus had chosen well.

They easily disabled the power generators since, contrary to their training, there were no personnel at the site. They quickly covered the distance between their first and second targets, the latter being the house and its contents. As they approached, everything about the house and its generators looked exactly like the last satellite photos. Any change would have been reason to believe they were expected. They split up in pairs and began the work of disabling the generators.

Ethan lay on his stomach, peering across the clearing and trying to see the rest of the team. Since they'd arrived on the site, he'd begun feeling uneasy—like something wasn't quite right. It was so quiet and still. The guards they'd expected to face were not there, and the security measures they'd been sure would be obvious were not.

Theo gave the signal, and all four generators detonated. The moldable plastic explosive they were using was designed to work quietly. Its blast was to act as a wide knife, slicing the generator cover and its connection from the concrete slab it sat upon. This happened in synchronization as planned, and as one man, the team ran toward the brick house, except for Barton and Pits. They would make sure the perimeter of the clearing remained quiet.

They entered the house expecting bursts of gunfire. Nothing. Ethan began to wonder if Cultus had just moved the computer and the vault to another location. After all, why would they leave it in a place that was now known to their enemies unless they had supreme confidence in its protection, its security? Barrett and Pits held their positions outside on the perimeter of the clearing. Leaving Casey, Cameron, and Vic on the main level, Theo, Robbie, and Ethan descended the basement stairs. As they set foot on the basement floor, they heard it.

"We've got company! From the southeast. About a dozen men." Barrett provided the warning on the radio.

"Barrett, any vehicles?" Theo asked.

"Negative. But we now have about a dozen more men coming in from the northeast."

"Barrett, Pits, you need to hold open the east end of that clearing. Give us five minutes."

"Yes, sir!"

"Ethan, can you do this in five minutes?" Theo was checking his watch.

"There's only one way to find out," Ethan replied.

Shots began to ring out over their heads as Vic, Cameron, and Casey added their firepower to Barrett's and Pits's. Ethan made his way to the corner and down into the sub-room containing the vault. Robbie stood at the top of the stairway.

"How does it look?" he asked.

"Heavy." Ethan switched off the communication link in his ear so he wouldn't be distracted. He bent down and grabbed the cold steel of the vault's exterior. He concentrated his entire being on lifting its lid. He strained against it and didn't feel it move at all. Undaunted, he gripped it tighter and tried again. Nothing. Beginning to get irritated, he grabbed the vault lid and with gritted teeth jerked up on the lid. It came up almost an inch. With a dull and thick clang, it fell back into place. Now Ethan's fire was up.

"Ethan, get that vault open now! We are under heavy fire, and by God if you don't—Fall back! Get back into the tree line! Give us two more minutes. Ethan, move!" Theo was trying to talk to everyone all at once.

"Robbie, you'd better get up there. I didn't need my radio to hear that," Ethan suggested.

"All right. But I'm not leaving this house without you."

Ethan looked back at the vault lid and decided there was nothing he couldn't move. He gripped the vault lid, and with a scream he pulled with all his strength. The lid came up and swung back to lean against the wall. Ethan moved quickly to grab the frame the computer was bolted to. He pulled with one arm while the other was braced against the wall. He could hear the computer frame straining against the idle hydraulics. Suddenly it broke loose, and Ethan lifted it from the vault. He turned on his communication link and checked in. "I've got it out. I'm coming up now!"

Ethan looked at what was supposed to be the computer and wondered how he would download what they needed. It didn't look like any computer he had seen before. Instead of a panel with ports to download the necessary information, Ethan was confronted with several hundred postage-stamp-sized chips each labeled with the word Milligraf. They were sandwiched together in rows of about twelve or fifteen. Below was a small box that appeared to link all the chips together. Without taking the time to try and figure it out, he pulled all the rows of computer chips off the frame and tucked them into the duffel he carried over his shoulder. He ascended the stairs and found the basement empty. He spoke into the radio.

"Where is everybody? I'm coming up to the main level." No answer. Ethan sprinted up the stairs and immediately saw Vic. He was sprawled out on the floor. "Man down! Man down!" Ethan shouted into the radio. He ran to Vic's side to check for a vital, but after a closer look, he realized there was no need. The bullet hole under his left eye told him everything he needed to know. Gunfire rattled toward the front of the house. He crouched and made his way toward it. Robbie and Theo were back to back behind a low window.

"Vic is gone."

"I know. Right now we're trying to establish an opening on the east end of the clearing. Barrett and Pits were down there, but when two dozen Afghans, or whoever, came storming in, they backed off. They had no choice."

"Afghanis or whoever? You mean we don't even know who we're fighting?" Ethan asked.

"Could be mercenaries. Could be Cultus. Hard to say. Bullets only speak one language."

"Where's that two dozen now?" Ethan shouted as more machine gun fire blasted the window opening and showered them with dust.

"Scattered around this perimeter. Barrett, Pits, Cameron, and Casey are still out there. The last time they

109

checked in, they had fallen back toward the river to the east and were looking for a way to surprise these guys."

"So we're trapped?"

"For the time being. Did you get it?"

"It's not what we expected. Here." He opened the duffel and let Theo glance inside at the rows of computer chips.

"We're not the computer experts. We're just the deliverymen. Pack it up."

Barrett checked in. "Theo, we're on the southeast side of the clearing. There's a tank coming from the south. I repeat, a tank coming from the south."

Theo was not pleased with Barrett's report. "Where were they hiding a tank?"

Robbie added, "I may have some choice words for Murrow at the debriefing."

"No time to think about it, Robbie. Listen."

Ethan heard the low rumble of a tank through the early morning air. All of his uneasiness had by now been confirmed. All had not been as it seemed. He also knew it was his time to act.

Theo was not optimistic. "When that tank breaks the clearing, we are out of time. This house will come down."

"I can disable the tank."

Theo and Robbie didn't say anything—at first. Then suddenly Theo blurted, "Give me your duffle."

Ethan raised an eyebrow. "The computer chips?"

"Give me the duffle. That's an order." Theo made it clear that Ethan could do what he wanted, but the core of their mission would not be compromised.

"Yes, sir," Ethan said as he lifted the strap over his head and shoved it at Theo.

"I don't know what you have in mind, Ethan, but if you

think you can make a way for us to get out of here, I'm all for it." His statement was punctuated with the sound of a screaming shell blowing through brick and mortar. The explosion showered all three with debris. Robbie grabbed Ethan by the gun strap around his shoulder and drew him close.

"Go, Ethan. Go now. I'll see you at the river."

Needing no further encouragement, Ethan sprinted to the door of the house and ran toward the gap in the clearing where the tank now sat, ready to take a second shot. When he got near what was left of the disabled generators, automatic gunfire revealed enemy positions encompassing three hundred-sixty degrees of the clearing. The shots kicked up dirt around his feet, and he felt bullets slapping the air near his face. He stared straight ahead at the tank, forming his plan as he ran.

Suddenly two men rushed from behind the tank to meet him. One of them shot at Ethan, and he could feel the bullet clang off his own weapon, which he held in front of him. The force of the bullet spun him to his left, and he began to lose his balance. Somehow he stayed on his feet, and his forward momentum carried him into his attacker. They both fell to the ground side by side. Then Ethan felt the weight of the other man he had seen pile on in an attempt to subdue and of course kill him. In the split second it took for Ethan to assess his situation, he felt his strength come upon him, and he grasped with both hands, grabbing whatever was within reach.

One hand held a belt near the small of one attacker's back while the other held a gun strap. He spread his arms apart, and the man atop him fell to the side. Ethan stood and, still hanging on to them, spun around once for momentum and sent both men spinning, sprawling, soaring toward the house. In the waning moonlight mixed with the coming dawn, he saw them clear the roof. Then Ethan turned to address the tank, which by now had fired again, making the front door considerably bigger than its builders had intended. He hoped Theo and Robbie had been clear.

Everyone was nervous when approaching Rolf Gallinger, but the bearer of bad news was doubly afraid. Gallinger was known alternately for his eerie calm when discussing the most terrible of plans and his raging temper over the smallest of interruptions. This would not be a small interruption. Dormand had worked for Gallinger for three years now. He had brought bad news before but nothing that threatened a plan like this. Dormand willed his five-foot-four-inch frame down the corridor and wiped nervous sweat off of his high brow. He had started as an accountant with Gallinger's enterprises and somehow over time became his personal assistant and messenger. Gallinger may have liked him because he was so short. No attempts at intimidation. Just the facts.

"Mr. Gallinger? Sir?"

"What is it, Dormand?"

"We have communication with our vanguard in Kunduz. They followed the team of Americans, special operations, to the mainframe storage facility."

"And they were all killed?"

"We have the facility surrounded. They had no idea we were there. A group went into the house, but we are almost positive they came out empty handed. We should have the situation contained by six a.m. local time."

"Almost positive, Dormand? Why almost? We knew they were coming."

"W-w-we haven't had a chance to go into the house to see, but the security system indicates that the vault has been opened. But it must be a mistake. There's no way anyone could've opened that vault without first engaging the hydraulics. Not to mention how we made the vault lid."

Gallinger's face was red with fury. "Do we have a connection with the computer or not?"

Dormand responded with a barely perceptible nod.

"Get in contact with our men on the ground and prepare to call a meeting of our investors. They will want to know what's happening."

"I will contact them again immediately and get an up-to-the-minute report, sir."

"Do that." Dormand turned to leave but was halted by Gallinger's last command. "Do bring back good news, Dormand."

There would not be good news forthcoming. Ethan climbed atop the tank and grabbed the top hatch. If the occupants knew he was above them, they didn't act like it. He twisted the handle and lifted the lid off the tank. If it had been locked, it now mattered very little. He reached inside and grabbed the first thing he could get his hands on. A collar. He lifted the shocked man out of the tank and literally threw him into the trees. Ethan thought there might be more men inside. He decided to drop in and find out.

He discovered two men. One, the gunner, was dispatched with Ethan's swift grasp of the back of his neck and a sharp push into his gun sight. The other, a driver, was thrown up through the opening overhead. Ethan didn't see him land. After making short work of those two, he decided it was time to carve a path out of the clearing and toward the river. Having never been inside a tank, he wasn't sure how to use it. The stench inside the tank was enough to speed him toward figuring it out. Whoever had been driving the vehicle had been in it for a long time and apparently hadn't bathed.

He figured out how to swing the cannon from side to side. He aimed it at the east side of the clearing and fired a low shot toward the brush and small trees on the edge. He turned the whole tank in that direction with the intent of simply bowling over everything in his path. His intentions went unfulfilled as gunfire began raining down on the tank.

From directly in front of him, he could make out three men running toward the tank. If any one of them had explosives, he was through. He pushed ahead hoping to do more to clear the path to the river and their extraction point. A moment later he poked his head through the hatch to check his direction and saw one man kneel in front of the tank less than fifty yards away. The piece of equipment he hoisted to his shoulders would put an end to Ethan's tank ride.

He quickly abandoned his plan and looked around for options. His eyes went to the hatch of the tank. He had nothing to protect himself and nothing but his strength for the offensive. It was time to get creative. With gunfire still erupting around the tank, he pushed his torso higher through the circular opening. He gripped the hatch with both hands and with all his strength wrenched it from its hinges. He now had a shield.

He stood with his new protection atop the tank, making himself an inviting target. Bullets clanged off the tank hatch as he jumped to the ground in time to greet two of the men who had been on their way to dislodge him from the vehicle. He swung the huge piece of metal at them and knocked them down. The third, who had prepared to fire the rocket-propelled grenade from his shoulder, had witnessed the creation of the shield and the way in which it had been wielded. He uttered something in his native tongue and ran for the trees without the weapon that had been intended to stop the tank. Ethan picked it up and walked toward the east end of the clearing, where some brush was still burning from the tank blast. He still held his "shield" in front of him. Gunfire continued from the northeast part of the clearing, and Ethan felt and heard several shots carom off the metal in front of him.

"Ethan! Ethan, over here!" Ethan could see Theo flagging him from just beyond the burning brush. It was at that moment Ethan realized his radio had not been working for the last few minutes. He ran to Theo and asked, "Where are the others? I haven't seen anyone else."

"They're here. All except Vic. Robbie carried his body out of the building. We all lost radio contact for a while. Someone was jamming our frequency. They could only do that if they knew what it was."

"Which means—"

"Which means someone connected to this mission is playing both sides. But we don't have time to discuss it right now. We need to move."

They began to run east by southeast toward their river rendezvous just under five miles away.

"Were you waiting for me?" Ethan asked Theo breathlessly as they ran.

"No. When we saw you make for the tank, we ran to the west side of the clearing and began working our way around. We were stuck until you blew that hole in the trees. They had set up a machine gun nest there. Like they knew our escape route."

More gunfire sounded from behind, and it spurred them on. Ethan knelt with the weapon he'd inherited and fired his one shot across the clearing toward the source of some of the gunfire. Low brush and fir trees burst into flame. Ethan took the heavy strap from his now useless weapon and wrapped it around the handle of the tank hatch. He then moved the circular piece of metal to his back where it hung by the strap held in his left hand.

"That's quite a shield you've got," Robbie remarked as they began to run.

"I didn't come this far to take one in the back," Ethan responded.

After two miles Theo said, "Barrett, Pits. Set up here and cover us until we reach the river. We'll be waiting for you."

"Ethan. You want to leave that for us? A little extra protection?" Pits gestured to the thick piece of steel.

"Sure." He slung it off his back and handed it, arms outstretched, to Pits who grabbed it and involuntarily let it drop to the ground. He said nothing but just stared at Ethan who shrugged and said, "You can roll it."

They continued to run, and before long they heard more gunfire. Barrett and Pits knew their job and would do it well. The rest of the team finally arrived at the river and set up a small perimeter. With only five of them, it was a tight semicircle. It wasn't until then that Ethan noticed Cameron limping. Mongezi caught the glance. "I've been shot in the leg. But I'm fine."

"If you just ran five miles, I guess you are."

Theo interrupted. "Quiet. Our radios are working

again. It must have been a short-range jamming frequency. Watch for Barrett and Pits. I'll radio our pickup."

Ethan was on the riverbank, the southernmost part of the semicircle. He looked out over the river. It was not a big river. And here, it was shallow. In the middle of the river, he could make out a wide sandbar. There was very little in the way of foliage. After leaving the brick house, the trees and brush surrounding it had given way to a mixture of mountain and high desert brush. It made their getaway much more difficult.

Gunfire continued and was getting closer. Ethan wished he knew how many men were out there. He had only heard of two dozen making their way into the clearing, but there may have been more in hiding. The thing that puzzled Ethan the most was how their opponents knew they were coming.

Minutes later Pits came down the dusty path. "Barrett's down," he said breathlessly. "They don't know he's alone yet."

Theo was calm. "Check your radio, Pits. It's working again. You need to get back down to him."

Casey spoke up. "I'll go."

"It's not far. They backed us up pretty good. Less than half a mile from here." Pits turned and started back toward Barton, reaching up and testing his radio as Theo had said.

"All right. Bring him back. Our pickup will be here in six minutes. Hurry." Theo didn't need to add that last encouragement. Casey had already started after Pits.

Ethan remained pressed against the banks of the river. Tension still ran high in his body. What had ignited his show of strength back in the clearing was still creating a buzz in his arms and legs. He felt sweat trickling down his back and forehead, the dirty sand beneath him cold and hard. He gripped his remaining gun as the tense minutes passed waiting for the helicopter. Finally he heard the hard slap of chopper blades in the distance. Theo ran across the shallow part of the river to the sandbar where the helicopter was going to perch. The team followed.

Moments later the helicopter appeared and following the contour of the river came to rest near the team.

"Robbie, get Vic in there first." Robbie carefully laid Vic's lifeless body on the floor of the chopper. Alright Cameron, you next. Ethan, you next. Pits, Linz, where are you?"

Casey came through on the radio. "Bringing him up the path. We've got about six or seven on our tail."

"We'll be ready." Theo and Robbie ran back across the shallows and waited on the river's edge. Almost immediately Pits, Casey, and Barrett appeared at the top of the small slope leading to the water's edge.

"Go! Go! Go!" Theo shouted at the trio. He scrambled to the top of the bank and fired a few warning shots at the pursuers. When Pits, Casey, and Barrett were halfway across the shallow part of the river, Ethan met them and helped Pits get Barrett in.

"Everybody in! We're coming!" Theo's voice came over the radio but could hardly be heard over the helicopter. On hearing this, Ethan noticed that the night had given way to dawn. They were falling behind schedule.

He watched Robbie and Theo pick themselves up from the bank and begin backpedaling toward the helicopter. Robbie made it and jumped in. Theo was still standing in the shallows when a lone gunman appeared on the riverbank. He and Theo fired almost simultaneously. Theo's gun arm jerked and then went limp at his side. More shots were fired, and he fell on his back. A shot rang out next to Ethan, and the man on the bank dropped out of sight.

"Theo!" Ethan lunged to get out of the helicopter, but Pits and Casey held him back. "What are you doing? We need to get him!"

"Where's the computer components?" They didn't want to risk losing the whole objective of their mission.

Ethan shouted back, "He has what we came for!"

It took a moment before they realized what he was saying. Then Casey shouted, "Go! We'll cover you."

Ethan ran to Theo. He was still alive. "Ethan, take the duffel. I only took it because I didn't think you'd make it. I didn't trust you."

"It's all right. Now if *you're* going to make it, we need to move."

"I'm not gonna make it. Just go."

Ethan grabbed the duffel and lifted Theo over his shoulder. Casey and Pits were periodically firing past him at the bank. He ran to the helicopter and placed Theo inside. It lifted off and started toward the south. On reaching a thousand feet, they could see the sun had broken the horizon. Vic was not going home, and they had no idea if what was in the duffel bag would actually mean anything when they got home.

"Mr. Gallinger. I just received word from Kunduz."

"Dormand. I can guess what you are going to tell me. What I want to know is how it happened."

Dormand spoke quickly, hoping to reduce the sting of his words. "The vault was opened, and the Milligraf chips were taken. Several of the men who tried to stop the Americans have a rather interesting story. You may be interested in one of the men on the American special ops team."

"And why is that?"

Dormand raised his eyebrows and leaned forward. "You're not going to believe this."

E than and Murrow walked past a group of soldiers being chewed on by an angry sergeant. A Humvee rumbled past them on the road, and the hum of cicadas provided mellow background music. Their walk had started at Murrow's office, but they made their way outside toward the training grounds.

"What happens now?"

"Well, Ethan, I need to speak with the federal judge who presided over your case."

"You think that will help? After all, he's the judge who denied all my appeals. He carried out the sentence handed down at the original trial."

"How do you think you got here in the first place? He's a friend of mine. The trick won't be convincing him to let you stay here. It will be getting him to forget the reason you were put away." Murrow cleared his throat. "Have you talked about that with anyone?"

"You mean gone up to someone and said, 'Hey, I'm a convicted murderer. Want to know how I did it?'"

"I know what happened, Ethan. No one wanted to convict you. They were just afraid."

"I could have walked out of that courtroom anytime. I could have left that prison too."

"I know. But you didn't. That speaks volumes to me about the kind of man you are. That's why I think we have a very good chance of dismissing the whole case."

"Time served?"

"Not exactly. More like reevaluate the evidence in light of the past few weeks with us." They began crossing a field where groups of recruits were enduring verbal abuse by a superior officer. Murrow smirked as he strolled by. Ethan wondered if he was remembering his early days in the military. "Stay here long enough, and we'll make you twice the soldier you are now, Ethan. If that's even possible." He turned and looked at Ethan. "You're not going back to prison. I'm going to make every effort to ensure that will not happen."

"Even if I get to stay, what am I going to do here? That mission was tailor-made for me."

"We can find other things for you to do. A man with your talents can be very useful. I am concerned, however, that you might present an inviting target for certain enemies. Perhaps even the one we just hurt badly while in Afghanistan."

"What would any of our enemies want with me? How would they even know about me?"

"You did some things while getting to your extraction point that normal humans can't do. You know that. All it takes is an eyewitness to report what they saw, and pretty soon the rumors start. Terrorist networks communicate, and they will know about you." They stopped at the officers club. "Ethan, sit tight. You'll be seeing me soon. We'll square things away with your favorite judge."

"Yes, sir." Ethan walked back the way he came, wondering if he should talk to someone about what had happened. The last thing he wanted was another target on his back.

As he walked, he thought of Theo and Barton. They were still in the infirmary. Ethan decided to make his way there knowing there were some things that needed to be said. Theo had taken several shots to the chest, but thanks to the body armor, he only experienced deep bruising. The shots that caused him to spend the last several days on his back had been in his legs and shoulder. It is a misconception that shots to the shoulder are only flesh wounds. Ethan had seen too many movies where the hero takes a bullet in the upper arm or shoulder only to momentarily flinch and then continue saving the day. Looking at Theo lying there in the river, it was clear there was more to a shoulder than flesh. It was possible he would miss the next assignment, depending on when it was. Barton, on the other hand, was recovering rapidly and would be ready for duty soon.

Ethan was directed to Theo's room. "Ethan?" Theo's eyes had opened, and it was clear he was surprised at his visitor. "What are you doing here?"

"I was in the neighborhood," Ethan said with a wry smile.

Theo gave him a slight nod. "I owe you one."

"You don't owe me anything. We all did what we had to do."

"I saw the notes from the debriefing. You did a lot more than you had to." Theo paused, but Ethan remained quiet, knowing he had more to say. "I underestimated you. I believe in order, discipline. There's a right way to do things. You kind of knocked the sides out of my box."

"I owe you an apology though. I'm not used to a team. All my life, it's been just me."

"I can understand that." A few seconds passed, and then Theo spoke again. "Oh yeah! Apology accepted. Forgot about that."

"Yeah, sure. Just heal up, all right?"

"You got it." A quick but firm grasp with Theo's good hand, and Ethan left. There really never was animosity between them. Just misunderstanding. The story of Ethan's life.

"Hey soldier! How was your first outing?"

Ethan turned and saw Sergeant Kaplan walking toward him. He had not seen her in a couple of weeks, but the effect she had on him had not changed. He didn't respond to her greeting until she said it a second time.

"I said how was your first outing?"

"Sorry, I—uh—outing? You make it sound like a third grade field trip."

"You and I are the only ones on this street who are supposed to know what you just did." She nodded at the group of recruits starting their PT nearby.

"So, the last time I saw you, I was disappointed we really didn't have much time to talk." Ethan tried to keep his voice low, even.

"Me too. But it's okay. I escorted you around this base for a week. I learn by observing." Kaplan lifted her eyes slightly.

"And what have you observed?"

"You're pretty harmless. And I find you very interesting."

"Interesting, how?"

She paused, bit her bottom lip, and then spoke directly. "Ethan, why don't we take a walk?"

Ethan didn't have to think long about this proposal. He had to admit to himself that he had thought about her quite a bit during his time in Afghanistan. He saw nothing wrong with a little stroll around the base. "I was just taking a walk with Murrow. I guess I can walk some more."

They strolled around the base making small talk until it was almost lunchtime. "You want to get something to eat? I know of a great place in town."

"I can't leave the base. Part of the parole agreement."

"You went to Afghanistan, but you can't leave the base? Are you kidding me?"

Ethan felt his face turn crimson. "It's a supervision thing. I—I don't know. It's probably not that big a deal."

Andrea leaned toward Ethan and smiled. "I'm teasing. I forgot about your restrictions. Come on, there's a great place right here on base. I'll buy."

"Is this a date?"

"No. Absolutely not. I don't date soldiers."

"Technically I'm not a soldier. Really."

A faint smile crept across Andrea's lips. "Then maybe I'll reconsider. But for now let's just get something to eat."

The restaurant was quiet and quaint. It served Southern comfort food, and Ethan wasn't too sure about it. Chicken and dumplings he could live with. Scrapple, grits, and okra were a different story.

"What do you mean you've never heard of scrapple?" Andrea prodded.

"I'm a city boy. I'm sure it's some kind of meat byproduct. But I'm not that brave."

"One would think you weren't afraid of anything."

"Just because I'm strong?"

"That's got to provide you with some sense of security."

"Not really. I don't know where the strength comes from, so I can never be sure how I'll lose it. *If* I'll lose it."

"When did you first know you had it—your strength?"

"Somewhere around age five. My parents knew before that. But I remember moving a couch for my parents—by picking it up and carrying it across the room. They didn't explain things to me until later, but I knew I was different." As Ethan spoke, Andrea leaned in, listening intently. He couldn't understand how he'd ended up here telling her this. He found her attractive but wasn't sure the feeling was mutual. She had smiled at him and said a few kind things, but he never thought her interest went beyond their work together. It could have been that he was just out of practice when it came to women. It all seemed a little awkward to Ethan. It became even more awkward when he realized that in some ways Andrea reminded him of Sarah. He took a deep breath to prevent the memory from assaulting him full force and instead asked her, "So what's your story? How did you end up in the military?" If the increase in his heart rate showed, Andrea didn't seem to notice.

"I wanted college paid for. I graduated, but I was doing so well I decided to stay. And now, here I am. You got here a little differently."

"I took the long way to get here, and believe me, if I could have avoided it, I would have."

"I put together your file. Studied your case online. They really went after you."

"They were scared. They didn't know what to do with

me. On one hand they wanted to applaud but on the other they wanted to lock me up and throw out the key."

"What really happened, Ethan? I read the reports but . . ."

He breathed a deep sigh, realizing what a burden it was for him to recount the story. There was bitterness toward the justice system but at the same time the old feelings from childhood that made him think he was a freak. They used the word "vigilante" in the trial. He was nothing of the sort. He merely stepped in where no one else would have. And he was punished for it; in more ways than one.

"Ethan? Are you okay?"

Ethan hadn't realized he'd been silent for half a minute. "Sorry. I was just thinking about where to start."

"Just tell me what happened."

Ethan took a long look into Andrea's eyes. He wanted to trust her with his past and perhaps have a friend for the first time in many years. She stared right back at him with compassion. He looked a moment more, trying to discern anything that would make her suspect. He wanted no pity, and he needed no therapy.

He thought for a moment about how to begin. There was no way to soften it. "Growing up, my neighborhood was a nice place. But by the time I was twenty, gangs had gained the upper hand, and lots of families were moving out. It bothered me. A few of my family's friends had already been robbed or assaulted after dark. I wanted to do something about what was happening right on my street, but I was never able to catch any of the gang members in the act."

"Didn't you know who they were?" Andrea asked.

"I knew the few who still dealt drugs at school. The others? We had educated guesses. We could see who was hanging out on this stoop or at that storefront, but we couldn't necessarily connect them to the crimes. Many of the people who had been robbed either couldn't or wouldn't make positive IDs. Especially after the first murder."

Andrea leaned toward him, listening closely.

"Mr. Emerson lived just one street over. He refused to give one of those thugs his car. He was found beaten to death lying half in the street and half on the curb. After that, a lot more people started to leave. The whole borough was changing, and law enforcement was being challenged everywhere. We just wanted our old neighborhood back."

"So where do you come in?"

"Well, I had a girlfriend at the time. We were planning on getting married."

Andrea sat back, surprised. "That didn't come up in my research."

"We'd only dated for a few months. I was sort of swept off my feet. She was the only girl in my life who saw more in me than my strength. Her name was Sarah."

"Was she part of what happened?"

"Not in the beginning. But my concern for her motivated me. With all that was going on, I didn't want her to get hurt—or worse." Ethan looked down at the table as he thought about Sarah. All that had happened was his fault, and he never stopped wondering what might have been.

Ethan continued. "I was on my way home from work. It was late. Close to midnight. There was a guy walking in front of me. I recognized him as a kid who worked at a bakery a couple blocks away. Nice kid. I was trying to catch up with him, thinking two together would be better than one. Before I could, I saw two men step through the glow of a streetlight, grab him, and pull him into an alley.

"They didn't see me, so I followed them into the alley. I followed the sounds of his shouts for help. I couldn't believe

128

they would assault and rob a boy who probably wasn't carrying any more than ten dollars. But then it occurred to me that he could help them break into the bakery, which would hold much more cash.

"I followed until I reached what looked like a dead-end alley. That was when I was taken by surprise. Instead of two men, I counted over ten. I figured I could at least distract them long enough for the kid to get away, so I grabbed a trash can and threw it over their heads into the end of the alley. When it crashed into the wall, I ran into the center of the group, grabbed him, put him on my shoulder, and made for the entrance of the alley, but there were at least six more gang members blocking the way out. I was trying to avoid a full-on conflict, but I was being hemmed in. I had at least fifteen or sixteen men closing in on me within this tiny alley. I remembered one shop that backed up to this alley was a small garage. The guy there did small engines, electric motors and stuff. I wasn't sure which door it was, but I kicked one open and found myself in his work area. Just seconds after entering, there were bodies crowding the doorway. I put the boy down and told him to hide. They just kept coming through the door. I had thought this gang was a group of five or six guys making trouble, but it looked more like a small army. One of them challenged me. Probably the leader. He said, 'Who are you, Superman? Are you tryin' to save the day or somethin'?'

"I said, 'I'm just making sure nobody else gets hurt. There's been too much hurting already.'"

"The leader answered, 'It's just starting.'

"That's when I heard several knives flick open. I was thankful it was dark. Otherwise they probably would have just shot me. Still, I knew I was in trouble. I started reaching around for something to defend myself with. There were several small engines on the floor, even a vacuum and a sewing machine. I had hoped an alarm would sound when I kicked in the back door. It didn't, and I needed to buy some more time. Finally my hand ran over a wrench. It was small. I found out later it was a half-inch box-end wrench. The thing was only seven, maybe eight inches long. But that was what I had to work with because as soon as my hand touched it, they came. Knives were being swung through the air. I couldn't make any sense of their attack. It just seemed like they were around me everywhere all at once. I started swinging that wrench, and then...I felt it come over me."

He stopped talking for moment as his breathing had become more rapid and his forehead began to perspire. "I'm sorry. I just put myself back there."

"It's okay. You can stop." Andrea reached out and put her hand on his.

"No. I want to finish." He moved his hand out from under hers. He took a deep breath before he continued. "It seemed like I could see every blade, every hand. I knew where to swing that wrench. I connected with it again and again. After just a few minutes, I couldn't move my feet easily without stepping on a body. One gang member leaped onto my back, so I reached around and grabbed a handful of shirt at the base of his neck and threw him through the front picture window of the garage. That's when we got the attention of someone in the neighborhood. The cops arrived, but by then the remaining gang members had disappeared. There were thirteen bodies on the floor of that small garage. Every one of them killed with a seven-inch wrench...swung by me."

Andrea was stunned. "You were defending yourself... and that boy."

"I went too far. I couldn't stop. And when I found out about the victims—"

"They weren't the victims. They committed the crime!"

"They were about to. But, Andrea, the youngest one killed was thirteen. Thirteen! The rest no older than twenty. Even the one that spoke to me, he was only twenty-one, and he got away. I thought they were men. Grown men; not boys playing games at night."

"What about Mr. Emerson? They weren't playing games with him."

"Maybe they didn't do that. Maybe it was another gang. Maybe it was the older members."

"If you hadn't done anything, you'd be dead along with that boy."

"If I hadn't done anything, everyone would be a lot better off, including Sarah."

"What happened to her?"

"She made the mistake of loving me. She paid for it with her life."

Andrea was quiet for a moment, trying to understand the weight of Ethan's words. "I don't think Sarah would want you to stop being who you are."

"I went too far. After I threw that boy through the window, one of the gang members got up off the floor and ran for the alley. I should have let him go. I chased him almost to the street and struck him down right there."

"You did what you had to do."

"But thirteen lives! They were right. It was monstrous. *I'm* a monster."

"Do you really believe that? Everyone on your team has killed someone in the course of battle. Doing their job. Are they monsters?"

"They had a job to do."

"So did you. Maybe it's what you're supposed to do."

Ethan thought back to his father's words. "Ethan, God has given you this gift for a reason. With it you can defend the weak. You can rescue people who are hurting and oppressed. We don't know the extent of this gift until you use it. Who knows how much power God has given you? Test him, Ethan. Let Him show you."

He felt at times that he had been given a piece of machinery to use but no instructions on what it was supposed to do or even how to operate it properly. Maybe Andrea was starting to understand the confusion inside his mind. He was startled when he heard her cell phone jangling some obnoxious new pop tune. She answered quickly.

"Yes, sir. I'll be right there." She snapped the phone shut. "We need to go. Murrow said they found something on those computer chips that should interest us."

"Why should it interest us? We're not really supposed to be in the know on these things."

"Maybe what they found is going to involve both of us in something else, something bigger and more important than what we just did."

She stood to go, but Ethan hesitated. He hadn't told her the cruelest part of the story. The part that filled him with so much rage and sadness that he wished prison had killed him.

Andrea moved close to Ethan. "Come on. They'll be waiting for us."

Murrow was waiting for them in his office. He seemed surprised to see Ethan and Kaplan together.

"Please. Sit down. Ethan, we're not entirely sure of everything that's on the computer chips you brought back from Afghanistan, but we have seen enough to know that we need you to stay here whether the state of New York wants you back or not."

"*Need* me to stay? As in, you need me for something else, or I should stay for my own good?"

"Before this is over, it might be both. I can't give you all the details right now, but I can fill you in a little. Cultus obviously never intended for us to open that vault. The only thing they didn't plan on was you, Ethan."

"It was a trap?"

"Lure us in with light security and attempt to send a message. Well, not only did they get more than they bargained for. So did we. Those computer chips are like nothing we've ever seen except in research and development labs in Silicon Valley. They're nanochips. An outfit in Switzerland calls them Millipedes." He held one up. It was slightly smaller than a postage stamp and only a little thicker. "This can hold two terabytes. That's the same amount of information as three thousand compact discs. It's rewritable, and a whole string of them can be powered by something as small as a double-A battery."

"What's a terabyte? And what's nano?" Ethan asked.

"There's kilobytes, megabytes, and gigabytes. A terabyte is one thousand gigabytes."

Ethan just shook his head.

Murrow tried again. "You know the Hubble space telescope? In twenty years it gathered forty-five terabytes of data. What I'm holding in my hand could record just over a year's worth of information from that telescope. And what we recovered from the vault is exactly what an organization would need to hold data from billions of credit transactions."

"And nano?"

"Nano is small. A nanometer is one-billionth of a meter. It's like comparing a marble to the size of the earth. Or an inch to four hundred miles. It's small. Really small."

"What's it used for?"

"There are a lot of practical and consumer related applications. Some in the military field as well."

"So what's on the chips?" Ethan inquired.

"So far, what we suspected. Details on how Cultus has paid off terrorist organizations in the Middle East to help carry out its agenda. Financial information. Encoding that enables Cultus to carry out their worldwide theft. But there was something else. That 'something else' is why we need you around. I'll be briefing the team again in a few days after I've talked to Washington."

[8]

Dormand hurried down the long corridor toward Gallinger's office. It seemed he was always hurrying. And why couldn't Gallinger choose an office closer to...everything else? He once spent an entire day outside the office door rather than make the long walk every ten minutes. When Gallinger discovered him out there, Dormand found a snub-nosed pistol shoved in his face and a hand roughly grabbing his designer tie, dragging him inside.

"What were you doing out there?" Gallinger had demanded.

"Waiting on you," was the choked-out reply.

"You have one minute to repeat back everything you overheard, or you will find yourself taking an unscheduled flight from my window. That or I will 'discover' you searching through my desk and will have no choice but to shoot you."

Dormand had never believed he could talk so fast. Nor had he realized how much he had overheard and retained throughout the day. Fortunately his fast talking had satisfied

Gallinger and also helped him to realize that if there was a leak, he would know who to ask first.

He arrived at the door. Gallinger had made it sound-proof the week after that incident. Entrance was granted not by knocking but by punching in a short code that alerted Gallinger to his presence.

A low buzz told Dormand the door was unlocked. He walked in and found his boss with his back to the door staring out over the city of Frankfurt, Germany. It was a beautiful skyline. Frankfurt had been badly bombed during World War II, but in the rebuilding phase, city planners had the opportunity to construct a city that was aesthetically pleasing and highly functional while still incorporating some of the historical elements that had made antebellum Germany so charming. Skyscrapers, like the one housing Hyperteq's headquarters, were common. But Gallinger had found a way to make his distinct, a tower atop the building that made it the tallest in Frankfurt. At the top of the tower was an observation deck he often used for time alone. And planning.

"Dormand. The loss of our main computer in Kunduz was difficult. We can certainly rebuild it, but it sets our plans back by several weeks. While we are rebuilding, I have another task for you."

A tone sounded from the door. Gallinger pressed a button on the remote in his hand, and the familiar buzz sounded. Dr. Kelso walked in with an aide by his side.

"Thank you for coming, Dr. Kelso. I was about to begin."

"My pleasure, Mr. Gallinger."

"Please. Be seated." Gallinger gestured to two chairs that faced the windows overlooking the city and then sat in one of them. Kelso's aide stood behind him ready to write.

"Losing the mainframe from the vault means that our enemies have a window into the technology we have unlocked. Others know nanotechnology but have been much more cautious in their research and also more consumer friendly. We have no such restraints. Self-funded research allows us that luxury. Dormand, please tell Dr. Kelso about the man who opened the vault." Gallinger stood and walked to a beautiful walnut liquor cabinet behind his desk and filled a glass from a short red bottle. He stood sipping while Dormand began to brief Kelso.

"We still aren't sure who he is. I mean, we know he's an American. He's exceptionally strong. Which may be an understatement. I mean, he opened the vault, so he must be. He tore the lid off a tank and used it as a shield. Some of our men there said he threw a soldier over the house."

"*Over* the house?"

"Yes. He was almost seventy-five yards from the point they saw him thrown."

"This is significant." He turned to Gallinger. "You are thinking what I am? He could be the one?"

"Of course, Doctor. The Americans can have a few computer parts. They've given us something much greater. They've given us the tool to accomplish our goal."

Kelso was excited. He stood. "It's been much too difficult to isolate each gene and mold it the way we want. If we could start with him as a template to build on, our task would be greatly simplified." He paced a few steps, in his own world, dreaming, planning. "How soon can we begin?"

Gallinger smiled. "I've done a few favors that need returning. Soon, Doctor. Very soon."

The briefing was shorter than Ethan expected. But shocking. He had learned a great deal about nanotechnology and its possible uses. But one he had never considered was what left him reeling. Genetic engineering. It was a great blur to him now. DNA, genetic manipulation, nanotech. He had never thought there might be something genetically that made him what he was. There wasn't anything extraordinary about his parents that could have been passed on to him. At least nothing he knew about. So what did that mean for him? What if he were to have a child? Would his offspring receive the same gifts as their dad? Ethan was hesitant to use the word *gifts* even in his thoughts. He hardly thought of his abilities that way.

More and more questions were developing in his mind, and he realized he now had at least three people he would consider talking to about them. Andrea, Robbie, and Dr. Remont. Murrow had reminded him he had another appointment with Remont tomorrow.

Ethan had no idea how long he would be with the military. After what he heard today, it was an indefinite amount of time, especially considering what the possibilities were. It was possible that the army could provide some protection for him from Cultus. As long as he was with the army, he figured he might as well see Remont. Even if the doctor talked as little in the future as had in the past, Ethan would gain just by being able to talk about what was going on in his head. He smiled to himself. That was certainly a turnaround in thinking from a few weeks ago when the last thing he wanted to do was talk to a psychologist.

"Another gorgeous Southern day," Remont began.

"Another boiling hot Southern day."

"How are you, Ethan? It's good to see you."

"You too, Doc."

"You can call me Erik, you know." Ethan quietly eased into one of Remont's chairs and got comfortable. "I've talked to Murrow. He was pleased not only with your performance on the mission but also with your conduct—among the men. Says you're a born leader. Good instincts."

"I was winging it," Ethan replied carelessly. He was not accustomed to compliments.

"Well, you winged it beautifully. I don't even know what you did or where you went, but Murrow liked it."

"We got what we went there for. You can't ask for much more. Although...we lost someone there."

"I'm sorry." Remont's eyes probed Ethan's face. "Has it been on your mind?"

"Some." Ethan took a long breath, thinking through the whole situation. "I hope our mission was worth it. And I don't know how to measure something like that."

"What is a life worth, Ethan? How much does it cost?"

"That's impossible to answer. Every life is precious. I was always told we're priceless."

"I would agree with that."

"But what about Vic? I talked to him about it you know. About why he served."

"What did he say?"

"I told him, I wish I had your kind of devotion to something. Your life means something. You're willing to fight and maybe die for your country. He said, no, I just want to make sure my enemy dies for his. Some response eh?"

"Your friend died for something," Remont assured.

"But looking back at it, it just doesn't seem important enough. When I die, I want it to mean something."

"Maybe there hasn't been enough time to know what his death meant. Maybe when you die, no one will see the immediate results. But it will mean something to someone. Someday."

"A meaningful death? I guess that makes a lot more sense if you've lived a meaningful life."

"Which would you rather have? A life of purpose or a death of meaning and purpose?"

"It *is* possible to have both, isn't it?"

"I think so. But each person has to figure that out for themselves. I personally believe that God gives purpose and significance to each life. But as an employee of the US Army, I am not allowed to state that officially."

"God? You sound a lot like my parents."

"I thought you'd say that. Based on what you've told me, I think they could be very helpful in showing you where to find meaning."

"I already know what they'll say. Didn't we talk about this already?"

"Have you ever asked your parents where you come from? Do you know your background?"

"I know I'm Jewish."

"What tribe?"

"What?" Ethan said with great surprise.

"I said what tribe?"

"You know there's tribes?"

"It *is* in the Bible, Ethan. Jacob and his twelve sons."

"Honestly I've never asked them. I didn't think it mattered. And as for my background, we're just a Jewish family from New York. Nothing special."

"I think there's more. The Jewish people have a rich

history and a written record of their past like few other people groups."

"How could there be more? What could my past possibly have to do with the here and now?"

"History has a way of repeating itself. It makes sense to look into the past. And for you it could unlock a few mysteries."

"Even if it could unlock mysteries, there's no way to find out any of that stuff. It's ancient history."

"Actually—"

"Oh come on, Erik! Are you gonna tell me it's in a book somewhere?"

Remont simply stared back at Ethan and slightly raised his eyebrows.

"I don't believe you," Ethan said. "What's your agenda anyway?"

"My only agenda is to help you find purpose in life. And I think I can do that if we look to the past."

"Why the past? I don't get it."

"People like you are born for a reason. I mean, we're all here for a reason, but I think sometimes God raises up people for a special purpose."

"But the past? My parents are normal people, who were born to other normal people, and so on as far back as we can remember."

"What if we could go further back than that?"

"Would you stop being mysterious! Just tell me what you're thinking."

"I have a hunch that's been nagging me. I want you to explore it."

"You want me to explore *your* hunch so you have peace of mind? Pretty selfless, Doc."

Erik chuckled at the sarcasm. "Ethan, if my hunch is

correct, it will change your perception of who you are. I believe it will give you meaning and purpose and you'll finally feel complete."

"And if your hunch is wrong?"

"Then we take another approach. But it can't hurt to check it out."

"At least tell me exactly what you're thinking so I can make a real decision—instead of being bullied by you." Ethan punctuated this sentence with a wry grin that revealed his half-hearted reluctance.

"They're called JGI—the Jewish Genealogical Institute. They research ancestry. Headquartered in Tel Aviv."

"Tel Aviv? I can't leave base. Too bad."

Remont stood and came from behind his desk. "Ethan. You want your death to mean something. That means your life has to have some kind of meaning. Don't you want to know? Do you want to keep stumbling through life with frustration? Not really knowing why you're here? I want you to have the opportunity to make your life all it can be."

It was a step that would take Ethan into unknown territory, but what Erik was saying resonated deep inside. He could say no. He could walk out of the office and forget the whole conversation. But somehow he knew he wouldn't forget and years from now he would still be wandering through life blaming everyone else for the way his life turned out, still frustrated that he had not found purpose.

"I'm willing to look a little. But just a little."

Smirking, Erik Remont said, "I was hoping you'd say that. Since you can't officially leave base we need to start online. And we also need to get in touch with your parents."

"My parents? I thought we covered that subject."

"Trust me. C'mon, let's figure out how to get started."

Murrow knew of a house on base that was about to become vacant and was willing to allow the Zabads to live in it as long as Ethan was US Army property. After the proper background checks, the way was clear for Ethan to invite his parents down. There was just one problem. Ethan was unable to do it at first. He asked Erik to make the call, but Erik refused.

Ethan hadn't talked to his parents in almost eight years. Ever since they walked out of the courtroom that day, he had feared seeing them again—their disapproving sadness. In the end the call was short. No apologies. No explanations. It was as if they already knew what was happening. Ethan wondered how much Murrow had to do with that.

They said they would come to the base. It was stated without judgment or fanfare. It left Ethan wondering what they must be thinking. They didn't even seem surprised. They had known he was transferred, but Ethan didn't think they'd been told where. They planned to meet Thursday, which was only two days away. After the call had been made, it was time to start on their next project.

Ethan was amazed at what could be found on the Internet. It was new to him only because he'd never bothered to look before and his access in prison was limited. Erik took him to websites that offered to reproduce his entire family tree. But what intrigued Ethan the most was the site sponsored by the Jewish Genealogical Institute. They claimed to have the most comprehensive Jewish genealogical records in the world. If Ethan could go there, he might be able to find out who his descendants were. When his parents arrived, he would at least know which tribe he belonged to. The next two days flew by, and then it was Thursday afternoon.

He waited in Remont's office. Erik was outside to greet Mr. and Mrs. Zabad. Ethan had decided it would be better to meet there than somewhere public on base. After all his parents had done for him. All they had tried to instill in him. And now he had to face them. He had tried to think of something to say but no words seemed to be appropriate. He was glad he only had two days to think about it.

Remont poked his head in the doorway and said, "Ethan. They're here."

Remont introduced himself, and Ethan could hear him attempt some small talk. From listening, it was clear the Zabads had only one thing on their mind. Seeing their son.

They entered the room, and Ethan was stunned to see how they'd aged. Tara Zabad looked shorter than Ethan remembered. She still had the limp from her accident so many years ago. There was much more gray hair, and her eyes were creased and worn with care.

"Ethan!" Tara Zabad ran to her son and hugged him. She held on to him tightly. He looked over her shoulder and watched his father tentatively walk into the room. Abraham Zabad looked the same as he remembered with the exception that his head was now covered in white hair. Their eyes met, and Abe Zabad smiled. Ethan released his grip on his mother and took one giant step and fell into his father's arms. Not a word had been exchanged, but much was being said. Tara wiped tears from her eyes. Ethan stepped back and was about to thank his parents for coming when he saw someone else come in the door. A small someone. A little boy who looked like he could be in kindergarten came in wide eyed with Erik at his side.

"Who is this?"

"Ethan, we should have given you some warning. We... well, we really should... Why don't we sit down?" Abe Zabad stumbled over his words, trying to say all the things at once that needed to be said.

Though it seemed awkward to Ethan, he pressed on with what he'd decided to say to his parents. "First, I need to apologize. I was wrong to shut you out of my life and—"

"Ethan," interrupted his mother. "We need—"

"No, Mother, I need to say this. I know you don't know all that's going on here, but this has been a good thing for me. It's helped me understand some things about my life that—"

"Ethan, please, your mother and I really need—"

"No, don't make this easy for me. I have to say these things. It's been so long since I listened to you and trusted you. Maybe if I'd listened all those years ago—"

The boy had walked into the office and was standing behind Remont's desk. Ethan glanced at him but gave little thought to him. He was more interested in squaring things with his parents.

"Please listen, Ethan," his mother begged again.

"Mother, I wish you would—"

"This is your son!" Ethan's mother shouted the words as she gestured to the boy behind the desk.

He was sure he had heard her wrong. A son? He took a stumbling step backward. His hand reached for something to lean on.

To say their news was unexpected would be a significant understatement. Abe and Tara could see that their son was woefully unprepared for the idea he was a father. "Sarah came to us after your sentencing. She didn't know what to do. She was scared. Her parents were so angry."

He wanted to ask them why he'd never known, why

they'd never told him. Why they had not written or visited. But it was his shame, his guilt that had refused every visit, left every letter unopened, and ignored them at each court appearance. He had lived in willful ignorance. Even memories of he and Sarah's night of indiscretion had been pushed aside. They had known it was wrong. Both he and Sarah were taught to reserve the physical relationship for the marriage bed. But they had vowed never to give in again. And they hadn't. Just a few months later, he had been arrested. And then he'd heard the news in prison. Sarah had been murdered.

Nothing in life compared to that awful moment. The news reported it as gang related, but Ethan knew exactly what had happened. Later it was confirmed that one of the victims of Ethan's stand in the storefront repair shop had an older brother. With Ethan incarcerated, Sarah had become the target of a revenge killing. If Sarah's killer had not himself been murdered shortly after, Ethan would have broken out of prison to kill him. He was planning to do just that when he heard the welcome news of his death.

While Ethan and Sarah had talked of the possibility that Sarah might be pregnant, she had never confirmed it, and Ethan simply assumed that with her death, any child she may have been carrying had died as well.

"She came to you?" Ethan managed to say.

"Her parents were furious that she had deceived them. They wanted nothing to do with her or the child. Their advice was to give the baby up for adoption. Sarah would be welcomed home when it was all over."

"Why didn't she tell me?" Ethan sat down, overwhelmed as the memories and the new reality swept over him.

"She wanted to, but she didn't want you to do anything that would get you into more trouble."

Ethan looked up at his mother, confused by this last statement.

"Ethan, if you had known she was pregnant, you would have peeled back the bars of that prison in a heartbeat. She knew you would only want one thing—to be with her and your child."

"But if I'd known, I—"

"If you had known, you'd have made yourself a fugitive."

"But I could have protected her! I could have stopped it." A burning tear traced its way down his cheek.

Tara looked into the eyes of her son and could see the pain, the regret. "No, Ethan. You couldn't have done anything. What happened was out of our control. But God was still able to bless us all." She glanced over at the boy, who was still sitting behind the desk, wide eyed. "We did try to tell you about him. After Sarah died. But then you never responded—never wanted our visits—we—" His mother swallowed the words. Then she changed the subject. "We told David about you. We just told him you've been away, but he doesn't know why. Would you like to meet him?"

He looked at the boy again. He could see it now. In his eyes, his lips. Sarah was looking back at him. A lump swelled in Ethan's throat as he looked into the eyes of the one woman who had loved him. He wiped his eyes as his mom motioned to the boy.

"David, come here. I want you to meet someone."

David walked to Mrs. Zabad obediently, giving no hint that he knew who he was about to meet. "David. This is your father."

David looked up at him with innocent eyes. "Hi. You're my dad?"

Ethan felt more tears starting in the corners of his eyes. His dad? In name only. He certainly hadn't been a father to him for his whole life. "Yes, David. I'm your dad. I know you don't know me, but I'm going to change that." He looked up at Remont. "Does Murrow know about all this?"

"He knew about your parents. Not David."

"He needs to know. This changes things."

Abe spoke up. "We're not trying to change anything. This was just the first opportunity we've had to see you. We didn't know if we'd get another. We thought it best to tell you everything."

"But this does change everything. I'll tell Murrow I can't stay. I'll go back and apply for parole next opportunity I get."

"He has been with us since birth. He will continue to stay with us. You have things you need to accomplish here. God has you here for a reason."

He put his hands on David's shoulders. "This is the reason I'm here. Alive. On this earth."

"Son, we're not going anywhere. You'll have time to get to know your son."

Ethan, through clouded, teary eyes, looked down at David, who was still looking up with wonder in his eyes. He couldn't believe he had a son. He looked up at his parents, who were now smiling. "How? How did he survive?"

"Sarah was thirty-two weeks when she was attacked. They were able to save David. He's our miracle grandson. He's been with us from day one."

"Have you formally adopted him?"

"No. He's *your* son."

Ethan looked again at his son. *I want to know all about*

you, he thought. No matter what his parents said, this did change everything. All of his questions about his past, all of the wondering about his strength and its origin. Now he needed those questions answered, not only for himself but for David. He glanced again at his parents.

Abe was beaming. "A father prays. I've been asking God for this for so long. It is so good to see you again. To be able to unite you with your son. I wish Sarah could be here today to see this. Now more than ever, I can see how David favors you in many ways."

Favors me? Ethan thought. He looked at the boy again and could only see Sarah. It would be difficult though to spot himself in the boy's features. He felt so nondescript.

Remont stepped up behind the family. "If you'd like, I can have someone drive you over to the house you'll be staying in."

"I think that would be good. It's been a long day." Abe stepped to Ethan and, with David between them, gave his son a hug. He whispered in his ear, "God bless you, Son. You have no idea what this means to me. I love you."

Ethan fought back the emotion again. Almost eight years since he'd heard those last three words. Tara stepped near Ethan and hugged him as well. She couldn't speak through her tears.

"I'll meet you all there later," Ethan whispered to her through his own emotion. The Zabads left and David followed, walking backwards, trying to see his new dad the whole way. Ethan watched him until he left the room.

A few hours later Ethan and Remont both went over to

the house where the Zabads had begun to unpack. They weren't moving, but they had brought enough things for an extended stay. Ethan called Robbie as well and asked if he'd like to come over. There was a shortage of friends in Ethan's life but that was beginning to change, and he wanted Robbie in on this major event. Robbie certainly made an impression on the Zabads. He towered over them all. And he seemed to make a special connection with David.

When the small group had been assembled and introductions had been made, Remont started out. "Abe, Tara, I've been talking with your son. One of my goals is to help every soldier on this base to be healthy emotionally and mentally." The Zabads' eyes went wide for a moment, but Erik caught it and quickly said, "Ethan's fine. But I think he would benefit greatly, given his unusual abilities, from learning more about his background. Anything you can tell him."

Ethan broke in. "That's part of the reason we contacted you. I've been wondering about my—our past, where we come from. I know you told me things when I was young, but I didn't always pay attention. I want to know. David will want to know." He nudged David, who was sitting next to him on the couch. David looked up at him and smiled.

"I can tell you what my father told me," Abe offered.

"I probably don't know as much as Abe, but I can tell you a few things," Tara added.

Remont slapped his knee and with a confident nod said, "Then let's get started."

Ethan learned some interesting things that day and the

days following. His family came to the United States in the late 1800s. They had left Russia as the czars were beginning to relocate Jews from the cities to the rural areas in an attempt to lessen their influence both financially and politically. They were able to get out, and they settled immediately in New York City as many of the immigrants did. But knowing when his family came to the country was only the start of his journey. There were many things they simply couldn't find on their own. They turned to JGI.

The Jewish Genealogical Institute or JGI was devoted to tracing the ancestry of Jews worldwide and linking them to the genealogies listed in the biblical books of 1 Chronicles and Ezra. First Chronicles recounts the ancestry of the Jews up until the time of the nations' monarchy and Ezra recounts the names of the exiles who return after Babylonian captivity. Of all the world's people groups, the Jews were the best when it came to tracking their history. No other people group had their genealogies printed in the bestselling book in the world, the Bible. JGI was slightly different from other genealogical services. Instead of just tracing a family name in a particular region, learning its origins and finding famous people in the lineage, JGI made it its goal to connect each living Jew with a biblical name. Regardless of who else might be in the family line, to be associated with a name from the Bible was an exciting enough prospect for people to pay any sum of money. Who wouldn't want to find out they were related to a person who helped build the temple, carry the ark, or perhaps served as king? JGI compiled the results of their search in a beautiful leather-bound book, and it became a family keepsake for generations to come.

Abe and Tara were just as excited to finally find out where they came from. Though concerned about the cost, they knew it was something that would help their son and grandson to know who they were. Abe and Tara had suspicions about their background, but it could not be confirmed without help. Tracing a genealogical line wasn't something that was done overnight. It took time to ask the right questions and look in the right places. Genealogical records were everywhere. One just had to find them. Many ancestral connections had been made from handwritten notes in the front of the family bible, inscriptions on tombstones and meeting records of small town assemblies. Painstakingly, research was done and whenever a breakthrough was made, JGI informed Ethan.

Weeks passed, and Ethan had the opportunity to reunite with his parents and get to know his son. It took time for him to overcome the fact that he even had a son. He and Sarah had never considered the consequences of what they had done only one time. Knowing what had happened when he went to jail confirmed the fact that she truly had loved him as much as he remembered. Everything she did was for their mutual benefit. He was sure she would have told him about David eventually.

Thinking back, it seemed at the time that she was the only one who understood him and was willing to put up with his differences. Maybe the prospect of a child scared her. She may have thought he would have the same qualities as Ethan and did not want to witness a life like his—full of frustration and confusion. But Sarah was gone, and it was now up to Ethan to raise this child. Of course, how involved he was really depended on circumstances beyond his control. There was the court system in New York State, Wade Murrow's ability to influence his friend, and the motives of the crime organization Cultus. It had been weeks since the strike on their stronghold in Afghanistan, and they had heard nothing. The immediate threat to world banking had been stalled or eliminated. The world went noisily on, unaware of how close they had come to devastation. The credit cards containing the nanovirus still needed to be dealt with but Cultus's ability to activate the virus had been destroyed for the time being. Cultus was still a target but there was the public image the world knew and the private crime that would have to be reconciled. Their hands needed to be caught fully in the cookie jar.

Ethan continued to meet with Remont every so often. As the JGI updates got more and more in depth and more distant from the present, Ethan began to wonder if they would ever find anything in the past that might give him a clue as to his future. As his father had told him, his birth was special and God wanted him to accomplish something significant. Turn the hearts of many people? It was a little too vague to give any kind of direction or meaning to his life.

Meanwhile, Ethan spent as much time as he could with David. The question that hung in the back of his mind was, "How do I explain what happened to his mother?" He hadn't had the chance yet to ask his parents what they'd told him. If there was time, Ethan told himself, he would do that himself. He knew better than anyone what had actually happened to Sarah and why.

9

Gallinger had always been driven. Had his work ethic been directed in more positive ways, he could have ended world hunger or brought peace to the Middle East. He was tireless and seemed never to sleep. As a result, Dormand never slept. Gallinger was in his office at 2:00 a.m. The Frankfort office was dimly lit as only a few brown-nosing staffers were still working. Dormand was dozing down the hall when the phone call came. Ever since the debacle in the Eastern Afghan mountains, Gallinger had had his men researching and looking everywhere for any evidence of a man like Ethan. Narrowing the search to the United States had been the first obvious step. The first break came with a search of all the major US newspapers. Almost eight years ago, front pages of the *New York Times*, *New York Post*, and *New York Daily News* all highlighted the shocking murders of thirteen gang youths. From there the search narrowed until this phone call.

"It's Dormand," he answered in a sleepy voice.

The voice on the other end was breathy and low. There

was obvious excitement. "It's him. He's in North Carolina. Military installation."

"I'll tell Gallinger right away," Dormand answered.

"I'm glad I could help. Tell him I'm here if he needs me," said the voice.

Dormand hung up the phone and began walking back down the corridor to Gallinger's office. The code, the buzz, and then the door opened. Dormand repeated the contents of the phone call.

"Wonderful. Cultus has provided us with a very competent network of agents." Gallinger was pleased.

"So do you want me to notify Dr. Kelso?"

"Not yet. I want to know everything there is to know about this man. We know where he is, have a name, but that's all. We do our homework. Then we act."

Dormand was ready to doze off again. He glanced at the clock. It now read 2:20 a.m. "What do you want from me now?"

"Start working with the name Zabad. I want everything we can find. Find out if he has relatives. Friends. Lovers. Anyone who can tell us his story. If he did even half the things our men witnessed at the vault location, he's the man we need to find and use."

Dormand was grateful to be dismissed and slowly walked back to his office at the other end of the hall. Zabad. New York City. That seemed like a logical place to start. He never dreamed where his search would lead him.

It had been over a month since Ethan had returned from Afghanistan. Murrow had summoned the team back together to review what had happened a month ago and to go over some new plans for their continued assault on the plans of Cultus. They met again in the unit's briefing room.

"If we think Cultus has been dealt a death blow, we're kidding ourselves," Murrow was saying. "They have experienced a major setback, but there is no way they are retreating."

"We demolished their computer system and cracked some of their technology. What's next?" Casey asked.

"The only lead we have as to their intentions lies with Ethan. Everything we could glean from those computer chips leads us to believe that the same person who was able to plant an electromagnetically activated nanovirus on plastic is able to genetically alter an individual's DNA."

"We've been able to manipulate DNA for years now. What's the difference?" Pits asked.

"Most DNA technologies deal with new growth, cloning, test tube production. With the advancements in nanotechnology, this manipulation can take place in a fully mature adult."

"Mutation?" Ethan blurted out.

"Basically yes. While most mutations are experimented on with embryos, this type of mutation can emerge in an adult overnight."

Cameron was intrigued. "I can see why this might be a problem, but it could have some positive applications. Liver, lung, or heart disease could all be cured. Genetic disorders, behaviors. It could change medicine forever."

Murrow agreed. "I think on the surface that's probably what Cultus has in mind. The public will hear about this soon as one of their attempts to help heal the world."

"So what's the problem?" Cameron pressed.

"There are two problems. One, Rolf Gallinger is all over

the information we've uncovered so far. Each of those milli-pedes, the chips you recovered, holds more information than even seems possible, so we have a long way to go. Most of it is code related to their electronic theft. But another interesting fact is that Rolf Gallinger is named over and over in different files related not only to the theft but to the nanotech project."

"You mean we finally have a name instead of a fronting organization?" Casey was excited.

"It's a start. But having seen things like this before, it often takes years to pin anything specifically on guys like Gallinger. That's a job for an investigative organization. We just follow orders."

"So much for there being a 'rogue element' in the orga-nization. I guess there's nothing we can do?" Casey inquired.

"Not yet anyway. But at least we know Gallinger isn't in the dark about what's going on. There's a second problem. One of the documents we pulled from the microchips outlines a plan to use this combination of DNA and nanotechnology to create a superhuman."

Casey was quick to respond. "Whoa, that's a throwback to another German I know."

"Man's desire to create a super race didn't die with Hitler. What's interesting is how far the desire has taken mankind. In Hitler's time, the objective was to destroy the unwanted leaving only the pure of the human race. Now, technology enables them to select the 'pure' and combine their abilities to create the perfect human."

Ethan could feel the prickles creeping up the back of his neck. "What would Gallinger want with this technology?" He asked the question, but deep down he already knew the answer.

"Two reasons. It's marketable, so it makes financial sense. If a rogue nation or element like Cultus was able to create a superhuman race of soldiers, what kind of damage could they do? Really, it's an old plot. Throughout history the one with the best technology, the best equipment, the best soldiers has won. Oh, there have been some exceptions, but more often than not, technology and material superiority wins out. Second reason, people the world over will pay incredible amounts of money to have genetic predispositions and diseases removed from their DNA. Gallinger is trying to get what he wants, whether by stealing the world's money or earning it with genetics and mutated mercenaries."

"Sir, maybe you should have considered a career as a professor," Casey offered.

"My skills as a colonel not up to your standard, soldier?"

"Said with respect, sir. All due respect." Casey could see the faint beginnings of a smile on Murrow's face.

"Okay, so let me summarize. Gallinger is now being investigated. He may be our next target. It all depends on where he goes from here. At this point we now know that there is another computer somewhere in a Gallinger or Cultus facility. Based on what is required to house one of these supercomputers we have narrowed its location down to five possibilities. We also know that their attention is obviously to create this 'super race.' That brings me to another issue." Murrow looked directly at Ethan.

That feeling on the back of his neck returned. "What? What is it, sir?"

"No one here knows why you are the way you are. Neither does Cultus. Surely they observed you in Afghanistan. Do you know why you're so strong?"

"Only some story about my parents having dreams and

hearing from God." Ethan felt his face flush red as the rest of the team looked at him. "It's just a story. A way my parents used to cope. I really don't know why I'm strong."

"If Cultus and Gallinger are out to build a super race, it would make sense to get some DNA and make people who have the same abilities as Ethan." Cameron turned to Ethan. "Has anyone ever tested your DNA for...abnormalities?"

"No. And only one person ever asked. Dr. Siegers."

"At the base hospital?" Casey chimed in this time. "That boy don't even know a femur from a fibula. And he thinks he knows DNA?" The others chuckled, but the thought of genetic manipulation was a sobering one, so the laughter didn't last long.

"I think we need to take a look at your DNA. We need to be one step ahead of our potential enemies," Murrow was saying now. "We may need to know what it is Cultus might be looking for."

Ethan thought for a moment. Somewhere in his gut, he knew they wouldn't find anything. What made him who he was wasn't genetics. "No," Ethan stated firmly. "We won't be doing any testing. If Cultus thinks there's something to find, let them come find it."

Murrow's eyes narrowed, and he leaned forward over his desk. "We could take blood from you if we wanted."

"Are you threatening me? If I'm not mistaken, you are trying to help me."

"Let me make something clear. You're helping us. We've made some allowances, helped you out with a few things, but I'm just letting you know that we will do whatever it takes to bring down this organization and its leader. With everything that's happening in the Middle East, the last thing we need is another wacko terrorizing the world. I want to bring him down, and if we need your DNA to do it, we'll take it."

Ethan said nothing in response, but the challenge had been laid. He thought if his destructive power was genetic, how could he let someone have access to its building blocks? Did he really want clones of himself or genetically manipulated humans roaming the earth?

"Now, Dr. Siegers? He asked you about DNA when you first arrived?" Murrow seemed surprised.

Ethan nodded.

"Why didn't you inform me of that?" Murrow asked.

"I didn't think it was important. Others have asked me throughout my life why I'm strong."

Robbie spoke up. "Anyone ever ask you if you were related to Samson?"

Why is he bringing that up here? Ethan thought. "Who?" Ethan answered, hoping to deflect whatever Robbie was throwing at him.

"You know. Samson. In the Bible?" Robbie was referring to a man with supernatural strength who rescued the nation of Israel from being enslaved by a neighboring country.

Great. He's not going to let this go. "What about him?"

"C'mon, Ethan. You can't tell me you never thought about it. You're strong, but you don't look it. And we know it can't be your actual physical strength. Just like Samson."

"What's that supposed to mean?"

"Look at you! You *might* be a hundred seventy pounds soaking wet."

"I *might* be getting ready to kick your—"

"Hey! If I want to see a fight I'll get pay-per-view." Murrow scanned the group of men. I want you to be ready at a moment's notice just like always. Until Gallinger makes his next move, this team is not to leave base. Dismissed." As everyone got up to leave, Murrow added, "Ethan, stay here please."

"I'll wait for you outside, man," Robbie offered to Ethan as he left.

Murrow shut the door behind Barton as he exited last. "Ethan, you lay low. No leaving base. I made a mistake letting you leave before. Your parents have their housing on base. You can stay with them of course. Until things are cleared up with the state of New York, you are confined to the grounds. I understand you have some personal matters to attend to as well. We weren't sure about that part of your life. Nothing official anyway. But your son may need our protection as well until we've assessed Cultus' next move."

"My son?"

"Why wouldn't he? If there's even a glimmer of hope that you have a certain gene, you can be certain Gallinger or Cultus will try to exploit it. He'll use whatever it takes to get it."

"What if we get to him first? Stop him before he gets to us?"

"That would be great, if we knew where he was."

"I thought he had a headquarters in Europe?"

"He does. And as of this morning he disappeared. No sign of him at any of his homes. His private jets are still on the ground, and his face hasn't turned up at any national checkpoints."

"Just now you made it sound like we were watching him. Like we'd know if he ordered take-out or scratched his nose. I thought you guys knew how to find people. You can't just find him and...take care of things?"

"This isn't Hollywood, Ethan, and you know the guys in

this room bleed for real. Vic's only been gone a month. When we do work like that, we'd better be sure. Very sure."

"You're right. My life has changed so much in the last sixty days I'm not always thinking straight. My life has become a lot more complicated, and part of me wishes it could just go back to normal."

"You mean you in prison with no family in your life? Seems to me things have improved in many ways. A little more dangerous maybe."

"I definitely don't want to go back to that tiny little cell, but it's a lot to process."

"Well, you've got time. It's a waiting game now." Murrow took a deep breath and looked at Ethan. "I want you to spend some time with your family. Get to know your son. Spend time with your parents. No sense waiting on pins and needles until you get a call from us."

"Thanks. I appreciate it." Ethan left Murrow's office with a new sense of direction. He didn't have to wait around for the next assignment. He could spend time with his family, renew his relationship with them. He knew deep down that he was not done playing soldier. There would be another mission, but this one wouldn't be to demolish a terrorist stronghold. Much more would be at stake.

"He kept you a while, didn't he?" Robbie was waiting just like he said he would.

"He just let me off the hook for a while. Wants me to spend time with the family."

"That'll give you time to finish your research." Robbie had been a great help so far in searching Ethan's background.

"Yeah, I'm hoping we have a breakthrough soon. I'm supposed to meet with Remont tomorrow. We should know more by then."

"I want to know if my theory is right."

"What? About Samson? You're crazy."

"I'm crazy? You're the one who thinks all that strength is hidden somewhere in there." Robbie poked Ethan in the chest. If he hadn't known Robbie was kidding around, he might have hurt him just to prove a point. "God does some pretty amazing things, Ethan. I know. I've seen it."

"Oh yeah? What did he do for you?"

"You're looking at a recovered drug abuser. An alcoholic who used to swear like a sailor. God changed all that."

"Were you *fixed* at some holy roller place?"

"No, man. I bottomed out and ended up at an inner city mission. I had no home, drank away all my cash, and lost my last friend when I beat him up for some drug money. I had no place else to go. Six months at that mission told me I needed something more. I found Jesus, man. He did it for me. I walked out of that place at twenty-two years old and had new desires in my life. I joined the service and kept learning about God. Here I am."

"Jesus? You know you're talking to a Jew here, right?"

"I know who you are! You're Jewish. That's okay with me." Robbie flashed a big white smile and put his arm around Ethan. "C'mon, let's go get something to eat."

He had set up on a high hill about three miles east of the base. He didn't have much equipment. Most of what he had was surveillance related. A high-powered set of binoculars, a scope set on a high-powered rifle, and a computer linked to a private satellite whose geosynchronous orbit could be altered by the touch of a keypad. All of these items would become very necessary once the target was in the right place. That depended on their person on the inside. If they could get Ethan to the right place, his...extraction would be complete in less than five minutes. Forty-eight hours of preparation for five minutes of action. Cultus had learned a great deal from the terrorists they had been funding. The Cultus operative was beginning to feel like he was in the military.

Ethan said good-bye to Robbie and went to the house on base Murrow had assigned his family. He walked in the plain steel door set in the garage wall, which opened into a small mudroom. He ditched the shoes and walked through to the living room. Part of him wished David would come running to him excited that he was here, but then he thought, *He doesn't even know me. I'm a perfect stranger. Have I exactly warmed up to him yet?* As he entered the living room, his father stood and gave him a hug. His mother sat in a comfortable armchair, eyes shining as Ethan walked in.

"I've been waiting for the day when you would walk through a doorway back to us. God bless you, my son," he whispered in Ethan's ear. "It's not the doorway I thought it would be or in the place I thought it would be but—" Emotion cut off his words. The short time of reunion was still very emotional for his parents.

"I'm here, Dad. I'm not going anywhere."

"I know. I just need to hear that."

"Where's David?"

"He's in the other room." His dad hesitated. "I talked to him. I tried to explain some things to him."

"It's been a few weeks, Dad. And didn't you tell him some of this before you arrived? He's lived with you for seven years."

Abe gave Ethan a look that told him he should know better than to ask questions like that. "What would you tell a three-year-old, a five-year-old? Would you tell him where his mama went or what his father is doing?"

"I would," Ethan said with some hesitation.

"Think about it, Son." Abe crossed back to the couch in the small living room and slowly sat down. "Think about our situation. You were in prison, and you wouldn't respond to our letters or give us a chance to visit."

"I've been meaning to talk to you about that. I always thought—"

"Later, Ethan. We understand more than you think we do." Abe gave him a knowing look and went on. "We didn't want to take anything away from you as his dad. Or his mom for that matter. It was easier to say that you were simply away."

"He never asked, 'Away doing what?'"

"Oh he asked. And we said you were away, trying to get back to him. And someday you would succeed. Although in reality we got back to you. He seems to be pleased that he now knows who you are. But now he needs to really know you. As Daddy."

"What did you mean a second ago? About understanding more than I thought you did?"

"We know you thought we were disappointed in you. We could see that in your face. You never gave us a chance to explain how we felt."

"But every time I saw you, the looks on your faces. All I saw was sadness."

"Ethan, of course there was sadness! God had told us of a very different future for you. Not killing and prison."

"But it wasn't my fault! I mean I—"

"No! That's not what I meant. We know what happened that night. I just mean we never anticipated God using those events to bring about his plan. It took us a long time to adjust to what God was doing. And then when Sarah showed up..." Abe trailed off, lost in thought.

"Dad?" Ethan began cautiously. "I just want you to know how sorry I am that I ignored you for all these years. I couldn't handle what I thought was disappointment in your eyes. It was too much. I made a huge mistake. I wasted so much time."

"But you have time now. Use it well." Abe smiled at his son. "We love you and will never stop loving you."

"I love you too, Dad."

Abe wiped a tear from the corner of his eye and chuckled. "I have become a big softie in that last few years." He looked up with moist eyes, still smiling. "Go spend some time with David."

Ethan went past the kitchen counter where some stools were lined up and walked around the corner to the door of the smallest of the three bedrooms. It was open a crack. "David? Can I come in?"

"Sure...Dad."

Ethan couldn't decide if the pause was out of uncertainty of who was at the door or just a continuation of the caution with which David had decided to pursue this new relationship.

"What are you doing?" It was a dumb question since Ethan could see the floor was strewn with a popular brick building toy. But David didn't seem to think it was a dumb question since he enthusiastically answered by zooming what looked like a spaceship right past Ethan's face, complete with engine noises and laser guns. Ethan squatted down on the floor.

"Can I help?"

"Sure. You be the bad guys. You have to use these." He handed Ethan about thirty odd shaped pieces and said, "Make them into a ship, and we'll fight."

Ethan was a natural at true combat, but he failed miserably when it came to building a weapon of war. After a few minutes he said, "I'm not very good at this, David."

"That's okay." He grabbed the feeble attempt from Ethan's hands, and in a minute or so refashioned it into something worthy of interstellar travel.

"You're pretty good at this."

"I know."

Ethan was unsure how to start any kind of meaningful conversation. He knew he needed to tell David where he had really been his whole life. He also needed to tell him about Sarah. And of course his unusual abilities. Once he started listing things in his mind, he decided maybe just one at a time. There really was no good way to say any of it.

"Uh, David. Do you know what prison is?"

"Yeah. It's where bad guys go." More ships zooming, engines roaring.

"Most of the time that's true." He paused, trying to figure out how to continue. He decided to just blurt it out. He could always clean up the mess later. "David, I've been in prison your whole life."

David stopped playing and looked up at Ethan. There was caution in his face, and he glanced at the door behind his dad. "Are you a bad guy?"

167

"No, David, I'm not."

"What did you do wrong?"

"I tried to protect someone from bad guys. I ended up hurting the bad guys and killing some of them."

David was quiet and Ethan could see he was trying to process this new information.

"I know it's hard to understand, but there were people who thought I was a dangerous person. They were afraid of me. But in my heart I just wanted to help someone."

"Did you save them?"

"The person I was protecting?" David nodded. "Yes, I did. I think he still lives by you in New York."

"You saved someone's life. I think you're a hero."

"I don't know about that, David."

David just shrugged and picked up a few more bricks. "David?" He looked back up at Ethan with anticipation. "Do you know what happened to your mom?"

"She died when I was a baby." Suddenly he jumped up and ran out of the room. Ethan rolled off his haunches and sat fully on the floor. He had pushed it too far. Sent his son out of the room overcome with grief. Ethan was shaking his head in frustration when he felt a hand on his shoulder. It was David. He thrust a picture frame out in front of Ethan's face. It was a picture of Sarah. She was sitting on the railing of the stairs leading into her house. Her head was tilted and her beautifully thick, dark hair hung to the side and over her shoulder. Her wide smile revealed the dimple in her left cheek, and Ethan remembered the sound of her laugh. He thought about the feel of her lips on his and what her small frame felt like wrapped in his arms. And that she truly loved him as he was. Hot tears burned their way down his cheeks as he stared into the picture. He had not been prepared for this.

Of all the ways he expected this talk to go, this was not one of them.

Ethan caught David's reflection in the glass of the frame. He could see that his son was not sure what to make of his dad crying. "I'm sorry. I loved your mom so much. Let me tell you about her."

"Grandma and Grandpa have told me a lot too."

"Did they tell you what happened to her?"

David shook his head.

"Remember those bad guys I told you I beat up?"

David nodded.

"Their families were very angry with me. They wanted to get me back for killing someone in their family. So after I went to jail, someone hurt your mom. They hurt her so bad that she died. And just before she died, you were born."

David looked at the picture in Ethan's hand. "She was pretty."

"Yes, she was. I miss her. I'll tell you as much about her as I can." David, with a serious look on his face, was now sitting on the floor again with the building bricks in front of him. "Why don't we build something together?" Ethan suggested.

David looked up and nodded.

His contact with the Cultus operative on base had been successful. Their target was having some kind of family reunion on base. More people didn't complicate matters. If they had to, they would just take someone else with them. But timing was crucial, and they still had not worked out the final details. Beyond timing, there was the issue of where to make the extraction and how to evade the pursuers who would surely materialize within minutes. The base had one runway that was quite distant from its center. That would not do. It had to be someplace closer to where Ethan would be during the course of a normal day. He began packing up his surveillance equipment to move to another spot. If he stayed too long in one place with all these instruments, no one would ever believe he was bird watching. He had good fields of view, but the base, being secluded as it was, seemed lax in it security measures. He'd only had to evade one sweep of the perimeter. Better safe than sorry. He decided to move east and try to find a line of sight to where their target, Ethan Zabad, was staying. Cultus might get a clue about the best time to take him. This was the most exciting assignment he'd ever had.

His talk with David had gone well. He still had some things to explain, but the time would come. After all, he was only seven. How much could a kid that age reasonably handle in one day? One month? Besides, as the weeks had gone on, there were other things happening that Ethan was sure he'd be able to share with David. He learned that JGI had traced his ancestors to the Jewish exile in 586 BC. Through biblical records and historical records that had been uncovered, they were able to piece together family lines. One problem in genealogies is that sometimes whole generations are skipped and only the clan or family leaders are named. Very rarely are women named, and any children that did not bear children of their own are also absent. He and Erik Remont were meeting on a regular basis and talking with their contact from JGI. Their contact was Mered Gederah. Mered had moved to Tel Aviv from Iraq after the US invasion and overthrow of Saddam Hussein. JGI was just starting up, and since Mered had a background in research, it was a perfect fit for him.

Ethan went to see Remont the next afternoon. With the research getting more distant from the present, the chance that the trail would end soon was a growing possibility. Ethan had learned so much already. His family was filled with people who had taken incredible risks and done daring things for their families and their God. There were craftsmen, merchants, men of state, soldiers, and farmers. The Zabad family had a varied and exciting past. Ethan wasn't sure if he'd found what he was looking for yet.

For Erik, the exercise had done for Ethan what he'd hoped. It had given him purpose and helped to fill in some of the gaps in his past. He was learning where he'd come from, and it strengthened the idea that he had purpose and worth. Erik made the call to Mered, first checking the time zone difference, hoping there was an update today.

"Good evening, Dr. Remont. Mr. Zabad," Mered answered. Sometimes his accent was too thick for Ethan to understand, but Erik never seemed to have trouble.

"Good afternoon, Mered. I wondered if you had any updates for us," Erik answered as he pushed the button on the phone to go to speaker mode.

"As a matter of fact I do. I sent you the document about your family being a part of the first exile to Babylon?"

"Yes, I received that. Very interesting. Is there still a trail beyond that?"

"This is possibly the greatest biblical connection we've ever had here at JGI and certainly one of the oldest."

Ethan felt his heart beat faster. He waited while he

heard papers being shuffled and Mered's distant voice over the phone.

"I have the report here from one of my researchers." His voice grew stronger as he returned to his end of the phone. "She was unable to find a definitive connection to the person we were hoping for. She has found a connection to the name Joreth."

"What does that tell us?"

"Are you familiar with the names Zorah and Eshtaol?"

"Not exactly. Who are they?"

"Not who but what. They are names for two ancient cities. Both are named in the Law. The Bible I mean. The Old Testament."

"Okay." Ethan glanced at Remont, who simply shrugged then turned and poured himself a cup of coffee from the small machine he had behind his desk.

"With the recent push to do exploratory drilling for oil here, many ancient sites once thought lost have been uncovered. A recent archaeological dig in the region where these two cities once stood has uncovered some information that helped with your search."

"What did you find?"

Mered was purposely holding out on Ethan. Ever the researcher, he wanted Ethan to understand where all the conclusions came from. He didn't want to just give the answer. That would take all the fun out of it.

"First, do you know where Zorah and Eshtaol are located?"

"No."

"They are located in territory once allocated to the tribe of Dan. This is your tribe, yes?"

"That's correct."

"Of course. That was one of the first things we established. In the Bible, Zorah and Eshtaol are mentioned in the book of Judges. It is the area where Samson was born and lived."

"I'm related to Samson!"

They heard Mered laugh. "We don't know that with certainty. But we did find an inscription in the town of Zorah that was written by a person named Joreth. In the inscription it mentions a brother who served as a judge over Israel. We have narrowed your lineage to this area of Israel, and there is circumstantial evidence linking you to this Joreth."

"Can it go any further? Is there any way to find who the brother is?

"We're still working, Ethan, but sometimes these trails just end. It would have ended sooner had it not been for these recent archaeological discoveries."

"So what do we really know? I *might* be related to the world's strongest man?"

Erik couldn't help himself. "Ethan. You *are* the world's strongest man, whether you're related to Samson or not."

Mered, listening in, offered his estimation. "I haven't seen you in action, Ethan, but everything you've said reminds me of Samson. We'll do everything we can to seal the connection, but I can't promise anything. After all, the Bible records no actual descendants of Samson."

"Thank you Mered. We'll be in touch." After they had hung up, Erik and Ethan were silent for a full minute.

"I never thought it was possible. I knew there were similarities, but I never expected to be connected this closely."

Remont had his own theories. "If you are a descendant, then it's almost certain you have a genetic connection as well. The problem would be isolating it to find the source of your strength. If you're not a descendant, then there's something else happening here. Something supernatural. Or it could be a combination of both."

"It's either supernatural or it's not." Ethan couldn't believe he was even allowing the possibility. "I know my limitations."

"We need to talk to your parents again. You told me what they experienced before your birth, but we need to ask them again. That's probably even more important than knowing your ancestry."

"So we just wasted a lot of time and money?"

"No. We had to explore every possibility. Even if no one said it to you, lots of people have been thinking it."

"That I'm related to someone in the Bible?"

"Maybe. C'mon, we need to talk to your parents."

Abe and Tara Zabad had rehearsed the story so many times they had no trouble recalling the details of that miraculous night. The only thing Ethan didn't tell them was the results of the JGI research.

"We were reeling from the death of a baby Tara had carried almost to term. There are no words to describe that loss. But when the dream came—"

"Dad, tell me again about the dream. There were things I was supposed to do."

"The One who spoke in the dream said you would be a healer. A restorer. One who would be a healer and restorer of many hearts. Your life would touch many others.

"And the instructions?"

"Prepare you for your mission."

"And the One in the dream never said what it was?"

"No. Healing and restoration are all we know."

"There were other instructions. About my life."

"Four things."

"Four? You only told me three. Obey God's laws about food. Master self-control. Learn to give generously."

Abe Zabad bowed his head. "You must understand, Ethan. We wanted to prepare you, but we didn't want to tell you too much. Burden you too much. You were so young."

"Just tell me what the fourth one was."

"It is difficult, Ethan. It changes everything."

"It won't change anything. Just tell me." What could be so earth shattering? So big that his own father would withhold it?

"You were never to cut your hair."

Ethan was silent for a moment. The fact that he was hearing it for the first time caused his mouth to fall open in dumbfounded amazement.

"Never cut my hair? Mom, I thought you did cut it growing up. It seemed to stay the same length over the years."

Tara Zabad seemed surprised he had asked about haircuts. "I never thought I would have to tell you this, but . . . I never cut your hair. That's why you never sat in front of a mirror as I did it. I kept some of my own hair when I had it cut and every few months I would drop it onto the floor as I pretended. I hated to lie to you, Ethan."

"But why didn't my hair keep growing?"

"It just stopped at this length," Tara replied as she touched the ends of his shoulder-length black hair.

"Do you know what this means?" Abe and Tara just looked at Ethan and waited for him to continue. They did know what it meant—what it had meant their whole lives. "It's the missing piece."

Abe tried to explain. "We were afraid that if you knew about that command you would walk a similar path to Samson. That you would face a similar death. We just - couldn't tell you everything."

"It's okay. I've made my own way. My own decisions. But there's more you need to hear." He quickly told them what they had learned from Mered Gederah and JGI.

"How can they know this, Son? How?" The Zabads knew their son resembled Samson in every way but never thought there was actually a family connection.

"Thousands of genealogical records, Dad. I don't really know, but that was their conclusion. They are sending a summary of their research to us so we can see for ourselves." The house was quiet as these facts began to sink in. "So what does this mean?"

"If you're anything like your ancestor, I think it means you will make enemies easily."

"But what about what Murrow said? My DNA, David's DNA? We're targets now."

"But you can't run. You have a mission to accomplish. That much is clear." Abe was firm.

"But I don't even know what it is! I've been told to have self-control, give generously, and who knows what else I haven't been told? What am I supposed to do?"

Abe Zabad had been waiting his entire life for this moment. Ethan was asking now instead of pushing away. It was his chance to speak truth into the life of his son. It wasn't that he knew exactly what his son was supposed to do. It was simply his chance to give guidance that had been rejected for so long. "My son, I don't know when you stopped doing it, but now is the time to pray. You must seek guidance from our Heavenly Father. He is the only one who can show you what it is you must do."

"Start praying? I don't know how to pray. It's been so long since I talked to God He probably doesn't even remember me."

"Son, that's foolish talk. He has chosen you to do something great. He knows your name. He knows exactly what you have been chosen to do."

"Well I sure wish he would share it with me."

"I don't know what this all means, Ethan. But I do know that through prayer God will reveal his purposes. You must trust Him."

"Okay, so I'm supposed to give generously, obey God's laws about food, master self-control. Well, I've pretty much thrown God's laws about food out the window, and David is proof that I haven't mastered self-control, so that leaves giving generously and keeping my hair long. Sounds like a recipe for success."

"Just because you failed in the past doesn't mean that you can't succeed in the future. Your ancestor had the chance to be great. He had to be brought low before he aspired to his potential. You need no such prodding. There is still work to be done."

"What work? Saving the world?"

"You've already done it once, Ethan, or haven't you been paying attention?" Abe was not giving his son an inch.

"Cultus and Gallinger are enemies that will stop at nothing to destroy you and take whatever they can. If you have something they want, then he'll take it. You can't let that happen. You must protect yourself and your son. And who knows? In the process you may just save the world."

"Look out, Superman. You've got some competition," Ethan said sarcastically.

10

Ethan found it hard to believe how far he had come since sitting in a jail cell just a couple months ago. He'd gone from thinking his life would be spent wandering the country looking for odd jobs to being highly sought after by friends and foes alike. And the thing he was being sought for was the very thing he'd spent most of his life trying to avoid and forget. It had taken some time to sink in. It was a reversal that he had not been expecting. But what had he expected? That searching his lineage would reveal a long line of superhuman freaks? That he was the descendant of a famous geneticist? He thought back to the conversation he'd had with Remont about significance. How important was it for a man to die for something that mattered? But more importantly, what was worth living for? And had Ethan found it?

He had read the story of Samson. That man had it all, everything he needed to be successful, and yet he had squandered it to his very last day. Was there redemption in his final act, pushing the pillars down on a bunch of partying heathens? Had he made his life all it could be?

His fatal flaws? Pride and women. Not really problems for Ethan, unless he counted that one night with Sarah. He cringed to even think of it that way. He had loved Sarah. It wasn't a pickup in a bar some lonely night. If only he had been stronger. Been able to resist temptation. Maybe she'd still be alive. And pride? He had always thought of himself as humble and unassuming. Maybe that was a false pride. Ethan shook himself out of his thoughts, wondering if it were possible to second-guess his own second guesses.

He spotted the target through the scope and dialed in so he could get a clear view of his face. The scope was equipped to take digital pictures, and he took some now. The photos were automatically transferred to the multi-function handheld in his side pocket and immediately sent halfway around the world.

"You're looking at Ethan Zabad. I was expecting someone bigger," he spoke into the radio.

The voice came back. "We're not interested in your commentary. Please confirm he is the target, and then tell our contact where we want to make the extraction."

"Copy that. Out."

He dialed the cell phone and waited for the answering beep. "We are ready. We need a positive ID on the image I'm sending. Please confirm and give us the exact time and location of the pickup." He uploaded the scope shot into the phone and pressed send. Now, more waiting. There was another team working on the method of extraction and yet another group working with their contact to get on base.

That would be the tricky part. As for surveillance, he got to just walk away when it was all done.

Andrea came to the house. He had called her on her cell phone as soon as he had a chance. He wanted her to know that he had made significant progress. The discoveries of the past few days had left him breathless, anxiously awaiting the next revelation. She seemed genuinely excited for him. Though not a church person, she had heard of Samson and was surprised JGI had been able to search back far enough in history to find such a connection. They talked about that and many other things. Ethan and Andrea had an easy way with one another. Not since that first meeting at Murrow's office had there been any tension. Andrea had melted from being all icy business to warm friendship. If that's all it was. And so Ethan spent the next few days with his family, with Andrea, with Robbie and Erik. People he had little to no connection with just a few months before and now they were becoming a tight-knit family in the sense Ethan had never known. He had his parents, yes, but his gifts always separated them from others—Ethan, because he felt like he stood out awkwardly and Abe and Tara because they didn't know how to act around others when they were carrying such a big secret. But now that things had come into the open and the words that needed to be said were spoken, there was a new freedom, an effortlessness to their interaction. It was a joyous time. Several times Ethan forgot where he was and what he was waiting for. Thoughts of Cultus, Gallinger, and danger were lost as the days went by. Gallinger was still missing and US intelligence had no leads. He had never completely disappeared before, not for this long. They had checked all of his normal hideouts. Houses in the French Riviera, tropical getaways off the coast of Africa, a Tibetan retreat. Gallinger knew how to spend his money. But somehow he had spent a great deal of money without anyone noticing.

Over the course of three years, Gallinger had tunneled from his building in Frankfort to a riverside dock. It incorporated parts of the sewer system, other buildings' foundations, and many other natural obstacles. The result was a tunnel that could never be perceived as such unless one knew where the next turn or hidden entrance was. Others in Frankfort could have discovered it for themselves had they known what to look for. On the night Gallinger disappeared, he had simply ridden the elevator to the third basement and begun walking the tunnel. Dormand had been along of course. From the exit point at the river, they got on a small speedboat belonging to one of Gallinger's top executives.

The Main River in Frankfort had many launching points. The one Gallinger chose had no connection to him in any way and was not watched. Rather than going downriver and meeting up with the Rhine, they went many miles up the Main River, docked, and then drove into the Bavarian countryside. It was a retreat Gallinger had built in case he ever needed to flee. He had houses too, but this was a special place unknown to prying eyes. At this time, however, he was not fleeing from danger or any person. He was leaving to think, to plan. To work without the eyes he knew were out there, watching him. He not only invited the scrutiny of the business world and the corporate spying that came with success, but the governments of several countries had set up surveillance in various buildings around his company headquarters. He didn't bother to deal with them. What could they find out? That he liked his English Breakfast tea at 8:1o a.m. each day. It was the only thing he liked about the English. They would learn that he never wasted a moment, a word, or a move. Everything was done with efficiency and speed. Even his failures were well executed. However, barring this latest setback and his new problem with Ethan Zabad, his failures had been few and far between. Gallinger was the consummate plotter. His journey to the top of Hyperteq had been one such plot. This time his response was not as clean but just as smooth and even more effective.

Rolf Gallinger grew up in the German countryside. It was a fitting place for his retreat. Whenever he looked out at the forests that shielded his home from most eyes, he was reminded of the days spent roaming through the woods. In these woods he had learned what it meant to survive, to do whatever it took to win.

He recalled to himself how he and a boyhood friend Janko had spent the afternoon playing army man or some such game. When the game had lost its appeal, they had looked around to realize they had wandered far from their normal playing area. The trees looked unfamiliar and the sun was low in the sky, not providing much help as far as their direction was concerned. They had begun walking, and the sun dipped lower until a hand could barely be seen in front of one's face. Rolf and his friend were terrified. They stayed close to one another, knowing that in these woods roamed bears, wolves, and other creatures that would not hesitate to make them into a meal. They decided to stop and try to create a lean-to between two fallen trees. There was shelter enough for them to pull in some other branches and leaves to create beds. They were two boys, very frightened, never having had to spend the night out of doors aside from campouts within sight of their houses. They couldn't know there were already people looking for them. Not knowing where they started from, they had actually walked away from the search parties in their quest to get home.

Once the darkness was complete, the searching had slowed as lights had to be brought in. It was the longest night of little Rolf Gallinger's life. He and his friend hardly slept. Every noise startled and woke them. When it was still gray, they left their shelter and continued to walk in what they thought was the right direction. Hunger began to make itself known, and fatigue was setting in after the long night. When they came across the stream, it confirmed they were headed in the wrong direction. They knew of no stream near their houses, and it frightened them to realize how far they had gone in the wrong direction—and how far they would have to walk to get back home. The stream meant some water however. What they did not realize was that in the gray dawn, many of the animals of the forest came to drink.

As they slid down the bank to get a drink, they saw the bear. It was not large, but to a ten-year-old a bear's size does not matter. It was no more than five yards away, and it was obvious that the boys had startled it. The wind was coming toward them, so they had not been detected. Rolf froze and stared at the bear. He wasn't sure if it was an instinct or just fear, but he slowly reversed his direction and began inching his way back up the bank. The bear stood stock still. Janko was less collected at the sight of the bear. Rather than inch his way back, he stood and began to scramble. Leaves slid out from under his feet as he tried to get traction. He clambered his way to the top of the bank and let out a shout of fear. At the top of the bank was a much smaller bear. A cub. He began to run.

The bear's head lifted sharply at the sound of the shout and broke into a run at the sight of Janko sprinting along the stream. Rolf knew he would have to run too. They had unknowingly wandered between a mother bear and her cub. He breathlessly climbed to the top of the bank and ran after Janko.

"Wait, Janko! Wait for me!" Rolf called.

Janko slowed just enough for Rolf to come within a few feet and then sped away again. He had run only twenty more feet when he lost his footing among some thick tree roots. He stumbled and fell at the base of a tree. Rolf, still behind, saw Janko fall and begin trying to pull himself up. Still at top speed, he ran past Janko.

"Rolf! Wait for me!" Janko called. The situation had reversed itself, and Rolf knew what he should do. He glanced back to see the bear had topped the bank of the stream and was heading their way. He stopped behind a tree. He cautiously thrust his head out from behind it to see where the bear was. For the two boys, the last few seconds had seemed like an eternity. They had gone from complete exhaustion to the burst of adrenaline that had propelled them up the bank and into the trees. They were wild with fear. A mother bear would not stop until the threat to her cub was eliminated. Rolf knew deep down that they could not outrun the bear. That they could not *both* outrun the bear. He came out from behind the tree and waved Janko on. "Come! We must hurry!"

Janko cried out again, "Wait! I'm hurt." He was holding his ankle, and there was blood on his knee.

From Rolf's vantage point behind the tree, the bear was closing in on his friend. He knew he should run to him. Help him. But Rolf wanted to *live*. He ran away with his hands over his ears and never looked back.

Rolf struggled to get over that day. He had rehearsed his explanation for when rescuers arrived. They learned that Janko had tried to approach the bear cub while Rolf wisely hid behind a tree. It seemed to satisfy everyone though some wondered how Rolf got away without so much as a scratch. And even though his decision bothered him at times, he learned that day that there was only one person he could worry about. Himself. To do any different would be foolishness. Let the weak take care of their own. Rolf Gallinger was not one of them. His tears over the incident were brief. The beating he received from his father that day reinforced the belief that weakness was not to be tolerated. Weakness, tears, sensitivity all invited more of the same. Rolf shoved the struggle of his decision that day deep down inside. He only cried about it once. He did it in private for fear that his father would ask why he cried and beat the truth from him. He knew tears would not be accepted in the Gallinger house. Neither would regret, though it was the driving force of his father's life. It was a lesson he would be taught many times by Hermann Gallinger. Lessons always delivered with a strap. After one such beating, Mr. Gallinger handed the short strap of leather he had been using to Rolf and said, "You will use this on your brother. I only have time to punish one of you. See that you do it, or tomorrow it will be your turn again." Rolf did as he was told.

The beatings were for minor offenses. Hermann Gallinger had been a proud officer in the restored German army of 1955. Too young to have fought in the war, he was eager to prove himself as a soldier and leader. His harsh manner and brutal treatment of others led to his dishonorable removal and a self-inflicted life of disgrace—disgrace and shame he took out on his sons every day. These were the forces that shaped Rolf Gallinger.

The day Cultus took shape in his mind, Rolf Gallinger was in Munich attending college. In a required religion class, he learned about the power of belief. He became intrigued by different belief systems and the rigid prescriptions for life many of them placed on their followers. But no matter how crazy some of them seemed, there were people who followed them. Some had to walk across hot coals barefoot, some prayed at all times of the day and even had to kneel in a certain way, others wore only certain types of clothing while still others could only eat certain types of vegetables. What if he could design a system of belief that brought others not into submission to some fabricated god but to a living, breathing person?

One religion he read about actually believed a living man was the true Jesus Christ. He was worshipped, lavished with offerings of money, food, and as crazy and contrary as it seemed, women. What if he could get people to worship a person? What if he could get people to worship him? It would be like having his own private religious army. If he could turn them into zealots they would obey him not out of loyalty but out of religious devotion. Loyalty was important, but intense religious devotion was legendary. The idea took shape over the next several years but nothing significant happened. Gallinger was busy finishing school and laying the foundations for his future corporate takeover. No one starts a religion in his spare time.

Yet that's exactly what he did. The charismatic and

charming Rolf Gallinger began meeting with a few "friends" in the evenings. There were only a few at first. People who looked up to Gallinger and wanted to be able to say they knew him. Their times began as social interactions, but eventually Gallinger began to propose some radical ideas. What kind of world could it be if people got behind one man? If people could unite in thought on the essentials, there could be peace. So during the day Rolf Gallinger finished school and worked his business contacts and at night started forming the foundation of what would be known as Cultus. He had chosen the name Cultus because he knew that any religion started by a man would be labeled a cult. By calling it Cultus, Gallinger hoped to achieve two things. One, its name would make it the anticult. After all, here was a religion willing to put cult in its name. Surely it's not a cult like so many others. A true cult is forever denying its existence as such. Two, it put the organization in the enviable place of having enough mystery to keep people engaged and enough facts to keep government and culture at large satisfied. As large as Cultus had become, it still did not have worldwide recognition. But it would come soon. The celebrities Gallinger needed to embrace him in order to break out were beginning to emerge. Scientology and Kabala had been fringe beliefs, known at worst as cults or at best as fringe denominations until a few Hollywood elite had placed their stamp of approval.

Having studied the greatest of the so-called religious wackos, Gallinger knew how they had manipulated and brainwashed their way to great power and riches. They were techniques anyone could observe and attempt, but it took someone especially gifted to make them work. He was such a person, and he made them work beautifully. From the few people he met with each week, Cultus grew to almost one hundred by the end of the first year. Realizing he would soon be overwhelmed with the administration of the finances and work of Cultus, he hired a business manager and a press representative. Questions were already being asked about this group of devotees. From that first year, they doubled in size every six months for the next two and half years. With over three thousand members, Gallinger was able to begin putting to action some of his plans.

There was no prayer in Cultus. Only a "bible" Gallinger himself had written. It contained a wild story of God speaking to him, bestowing on him the rights and privileges of godhood, and commissioning him to lead a band of a faithful few to take over the world and make it the kind of place He'd always wanted it to be. So no one needed to pray. Gallinger was there. There was worship, however. Gallinger had made sure when he wrote his bible to include how he wanted his followers to make sacrifices. And sacrifice they did, to the tune of almost three million dollars in their third year. Some of his followers had even written some songs for him. Everything about Cultus made Gallinger proud of what he had done, but the songs made even him cringe. But he had to admit, he had opened the door for that based on the way he had written his bible.

Everything offered to Gallinger went toward raising a person's level of spirituality. With each level they supposedly were given more spiritual insight, greater spiritual powers, and some monetary reward. He couldn't vouch for the first two, but the monetary reward portion came to him in a moment of pure brilliance. Why not turn membership into a simple pyramid scheme? As people were inducted into Cultus's membership, they paid a small fee, which was meted out one level at a time. The oldest members received the largest portion, of course, with smaller amounts being distributed throughout the organization. The beauty of it was, they weren't "selling" anything. There was no product. Only the promise of spiritual transformation sometime in the future. And the organization held no responsibility. Advancement and growth were dependent entirely on the individual's desire to learn, not the organization's ability to deliver.

Like any organization, there were many who signed on and a percentage who gave up after some time, but with their money in the bank and another percentage who became fanatical devotees, Gallinger was unworried. He knew after so many years in leadership, he had the ability to make them drink the Kool-Aid, wait for aliens, or burn themselves to death in their own houses if he commanded it. And he could also order them to help him control the world in every way. Financially, militarily, and politically.

Joining forces with the terrorist networks had been a stroke of genius. In many ways his goals were similar to those of the radical jihadists. They thought of Gallinger as a help to them, but in reality they were the ones being used. Gallinger didn't operate that way. The phrase "give and take" was not in his vocabulary.

Recent events made his plan so much easier to accomplish. The economy was globalized. A downturn in one part of the world affected every other. It was just a matter of time before his takeover was complete.

Rolf Gallinger paced in his characteristic manner. Even

when he was pacing, it looked purposeful. "We have been here for over a week. Is everything ready?"

Dormand looked hopeful. "The team is in place. We are just waiting for a call from our contact."

"I knew Cultus was growing, but I never thought we had reached some rural areas in the States."

"Power of the Internet, sir. The website registers almost eight thousand new hits a day. That doesn't include the thousands of followers getting their 'spiritual illumination for the day.'"

"Fascinating. I wish I'd had the Internet when I was just getting started." Gallinger stared out a broad window onto a thick stand of trees on the south edge of his property. "This is going to work, Dormand. Our setback with our financial plans is temporary. This could actually work to our advantage."

"How so? Don't we have to redevelop the nanochips for the computer and redesign its security system?"

"Yes, but it gives us time to develop other areas." Gallinger stepped around the couch to the stone fireplace across from the window and picked up the poker. He began to gently stoke the fire. "Dormand, we have an unprece-dented opportunity. With the thousands of followers of Cultus already devoted to me and their beliefs, we have a ready audience. With the technology we've harnessed and the young man we will soon have at our research facility, we may be able to accelerate our plans past our original timeline."

"If things go according to plan."

"Even when they don't, we adjust, don't we?" Gallinger said coldly. "We've taken every precaution based on the information we have. He's not a comic book hero. He's flesh and blood."

Dormand shifted his weight and looked at his watch. "It's three p.m. in the eastern US right now. We should be getting a call soon."

"Thank you, Dormand. Your attention to detail is appreciated." Gallinger left the room appreciating the efficiency but despising the sniveling weakling who provided it.

"Dr. Siegers has asked to see you, Ethan." Murrow had stopped by the house on base.

"What does he want to see me for?"

"He knows about what you discovered. He just wants to ask a few questions." Murrow seemed unconcerned.

"He already asked a few questions. The first day I was here, he was trying to take my blood so he could test it!"

"He's just curious about things like that. I'm actually interested myself. Look, I know you didn't have a family physician growing up, so let him take a look at you, and you can start a medical record."

"What about my prison records?"

"From those state doctors? Their charts are sketchy. Mostly your stats. Oh, that reminds me. I talked to the judge that presided over your case. They've been informed as to your involvement here. They are setting up a court date so they can formally lay it to rest."

"You mean I'm out?"

Murrow smiled. "They will consider your time served, and most likely you will be released with a conditional parole."

"Conditional?"

"Normally you are confined to a state or county. In this case, you will be confined to military oversight. That means where you go, we go."

"For how long?" Ethan was sure that after a while military life wouldn't be so different from prison life.

"Don't know yet, but it could be two years. We could use a man like you around here."

Ethan could feel the fences closing in around him again. He needed to leave. Even leaving the room would be a start. "I need to go see Siegers." He turned and spoke loudly into the adjoining hallway, "Dad, would you let David know I'll be back later? Oh, and if you see Andrea, tell her I went to see Siegers."

Abe Zabad's voice floated back down the hall. "Of course, Son."

Ethan turned back to Murrow. "Thanks for delivering the message."

"No problem, Ethan. No problem. I would have called, but with news like this, I thought I should deliver it in person." Murrow watched as he strolled away from the house. Ethan could feel eyes on his back as he made his way down the street. Murrow had seemed a little different since hearing the news about his past and about his family. Maybe he was just imagining things.

They did it over the course of a few days. Each time the contact left base, one of them returned inside the trunk of the contact's car. An unused portion of hangar at the airstrip served well as a hideout for forty-eight hours. The runway was used just once or twice a week, and no one bothered to plumb the depths of the hangar where plane parts and surplus gear were stored. When the flight team was in place, their contact helped them find a place to wait closer to the center of the base. When it was time, it would happen quickly. Ethan Zabad would have no idea what hit him.

Dr. Siegers's office looked and smelled the same as the last time he had been there. His visit that first night on base seemed like an eternity ago.

"Ah, Mr. Zabad, I've been waiting for you." Dr. Siegers walked to the middle of the waiting area and shook Ethan's hand. "I told Murrow I wanted to see you. Don't worry; I'm not going to take any of your blood. That's not really my job today. I just wanted to ask you some questions and get a sense of your medical history. If you're going to be with us for a while, we need to know some of this information." Dr. Siegers pulled out his cell phone and pushed one button then snapped it back to his hip.

Ethan shook his head and followed Dr. Siegers through the door into his office where he had bandaged Ethan's ribs almost two months ago. As soon as he walked through the door, someone from behind it dressed in black reached back and swung something hard over Ethan's head. He had time to think just one thought before the lights went out—*David* —and then Ethan slumped to the floor.

Three men in black grabbed Ethan's limp form and ran quickly out of the office. They went directly to the intersection in front of Dr. Siegers's office. The helicopter swooped in right on schedule. It hovered inches above the pavement for no more than ten seconds as the obviously highly trained team loaded the package into the helicopter and also hitched a ride as it took off again and headed east.

Personnel on base were shocked to see the helicopter swoop in so low and even more shocked when they saw it land within the base itself. More disturbing was what some of the men on base realized. Knowing military aircraft, they recognized it as an NH Industries NH 90 that was housed at Pope Air Force Base just a few miles away. It had been purchased in France by a private citizen and then bought by the US Air Force for training purposes. Whoever was responsible had not only known where the helicopter was but was skilled in flying it.

People from all over the base converged on the landing site, but the chopper had long since departed. When they came looking for Ethan, there was no trace of him in Dr. Siegers's office, but the doctor was there. He had a single knife wound to his neck and had been dead for less than an hour. The helicopter had been on the roster of scheduled flights. The real pilot was found dead in a hangar at the airfield where the chopper had taken off. The deviation from the flight path had been less than a minute. After it returned to course, it deviated again and then disappeared.

In less than an hour, Ethan had disappeared from the base and, for all intents and purposes, the planet. A search was made, but everyone knew who had taken him. Surely, Cultus and Rolf Gallinger were behind it. But it could not be proven, nor could it be shown exactly how it happened. The most obvious answer was that Dr. Siegers had somehow betrayed him. But why would he? And it was very clear that if he had betrayed him, he had gained nothing by it. Though the disappearance raised many questions, it also answered a few. Gallinger wanted Ethan and apparently had gone to great lengths to make sure he got him. Ethan was in great danger, and he was on his own.

[11]

He wasn't sure if he'd ever been hit quite that hard. His head was swimming, and there was a throbbing knot at the back of his head. There was a buzzing so loud he struggled to focus on a clear thought. His body felt jolted and rocked back and forth. His eyes opened, and he tried to get his bearings. He was lying on his side. The floor beneath him was ridged, cold steel. He could feel how its coldness had penetrated his face and, on moving his jaw, could tell it had left its grooves in his skin.

Across from him were two figures in black except their faces were exposed. He couldn't identify their nationality. They had automatic weapons across their laps. They seemed relaxed. Seeing ahead of them, Ethan finally realized why he was being jolted and rocked. A figure was sitting, his face lit up by an instrument panel, looking out on a broad panorama through the front windows of a helicopter. Ethan was on the floor and couldn't see the ground below, but if he could sit up, there was enough light that he may be able to see the terrain below. But more important than knowing where he was, was getting away and back to where he needed to be—with his family.

Plans for escape began to filter through the fog that was slowly beginning to lift in his mind. He was unsure if he was still recovering from the blow to the head or if they had drugged him. Either way he began to methodically think through his options. He could snap whatever bound him and take out the two armed men sitting nearby, but then he'd have to deal with the pilot. If he disabled the pilot, he would be unable to fly the craft himself. He was at his mercy. Not only that, but Ethan couldn't force him to go in any particular direction. He didn't know which way was *back* to where he came from.

Perhaps there would be an opportunity when he landed. He would have to get out of the helicopter eventually. He would be transferred to a car or a van or maybe directly into a building. At least on the ground, he didn't have the added liability of falling to his death. And so his mind raced on and on, trying to think through every option. He also had no idea how long he had to wait. Act too soon and they would be ready for him on the ground. Too late and he may lose his opportunity.

Suddenly he became acutely aware that he could not feel his hands. They had been bound too long and too tightly. He decided to test the strength of his bonds. He flexed his left arm and began to pull against whatever held his wrists together. There was a moment of tension and then the bonds gave way. His arm flew up in reaction to the sudden release, and one of the men dressed in black caught a glimpse of it in the now waning light. He shifted his left leg and swung the gun from where it lay and pointed it at Ethan.

"I wouldn't move any more if I were you." He spoke in

perfect English but with a European accent Ethan couldn't place.

The blood began to rush back into Ethan's arms, causing more pain. He sat up so his arms could regain their feeling. This caused the other man in black to shift his gun to Ethan as well. Ethan knew he was strong, but was pretty sure he couldn't stop a bullet. Though he'd never tried. Also, sitting up allowed him to see that there was another man sitting in the front of the aircraft. So there were four.

They sat now, staring at each other as the helicopter droned on. The light was now fading fast. Ethan had thought they were heading west at first but now was unsure of any kind of direction. It was hard to tell even though he was now sitting up and could see out the front windows a little better. He looked around at the chopper. It had two side sliding doors. Having experience with only one heli-copter, Ethan guessed he was sitting in a military one.

He decided to take a stab at conversation. "So where are we going?" They just looked at him. "Been working here long? How's the pay?"

Nothing. Ethan put a hand to his face to feel if the imprint of the floor was still there. It felt less pronounced. The move made both men flinch and raise their guns off their laps a few inches. "Relax, guys. Just checking my corduroy face."

"Wasn't he bound?" Ethan's captor to the right said to the other. The captor on the left nodded and trained his gun on Ethan. The man who had spoken now leaned toward the front of the helicopter and spoke. "He's loose. Land at the alternate site."

Alternate site? Ethan wondered if he could attempt an escape with guns trained on him. There would probably be more guns once they arrived.

He was soon to find out as he felt the craft descending. His stomach leapt up into his chest, and he felt lightheaded. It was now completely dark except for the light from the instrument panel a few feet away. They continued to descend, and Ethan began to ready himself for whatever was coming. His head had stopped hurting though the point of impact was still very tender and his hands and arms had regained their feeling.

When the chopper finally touched down with a bump, the door to his left was pulled open, and more men in black awaited him. They would escort him en masse. This was exactly what he needed. One man grabbed Ethan's wrist to shackle it again but instead had his own gripped. Ethan yanked the man off the ground and tossed him. He was sure the man had a nice view of the small group of men huddled near the chopper. Any higher and Ethan would have tossed him right into the blades. It was easy for Ethan. He was already among them.

He grabbed left then right, and whenever he was able to get a handhold, a body went flying. They pulled out sticks and tasers but never had the chance to use them. After dispatching four of the black-clad mob, he was hit from the left side by a sprawling tackle. Though knocked to the ground, he was still in the fight.

As angry pseudo-soldiers leapt onto him to hold him down, he held himself in reserve. They thought they had subdued him, and they pulled him to his feet. They took a few steps, and Ethan let them believe they were in control. He needed time to get his bearings. He looked around, trying to see another vehicle, a building, something. A few more steps and Ethan began to feel his opportunity slipping away. He had no plan, nowhere to go. Still, he walked another few steps, felt his strength come on him, and then he exploded.

He was all fist and brute force. He felt bones crunching under his knuckles and gasps as wind left lungs. He would escape. They couldn't hold him. He was too powerful. He cleared himself of six, ten, fifteen men. He lost count in his fury. Then he began to run.

The tarmac where the helicopter sat gave way to deep sand, and Ethan began to run uphill. The helicopter behind him had powered down during the fight, and at first all he could hear was the distant groans and cursing of the battered men behind him. As he trudged farther on, he heard a new sound. Not greatly familiar to a city boy but still well known. Waves crashing to shore.

He turned to his right, and the incline he had ascended began to slope away again. He continued to hear the waves. He bore right again, now looping back toward the tarmac. The sound of waves persisted, always to his left. The terrible truth began to creep over him. It appeared as though he would either need to dig a very deep hole to hide in or learn to love swimming. As it happened, neither was necessary. He ran toward the beach, which was now somewhat visible as the moon had appeared from under cloud cover. As he reached water's edge, mind racing, debating his next move, he heard voices behind him. Those men in black.

Ethan ran along the shore seeking cover of any kind. So far only sand lay on this island. And then he heard and felt two things almost simultaneously. The sound of a gunshot. And a sharp sting in his back. *Odd*, he thought. Not the explosive gunfire he'd heard in...where did he go last month? And not at all like he thought a bullet would feel... sharper...and he faded into unconsciousness.

He awoke cold. He was lying facedown on hard packed sand. This was the second time in who knew how many days he'd awoken with a throbbing headache. He sat up slowly, feeling again the sharp pain in his side that he vaguely remembered from his run on the beach. He reached around his back to feel where the pain was coming from. There was a small bloody wound. It felt like a puncture rather than a scratch. But he knew from the sound he'd heard that it wasn't a bullet wound. A tranquilizer most likely. He took a long look around at his surroundings. The floor was sand. He was surrounded by four steel walls. Rivets connected the steel plates forming each wall. Above him was also steel. The door allowing entry to this tiny room was steel with a tiny window in it, perhaps three inches square. Ethan slowly stood and moved to the door to look out. His field of vision was seriously limited. He could see more sand. A long hill rising away from the cell and most likely dropping down the other side to the beach. Even if he breached the cell, where would he go? Hemmed in by water, he was once again reduced to running circles in the sand. The familiar claustrophobic feelings returned as he contemplated the small cell. It was even smaller then his cell in Attica. He tried to redirect his anxious thoughts to something more productive.

How had they found him? He had no doubt he was in the hands of Cultus. How did they know where he was? His first thought was Dr. Siegers. He seemed interested in Ethan but not enough to betray his country. After all that's what had been done, wasn't it? Fort Bragg was large with many new recruits training there, not to mention all the military families and higher-ranking officers. Whoever aided Cultus was on the inside and had information about protocols that would help an unseen force infiltrate the place. That meant that there were more people in danger than himself. He had to get out of this cell. Then he remembered the helicopter. What if he could commandeer a helicopter? It was an idea he had dismissed earlier when fleeing, but with no other bright ideas forthcoming, he fell back on this wishful, albeit dim idea.

Surely they were watching him. Cameras were probably everywhere. Where exactly he couldn't see, but they must be watching him. Maybe making a move would cause them to reveal their hand and give him some information he could use in the future. He reached out to try his strength against the door and a piercing shock shot through his body and literally threw him into the opposite wall with terrific force. The door was electrically charged. That would have been nice to know before he tried to escape. His fingers tingled and buzzed, and his back ached even more now. He had only touched the door, but it stood to reason that the walls were charged as well.

"I wouldn't try that again if I were you. We've prepared for your arrival." The voice came from somewhere above him.

There were speakers in the cell, but Ethan couldn't see them. He tested for two-way communication. "Who are you? Where am I?"

"You'll be with us in just a moment. Don't hurt yourself anymore. We need you healthy."

So they could hear him and see him. "You're Gallinger, aren't you? Who else would do this to me?"

No answer. Ethan's mind began to race. Could he overpower them when they opened the door? He still had shoes on. Rubber soled. He could kick the door out as they got there. Maybe take out a few of them in the process. He got positioned in front of the door and decided to test it once. He knew they could probably see him, but he had little to lose.

He began to summon his strength when suddenly the hard packed sand floor gave way and started to drop. Ethan's instinct was to reach to the wall, but the recent memory of pain stopped him. Instead he slid with the sand down a long chute. When he hit solid ground again, he realized he had been standing all along on a trap door covered in about three inches of sand. His captors had thought of everything. No chance for him to kick a door out or overpower anyone. He found himself in another cell of sorts. This one had no windows and only a dim light from a naked bulb hanging in the middle of the ceiling. The contrast of the light from the bulb with the darkness around him prevented him from seeing the walls clearly and the ceiling above him at all.

"What do you want?" Ethan hated talking into the dark. The only reason he could think of for this voice not showing itself was fear. He must know Ethan could rip him into pieces if he were to lay a hand on him.

"Please relax," the voice replied.

"You're not getting anything from me!" Ethan shouted at the unseen owner of the voice.

Ethan was done listening to this voice. He cautiously made his way outside of the light cast by the naked bulb. He strained to see how big the room was or if there was any way out. And then he heard the hiss of air being leaked. His first thought was that it was a sedative, but he couldn't know unless he took a deep breath of whatever was leaking into the room. His best bet was to hold his breath. If it was some kind of knockout drug, it proved one thing: these people were really afraid of him. They didn't even send someone with a needle. Ethan held his breath and continued toward the unseen wall. He reached out with his hands and finally felt cold steel. He felt along until he reached what felt like the outline of a door. In the dark it was difficult to make it out but he felt around quickly until he grasped a hinge. With time limiting him, he grasped the hinge with as much of his hand as could fit on it and began to twist. As he bore down on it, he absent-mindedly thanked God they hadn't electrified this wall and door.

He twisted off the first hinge and began feeling up and down for the next. He had been holding his breath for at least thirty seconds. He wasn't sure he could keep it up long enough to get out. Every time he exerted himself, he expended more oxygen. He found the second hinge and twisted it off. He wedged his fingers into the groove below the hinge and began to lift and pry the door out of place. His lungs were burning now, and he felt a frantic urgency to get out of the room without breathing.

He felt the door give, and he pulled hard to dislodge it from the frame. Light broke through the gap as he yanked it completely free. He leaned the door against the wall, then stepped from darkness into light and into a man in black holding a strange weapon. Ethan moved toward him, still not having taken a breath, when suddenly two coiled wires sprang toward him and attached themselves to his chest. His body jerked spasmodically as electric current tore through him. He was thrown backward onto the ground just inside the doorway. He was trying to focus his body on jerking out the wires, but the current was too strong. He instinctively breathed and began to suck in the sedative that had been forced into the room. Within seconds, his body relaxed.

Waking up disoriented and groggy was beginning to wear on him. Standing over him was a man in a white coat. He was saying something, but it was as if Ethan's eyes were working at half power and his ears were turned off completely. He heard nothing this man was saying and could barely make out his face. Then he felt an electric shock rock his body to consciousness. Reflexively he shouted in pain. And then everything became clear.

"—showing you that if you try to escape we will shock you. It hurts, doesn't it? Now where were we?" The man in the white coat was now audible.

"How should I know? I just woke up." Ethan shot back.

"I wasn't talking to you." The man in the white coat glanced to his right and left and then back to Ethan with raised eyebrows.

Ethan looked as well and realized he was surrounded by people in white coats who all seemed busy with something. He was in a room that looked like it might be in a top hospital in the United States. There were lab stations, computer monitors, and projectors linked to microscopes. He could see on the far wall an image being displayed of something under magnification. Whatever it was it was squirming. He was able to lift his head just about an inch. He looked down and saw that he was dressed in white scrubs and inside each elbow was a bandage indicating they'd taken the blood they wanted. "I see you took my blood."

"Yes. We did. I'm Dr. Kelso. I'll be working with you."

"You're not doing anything with me."

"Ah, but you are the one tied to a table yes? No more foolish remarks. We have work to do, and I do not do small talk very well."

Ethan looked Kelso over. He was a short man with dark hair that had been slicked down into a part that had no doubt been that way since he was a boy. He wore bifocals with thick black rims, and he wore them halfway down his nose. He carried extra weight on his small frame, evidenced by the jowls, a double chin, and a flabby neck that looked like it belonged on a much bigger man.

A white-coated assistant came and whispered something to Kelso and handed him a piece of paper. Kelso glanced at Ethan and then stepped close to him. "At first glance it looks as if there is nothing in your DNA that makes you special. Maybe you're not special at all. Gallinger will be unhappy. He will want to know where your strength comes from."

"He can kiss my—"

Kelso's head snapped up from the paper. "I remember saying 'no more foolish remarks.' Isn't that what I said?" His manner reminded Ethan of his third grade teacher when she was irritated. "We will find out where your strength comes from."

Kelso turned and grabbed something off a silver tray about two feet from Ethan. It was a syringe. He plunged it into Ethan's arm and unloaded its contents.

"Now, Ethan. Let's be friends, shall we? Tell me everything about yourself. Let's start with your childhood."

Ethan began to come to consciousness. His blurred vision slowly gave way to clarity, and he started to remember where he'd been. He reached up to rake his hair out of his face with his fingers when a shiver went through him. His head had been shaved down to the scalp. Ethan did not know all that he had told Kelso, but he knew that whatever drug he'd been given was intended to loosen his tongue. He was back in his sandy-bottomed cell above ground still wearing only the white scrubs. He tried to remember what he'd said, but it was no use. The drug had scrambled his memory.

Hours passed, and Ethan did not hear from anyone or see anyone. He checked the window occasionally, being careful not to touch the door or the walls. That made sleeping tricky. The cell was only four by eight, so there was still a chance he could roll into the wall while he slept. He had no idea how long he'd been there now. The numerous times he'd been knocked out or drugged left him unsure of anything anymore. And then a thought entered his mind. Something Robbie had told him. "I'll pray for you, Ethan." He could still see him saying it. Was he praying for him now? Was that Ethan's answer? Prayer? He'd never really tried it. He didn't know how to talk to someone or something he'd never seen. Why had he never tried it growing up? Why had he never embraced his parent's beliefs? His anger at God for making him this way had prevented him from fully adopting a religious attachment to Him. He maintained that anger all through his prison sentence. And now, here he was in an infinitely worse predicament than prison and he was thinking about God.

Samson pushed God away because of pride, Ethan because of selfish anger. Different flaws, same result.

He decided to try to pray. He would pray silently. No

sense tipping anyone off that he was calling for backup. He smiled at the thought that God would come in like the cavalry and bail him out. No, the only cavalry he expected was someone like Robbie or Cameron to burst through the door. But he would give God a try.

"Dear God." *This isn't a letter*, Ethan thought to himself. "Uh, God. I don't really know you," he started again. "I don't even know much about you. I know what you did to me—what you gave me. I—I guess I'm just asking if you could help me use it to get out of this. I don't know how you do...whatever it is you do, but—just do it please. Okay?"

Ethan prayed similar prayers throughout that day and the next, never really expecting anything. He was surprised they had left him alone so long. The only sign that someone was still out there was once each day for the last two days someone had thrown a tin of food through a slot in the door Ethan had not noticed before.

On the second night, Ethan had a dream. In it he could see his father, Abe, waving at him. They were standing in a warehouse of some kind. His father was up high near the ceiling while Ethan was trapped near the floor. Something was holding him back. He tried to reach his father but could not. Abe's wave was not a friendly one. It was more frantic and distressed. He was pointing at something. Then something shook the building they were in, and Abe fell from the catwalk he was standing on and hit the floor with an appalling thud.

A man in gray walked out from the shadows behind Abe and stood over him. Ethan strained to see the face of this man. When he looked up at him, Ethan was shaken to find that he had no face. Smooth skin where a person's features should be.

He awoke in a cold sweat. Was this an answer to his

prayer? Or the food they put through the slot? It had been cold, gray, and mealy with no real flavor. Is that why they were leaving him alone? They were after his father?

He tried to get comfortable again and go back to sleep. He did, but the dream began again. He was back in the warehouse only this time he was standing on the catwalk, and below he could see his son, David, straining to reach him. Something shook the warehouse, and the catwalk shuddered then broke free, and Ethan began to fall. He caught himself on one of the handrail supports and hung there only to watch what looked like a heating unit detach from the ceiling and fall directly onto David, burying him under a mound of twisted metal. From behind this mound came the man in gray, again with no face. In his dream Ethan let go of the catwalk. He awoke just before he hit the ground. He jumped to his feet in the tiny cell. His mind racing. A dim light came through the tiny window, telling him it was early morning.

Just months ago he didn't care. He had no attachments. No expectations. His life would play out the sad way he'd expected. Now it was different. There were lives at stake other than his. Why these visions? Why now? Ethan asked the questions, but deep down he knew the answer. God had answered. "Do whatever it is you do." Isn't this what God did? He'd given his parents a vision. Now a vision had been given to Ethan. But the old cynicism crept up and asked, "Isn't this just God using the people you love as leverage?" But Ethan knew the answer to that too. God was showing him what could happen, not as leverage but as grace. It could be prevented. There was still time. Do nothing, and it was on him. Do something and fail, and it was on Cultus or whoever was in that dream. Do what God wanted him to do, and there was a chance for success.

Ethan dropped back to his knees and began to pray again. "God, I still don't have a clue who you are or why you chose me, but I'll do what you want. I'll do it. I'm sorry I ignored you for so long and for the time I've wasted. Give me strength." He rocked slowly on his knees, wondering if he should be expecting something. And then he felt it.

It started slowly, in Ethan's chest. A swelling sensation, a tingling that escaped from his chest up his arms and into his legs. Ethan looked at his body to see if it was actually getting bigger then reached up and touched his head to feel if his hair had suddenly grown. Neither had happened, but something had just brought new life into his veins. He felt similar to times past when he'd summoned all his strength, but this went beyond that by leaps and bounds. He felt—and he was afraid to think the word—invincible. He turned and looked at the door he'd been staring at for the last two days. He didn't have to consider options. He knew what to do. He reared back and kicked the door with everything he had. He barely felt the electricity that was still coursing through the steel. The door sailed away from the cell at a high rate of speed and then skidded up over the rise in the sand. He stepped into the fresh air of the morning and strode purposefully up over the rise the door had gone over. He glanced back and saw they had triggered the trap door floor hoping to catch him before he left. He walked on and saw he had been right. Below him was the ocean. To his right was a dock, and beyond that on the beach a rock formation rose up about forty feet into the air. It started at the shore and curved out about a hundred yards, providing a somewhat sheltered area for the boats that were docked there. Several speedboats were docked, and they were not your average ski boats. They looked high powered and designed for big seas.

He walked to the docks expecting those men in black to come swarming over the hill at any moment. He found the door he'd kicked out and carried it with him on his back just in case. As he reached the docks, he began to think through his plan. If he could steal one of the boats, he could head west and run into land. He might be speaking a different language if he was west of Florida, but it was better than heading east and risking a suicide run into the middle of the Atlantic. There were really no other options he could think of. His mind was unusually clear. If God was empowering him, there was only one option anyway. Go where He led.

He was about to check out the boats when he saw movement at the end of the dock. Someone going down a ladder to a boat. "Wait!" Ethan shouted. All he needed was someone taking a boat or alerting someone else that he was escaping. He ran to the end of the dock and found a man trying to hide himself in one of the boat's storage compartments. "Hey, get up here." The man turned and looked at Ethan. He was tiny. Just over five feet. His hairline had receded past the top of his forehead. He was skinny and even as an adult looked like he'd still make great fodder for high school bullies.

"Who are you?" Ethan demanded. He reached out, grabbed the man's collar, and pulled him over the side of the boat.

"No one you should be worried about."

"Where are we? What island is this?"

"An island near the Bahamas. Rolf Gallinger owns it."

"Owns it? Well, how do I get to the mainland?"

The man just laughed. "How should I know? I take the orders. I don't watch the street signs."

Ethan wasn't sure if he could just leave this man here.

Would it come back to haunt him? "I could kill you now," Ethan said menacingly.

"You could. And while you were doing that I'd be alerting everyone on this island where you are."

"How—?"

And the man held up a cell phone in his left hand. Ethan could see he had dialed a number that must have meant something because he heard an engine roar to life in the distance. Time was short. He snatched the phone from the man's hand and snapped it shut. "I ought to kill you."

"Me!? Like I said. I just take the orders."

"Well, take this one to your boss." He pulled the man's face close to his and said, "Leave me alone." And with that he picked the man up and threw him thirty feet or so away into the lagoon formed by the rock formation.

He quickly scanned the five boats. They all looked fast, but he needed one that wouldn't look like he was trouble to the coast guard or anyone else. He spotted one that looked a little older. On approaching it he realized they'd probably been using it more for cargo and storage than simple transport or pleasure. He dropped the steel door and jumped in. The moment his feet hit the deck, he heard gunshots. He ducked, and the windshield shattered above him. He nimbly got back onto the dock. He snatched up the steel door, stood, and flung it like a Frisbee at the approaching black-garbed security officers. The door's long edge caught three of them in the midsection. He leapt back into the boat and crouched down under the steering wheel, reached up, and turned the key, praying it would start. The engine roared to life, and Ethan grabbed the throttle to ease it out of the dock.

More gunshots shattered the rest of the windshield, and he could hear bullets spraying the water and plunking the side of the boat. He could barely see where he was going. He had to stay low enough to avoid gunfire but get high enough to drive the boat. Suddenly he heard heavy footsteps on the aluminum dock that ran between the boats. He stood and saw a man in black fire that same strange weapon at Ethan. The coiled wires sprang out at him, and he let them hit his chest. This time he reached up pulled them off even as the current began to come through. It felt like a bee sting. Then he was yanking the wires and the unfortunate man at the end of them into the water. A Range Rover had growled over the sandy rise but had stopped to unload. The security officers in black had stopped firing. Clearly they wanted him captured rather than dead. They must have decided on a different approach. Ethan turned the boat and roared out into the sea.

The sun was behind him, and he turned the boat into the wind. If the compass on the boat above the steering wheel was accurate, he was heading in the right direction. He had been going for at least an hour now. He found that at full throttle the boat couldn't take the pounding of the waves. He had no idea what kind of ride he was in for. Not knowing how far from land he was, exactly which direction he should be going, and if he even had supplies to make the distance all weighed on his mind. After another hour or so, he eased the throttle down and began to search the boat. There were no food stores. Ethan realized now how long it had been since he'd had a real meal. There were some lengths of rope, some fishing gear, a few life vests and several propane tanks he could only assume were used on the island as a backup energy source. There were also some extra cans of gas. He topped off the tank immediately.

He was just beginning to sort the rest of the materials when he heard the helicopter. If it was from the island, he was in trouble. He upped the throttle all the way and began leaping over the waves. He couldn't outrun a helicopter, but he could make it work a little harder. He quickly grabbed a length of rope and tied the steering wheel to the seat, so he could maneuver in the boat, making sure the compass heading was where he wanted it. The helicopter was almost upon him now. He was wishing for a gun, a harpoon, anything to shoot. He decided to put on two life jackets. It wouldn't stop a bullet but it might foil a shot from a taser or a dart. And if he ended up in the water at least he wouldn't drown. The helicopter slowed directly overhead and kept pace with the boat. He could make out their faces they were so low. They could take a shot at him and kill him right now.

The other scenario was another tranquilizer. The thought of being unconscious and taken back to that island made him icy with sweat in spite of the warm wind on him. He heard a shot and saw there was a small metal dart lodged in the deck of the boat. It looked easy in the movies, but shooting from a helicopter to a bouncing, moving boat was tough. But the dart told him one thing. They definitely wanted him alive. He pulled some of the fishing net he'd found up over him while they took shots at him and the engine. He cowered under the steering wheel thinking. There had to be a way to get clear of them.

His eyes scanned the boat again and came to rest on the propane tanks sitting at the rear of the boat. He didn't hesitate. He moved out from under his flimsy protection, grabbed two of the twenty-pound tanks and launched them straight up into the blades of the chopper. They must have guessed what he was thinking because when he moved they had too. The chopper moved off to his left. The man in the side door still had a gun trained on him. They were having difficulty navigating the wind and the waves looking for a clear shot. The tanks fell harmlessly into the sea. He reached for another tank. That's when he felt the sting of a dart in his calf. Lucky shot. He knew he only had moments before it overcame him. He took careful aim, trying to compensate for the bouncing boat. The chopper had started to move in anticipation of the makeshift weapon, but it was too late. Ethan fired the fuel tank at the chopper, and this time he connected just below the blades. The tank bounced up into them, and the chopper exploded in a mass of roiling flame and smoke. He leapt back to the wheel and turned it left to escape any debris. Then the tranquilizer took over, and he passed out on the floor of the boat.

[12]

He awoke to the sound of waves. Distant waves. He wasn't moving. He put his hands under his chest and pushed up from the floor of the boat. He stood to find that he was on a vast beach. He must have beached at high tide and then been left high and dry. The beach was empty, and he couldn't see any houses. Looking down, he realized he looked like he had escaped a mental institution since he was still wearing the white, though now less white, scrubs. He was groggy, a familiar state to him now. He tried to come up with his next move. He had escaped Cultus, or Gallinger, whoever was represented on that island. But now he was on a remote beach, possibly in the middle of nowhere, with no way to contact anyone. Unless—he remembered the cell phone he'd taken from that man on the dock.

He searched the floor of the boat and found it behind the remaining propane tanks. He flipped it open and checked for service. None. He began searching through it for information. The phone's owner was named Reginald Dormand. This could come in handy. He took off the life vests he'd put on, tucked the phone in his waistband, and hopped out of the boat onto the wet sand. He began walking up to the low brush and grasses that topped the slope leading to the beach. On reaching the top, he looked out over the marshy grasslands that mixed with dunes and realized he had quite a hike ahead of him. He had only walked an hour or so before he realized the crushing thirst and hunger he felt. When had he last had a drink of water? A bit of food? Just the thought of it seemed to weigh him down, and he staggered over the next dune only to fall. His adrenaline was gone. His surge of strength from God was gone. He had nothing left. As his eyes closed, he breathed one last prayer of desperation. "God, help me." It was all he could get out before he slipped away.

The voice was loud and twangy. "I was just walking along, and here's this guy in white stretched out on the sand. If I hadn't seen the footprints, I'd have thought he just fell from the sky."

Another voice, more calm, soothing. "Thanks for bringing him in. We'll take it from here."

Ethan cracked his eyelids and saw bright fluorescent lights whizzing by overhead. He was being wheeled through a doorway on a bed. He sat up only to be forced back down by a flowered-scrubs-clad nurse along with a wave of nausea and dizziness. "No, you don't. Not till we're finished with you." *Another answer to prayer?* Ethan thought.

"Who brought me here?" Ethan asked the nurse.

"Funny thing. He said his name was Karlson and he

lived on Duneshore Drive. Thing is I've never even heard of Duneshore Drive."

"You didn't know him?" Ethan asked as the nurse strapped on a blood pressure cuff.

"Never seen him before. But what's even stranger is how he found you. Who are you?" She stripped off the cuff and stuck a thermometer in his mouth. "Well?"

Ethan gave her a look that said, "Do I answer you with this in my mouth or make you wait?" The small tan box beeped indicating he was the right temperature, and he was able to say, "Ethan Zabad. Where am I?"

"You're in Port Salerno."

"Port Salerno? Where's that?"

"We're about twenty-five miles north of West Palm Beach."

"Florida?"

"That's the one. That Karlson fella said he found you in the St. Lucie Inlet Park. It's only accessible by boat. I don't know how he found you, and I don't know what you were doing in there." She grabbed a light and looked in his ears, eyes, and mouth as she talked. "You look okay. Temperature's good. You're severely dehydrated. We'll take care of that right now." She proceeded to hook him up to a bag of dripping solution.

"The state police are coming down to talk to you. They'll want a statement."

Ethan began to think through what he might say. This would force him to be creative, which was not his strong suit. He was making up a fish story when he saw the police officers come to the nurse station just outside his door. Then he realized he could just tell them he was from Fort Bragg and see what they say. If they didn't believe him, they would think he was crazy or a terrorist or something. After all, with his hair gone, he looked even more Middle Eastern. All the sensitivity training and laws against stereotyping terrorists as young Middle Eastern men had not stopped law enforcement from leaning that way. It was human nature, and in most cases it couldn't be trained out of people.

Ethan glimpsed uniformed officers through the open door. They started to walk through but were interrupted by a voice saying, "Wait! He's with me. I need to see him first." At first the officers tried to restrain her until she flashed some ID at them, and they melted away. It was Kaplan. She was in street clothes, and her hair was down. Ethan was grateful to see her and amazed again by how attractive she was.

"Nice hairdo," she said to Ethan. Her smile was better medicine than anything the hospital had.

The hospital was reluctant to let Ethan go because of his condition, but Andrea assured them he would get better care where he was going. They walked into the parking lot, and Andrea opened the passenger door for Ethan on a new model Lexus.

"We're driving?"

"Only to the airport. Besides, it's less conspicuous than flying." Andrea looked at him. "Do you really want to get in another helicopter?"

"What's with the new car?"

"I rented it. It's on the government dime. Why not?"

They settled in for the seventy-five-minute drive, and Ethan recounted his tale to Andrea. After telling her how he escaped, he realized he hadn't asked some very crucial questions.

"How long have I been gone?"

"Six days. We've been looking the whole time. They

came so fast that by the time we got choppers in the air it was too late. We even sent out a recon jet, but they had disappeared. They must've stayed low and fast. It's also possible they have radar-jamming technology."

"I didn't realize I had been brought so far south."

"The helicopter they stole had a flight radius of over seven hundred miles. With extra fuel they could go even farther."

"I talked to a man just before I escaped who said Rolf Gallinger had bought the island."

"Bought it? He would have to be talking about the Bahamas then."

"Aren't those too far away for me to have made it to the coast?"

"I'm not sure, Ethan, but we'll work backwards from the boat you came in on. We'll establish the radius and pinpoint its location."

"The island looked normal from the surface, but underneath it there were structures built into the sand." Ethan tried to explain it as best he could.

"Maybe it wasn't an island at all, but something built to look like one."

"I guess it's possible. He probably has enough money to do something like that."

"Who was the man who said Gallinger had bought it?"

"Reginald Dormand. I gave him a message to take to Gallinger."

"A message? You had time to write a message?"

Ethan felt a little foolish as he recalled what he had done. He also felt a twinge of regret. "I told him to tell Gallinger to leave me alone. Then I threw him into the lagoon."

"Good one," Andrea said with a smirk.

"It was all I had time for."

"Hey, do you want something to eat?" Andrea said suddenly.

Ethan wasn't sure if he should eat something after being so dehydrated. "I guess if you need something. I think I'll keep drinking this Gatorade-wannabe stuff. Tastes like flat soda, but I guess it does the trick."

"Suit yourself." Andrea pulled off the road and parked in front of the Kwik-E Mart. "Be right back. Why don't you take a little rest? The seat reclines all the way!" She flashed him a gorgeous smile and walked inside. He followed her with his eyes. She wasn't in uniform today and instead wore a well-fitting pair of jeans and a short-sleeve pullover that gave plenty of fuel to his imagination. He reclined the seat and put his head back. He found himself wondering again what a woman like that was doing in the military. He shook his head and realized he shouldn't be thinking like that. He sat up to look back at the gas station and noticed that she was on her cell phone. Must be checking in with Morrow. Then suddenly he remembered the cell phone he had found. Where was it? He checked his waistband. *Maybe Kaplan had gotten it from the front desk at the hospital. Or maybe stashed it in the car.* He opened the glove box and rifled through it. He pulled out the registration and insurance and threw it aside. Nothing. He began putting things back in the glove box and noticed the vehicle's registration. The name on it was not a rental company but Andrea Kaplan. Why had she lied to him? He threw everything back in the box and decided to lie down again in case she came back and saw him.

A few minutes later, he heard the door open. He sat up, and as she put her hand on the gear shifter, he put his hand on top of hers. "Where's the phone I had on me?"

"What phone?" she responded, glancing down at his hand.

"I took a phone from that man I told you about. It's how I found out his name. It had all kinds of numbers in it. Numbers for Gallinger and others. Names I've heard in our briefings."

"A phone like that could be really valuable to us. Are you sure you had it with you after you got out of the boat?"

"I tucked it into my waistband. Did you ask the hospital it they had any of my personal belongings?"

"They said you were brought in with the clothes on your back. I'm sorry, Ethan. Do you want me to call them again?"

"Would you? I feel like I should bring that back with me. I have to have something to show for my six days in captivity." He finished with an apologetic smile at her. She leaned toward him and, freeing her hand from under his, touched his face.

"I'm so glad you're okay, Ethan." She leaned in even closer and gently kissed him on the lips. Ethan wanted to jerk back and press in at the same time. The latter urge won, and the way he kissed her back gave away how badly he'd wanted to do that ever since he'd seen her that first day on base. He never admitted it to himself, but she reminded him of Sarah in many ways. Ways that made him want spend time with her and see how far their relationship could go. They kissed another moment. "We should go. I'll call, and if we have to go back, we're still close enough we won't lose much time."

Andrea dialed the number as they pulled out of the gas station lot and headed back onto the road. It was a fruitless call. "They say you came in with nothing on you. If we can figure out where you were found, we can always go back and look."

"No. That place is huge. I could never retrace my steps. Most of them were taken in a dehydrated and hungry stupor." Ethan laid his head back on the seat and tried to get comfortable. Something was nagging him at the back of his mind. He couldn't quite put words to it. He drifted into a fitful sleep. Suddenly he jerked awake. It came to him. He looked over at Andrea, who looked startled to see him awaken so quickly.

"What's wrong?"

"How long have I been sleeping?"

Glancing at the car's digital clock, Andrea reported, "About forty-five minutes. Why?"

"How far away are we from the airport?"

"I guess about ten minutes. Why, Ethan? What's wrong?"

The wheels were turning. How could he ask her without accusing? But how could he not ask her and blindly go on? He almost started praying again but went on what he felt his gut telling him. Or maybe just the thought of praying was enough for God to acknowledge there was a need, and He was answering with that twinge in his gut. Did God speak or lead that way? It was all new to Ethan. He pressed forward.

"Andrea. How did you know I was in Port Salerno, that tiny little hospital?"

"What? What do you mean?"

"I mean how did you know I was there? I could have been anywhere in the world after six days. You showed up fast. Really fast."

"I—I—I don't see what difference it makes."

"It makes a difference to me."

"I was listening to the police scanners. State police scanners. They said something about a man found on the coast, so I thought I'd take a chance."

"Murrow know you 'took a chance'?"

"I called him while you were being discharged." She paused, and Ethan could see her set her jaw. "Why would you ask me questions like that? If I hadn't showed up, you'd still be back there getting grilled about everything. I expect you to trust me."

"I'm sorry, Andrea. I had to know. I've seen and heard things the last few months that make it hard for me to trust anyone. And I can't help but think someone at that base is playing both sides. How else would they have known exactly where to find me?"

"We believe Siegers was working with Cultus to compromise you," Andrea responded quickly.

"Has it been proven?"

"Yes," she answered. "And no." She added. "Not with absolute certainty. It can't be proven. He's dead."

"Dead? Is my family okay? David, my parents?"

"They're all fine. Just worried about you. Why don't you rest some more? We'll be there soon."

Ethan put his head back and tried to rest some more but could not. Scenarios kept racing through his mind, and he tried to unravel the mystery that was sitting next to him.

His reunion with his parents was wonderful. In some ways it was better than his reunion with them over a month ago. This time he knew how thin the line was between closeness and separation, and he never wanted to cross it again. His reunion with David was even more special. He knew now more than ever how precious time was with his son. He had already missed seven years, and he didn't want to miss anymore. He spent the next few days recovering with his family. He and his father were sitting in the living room relaxing when Ethan decided to tell him about what had happened in that cell on the island.

"You prayed to God?" Abe asked. He was thrilled, but Ethan could tell he was trying to hide it.

"Yes. At least it was sort of like a prayer. I just talked to him. Asked for his help."

Abe smiled. "Sounds like prayer to me. What did God tell you?"

"He didn't tell me anything. I just knew He was there. I felt His power."

"What did you tell Him?"

"I told him I would do what He asked. That I would be who He wanted me to be."

Abe smiled again. "I have been asking God for that for many years. That you would fulfill your calling."

"What are the four things again?"

"God's laws about food. Master self-control. Give generously. And leave that hair alone."

Abe finished this list with a chuckle. "I never understood them, Ethan, but I knew that if you obeyed, He would do amazing things with you."

"What hair?"

"God is not like us Ethan. It could be that he allowed your head to be shaved so that you would go to Him as your last resort. He wants you to trust *Him*, not your obedience or good works."

"You may be right. I've started doing those other three

225

things. It's only been a day and half, and already I feel different. I can't explain it."

"I can. It's obedience, Son. God blesses it."

Gallinger was livid. "Is anyone here going to tell me what happened?"

Kelso's staff, along with Dormand, were cowering in the lab below Gallinger's private island. "All of our precautions were pointless. You told me we could contain him. And how in God's name did he get his hands on a boat?" He slammed his fist down on one the lab tables. It shook, and several glass beakers fell over. "Kelso, I have put great faith in you." Gallinger trembled as he tried to regain control of himself. He had to remain in control. He needed these people to make this happen. He hated needing them. Hated being dependent. He must remain in control of himself. His inclination at this moment was to leave by helicopter and detonate the island along with everyone on it. "Get my computer operations up and running again. Recode the virus logarithms and prepare to launch our original plan. I want everything the way it was before this Zabad character. He's been a damaging and distracting detour. Prepare the storage facility for the mainframe as before. Let's put it in our facility near Sao Paulo. Add a few surprises for Mr. Zabad in case he attempts an encore performance. Dormand, call the board of directors, and tell them I will be back in Frankfort tomorrow night. I want them all there for the launch."

"Uh, sir. I can't do that."

"Oh yes. Your phone." He stared down at Dormand.

"You are lucky we had help on the mainland. I ought to kill you myself for your stupidity. Ask Kelso's staff to reprogram a phone for you. I want the media package released to international media two weeks from today at noon Frankfort time." Gallinger let out a disgusted sigh. "We should have been doing this months ago."

Gallinger was already more rich than he had any right to be. Before Ethan had destroyed the computer system in the mountains of Afghanistan, Gallinger was reaping thousands of dollars a minute from his intricate system of algorithms designed to skim a small percentage of worldwide credit transactions. This next step wasn't about money. It was about power. Ever since Kelso had harnessed the power and possibilities of nanotechnology, Gallinger had been ready to take this next step. Money was the universal language. If he could show them that defiance would get them killed, they would quickly bend to his demands. The demands were simple. Control of every international banking institution. A consolidated worldwide bank run by none other than Rolf Gallinger.

Once the warning was issued, the world banking elite would have hours to decide before Gallinger activated the first set of algorithms, which would randomly activate the virus on a set number of credit cards worldwide. People would die en masse until control was handed over. If control of the banking sector was successful, Gallinger would turn his attention to governments. Just knowing he could influence the entire world provided him a rush like the drugs he'd experimented with in college. He didn't take them anymore. He got too much of a thrill out of everyday business. Cutthroat takeovers, behind the scenes power plays. It all got his blood pumping.

He hadn't started out in life to control the world. But as

his attempts at false religion became successful and his business ventures grew, he began to believe he was destined to have control. After all, he had the resources, the know-how, and the personnel. Almost everyone working in Qualtech was also a member of Cultus. His dreams of a loyalty inspired by religious belief were coming true. There were many members of his organization willing to die for their belief. For him.

The radical terrorist networks he had been using were also willing to die for their beliefs. But once this plan went into motion, he would no longer have any use for them. They had failed in Afghanistan anyway. But it certainly paid dividends to fund their activities in other parts of the world. It kept whole governments focused on the war on terror while Gallinger plotted his own version of terror unseen.

He had the world in his grip. Their dependence on credit would be their downfall. He was imagining the run on banks once people learned they could not use their cards without putting themselves in danger. Cash would run short; the economy would slow. Everyone would panic. Except Gallinger. He would not only be their demise. He would be their savior. That was the coup that made his plan brilliant. He would bring the world to its knees only to step in and save it, at a cost of course. His message to the world and its banking systems said nothing of Qualtech or Cultus. In fact it said nothing even of Gallinger. A nameless, faceless enemy to the world. The unknown terror that would strike. There would be no way of tracking the virus's origin or which cards carried it and which did not. Most of the world did not have the technology to understand let alone investigate his brand of nanotechnology. It all felt right. He never even gave a thought to the lives that might be lost in the process. They were cattle to him.

He had two weeks to prepare. One thing still seemed undone. He had walked to the surface while he had been lost in thought and realized he needed Dormand. Where was that idiot? "Dormand!" he shouted as he made his way back down the corridor to the lab.

Dormand appeared, breathless, at the bottom of the ramp, not far from where Ethan had torn the hinges off the steel door in the lab.

Without preface Gallinger stated, "I want Ethan Zabad dead, and I want his father and son in my custody. If Ethan had no DNA that gave him his ability, it's possible that his father has something we missed. Or perhaps his son carries something. As long they are a possible resource to me, I want them alive."

"Do you want our contact to do it?"

Gallinger thought for a moment. It was a useful contact and had provided useful information. He didn't want to throw it away in a moment of carelessness. But on the other hand, once he started next week's events, he wouldn't have much time for maintaining contacts. It might become useless to him.

"Yes. I want him dead before next week's announcement. I'm not taking any chances this time."

13

Though security was heightened at the base, there was still a great deal of speculation about how Ethan had been kidnapped in the first place and whether something like that could happen again. There was talk that they should move Ethan's family to a more secure location, but they decided against it based on the last invasion. Another strike like that was unlikely. With the ground approaches covered and better attention being paid to the skies, the Zabad family felt safe.

Ethan walked with a cup of hot tea out to the front porch. The house the family was living in was small but well maintained and cozy. David was beginning to enjoy living on the base with all the constant activity. He had taken to Robbie and had the privilege of going with him to the firing range. They had also observed a live munitions demonstration. David loved watching things blow up. He was really no different from any other boy his age. While Ethan had been a captive, Robbie tried to keep David's mind off his father's absence by spending time with him.

Ethan remembered imagining Robbie coming through the door to his cell on the island but now realized that Robbie had been helping him in a way he could never have imagined. He was taking care of Ethan's family. Ethan was appreciative of this, and once he had returned he started once again making up for lost time. He kept thinking of the day he could just go home with his family and start a new life. It didn't seem possible that one day he could live without fear of an enemy or himself. He was learning what God expected of him and therefore understanding how to control himself. Rather than just acting in his self-interests or in whatever way seemed right at the time, he was learning to act according to his strengths, according to a leading from outside himself. The last time he'd acted for someone else he'd ended up in jail. It made one a little reticent to help others.

While he was in prison, he had read quite a bit. Fiction of course but many biographies. He was drawn to stories of great men. And strangely enough, stories of men who had the potential to be great, to be remembered by history, yet failed and ended their lives in obscurity and poverty. In some ways this prospect scared him more than death. He knew he had the potential to be great. And it wasn't some prideful notion or him patting himself on the back. He was beginning to understand his purpose. He was beginning to see the parallels between himself and his ancestor, Samson. It still was amazing to him to think that he had some connection, even if remote, to that man of the Bible. How many of his people could say they had a known biblical ancestor?

The parallels were interesting. His predicted birth, conditions on his diet, difficulty controlling himself in tense situations. Of course one element that he hadn't seen in his own life was Samson's weakness for women. Ethan had one relationship with Sarah, but that was it. He didn't have issues with women. There was Andrea. What was that relationship? Platonic? Growing? Close to commitment? He knew there was something there, but what? He definitely felt an attraction to her, but they were in completely different situations in life. His ultimate goal was to finish with this Cultus and military business and then get on with life. What that life might consist of he had no idea. He hadn't been trained in anything so far except what he'd experienced here. Before that it was the odd jobs he'd held in New York City. Now that he was seeking a leading in life outside himself he was a little more confident that guidance would come.

A week had gone by since he had returned from Florida with Andrea Kaplan. He was feeling good. Better, in fact, than he ever had. He wondered if he would have felt this way all his life if he had taken seriously the conditions his parents gave to him as a young man. He stood on the front porch of the little house and stared over the nearby housetops to the horizon. He felt a tug on his arm. David.

"Good morning, Son. How did you sleep?"

"Good." It was quiet for a few seconds as they both took the morning in. "I'm glad you're back."

"Me too. Robbie tells me you're a pretty good shot. You did some destruction while I was gone?"

David grinned ear to ear. "Yeah. I got to push a button, and stuff just blew up."

They both chuckled softly. "Dad? How long are we going to be here? I mean, I like it, but I miss some things."

"I know. This will all be over soon."

"What's going on?"

Ethan knew the whole story would overwhelm David and scare him, but there were some things he should know about. "There are some people in this world that want to hurt me, and I need to stay hidden for a while."

"Why do they want to hurt you?"

"They think I have something they want. And they've tried to do some bad things, and I stopped them."

David considered this. "Are you like Batman?"

"No, David. God gave me some special abilities. I work for Him."

"But why do I have to stay?"

"The people who want to hurt me would hurt the people I love just to get to me. We need to keep you safe, too."

"Is anything going to happen to me?"

"No. I won't let it."

"You promise?"

Ethan hated to make a promise that he wasn't sure he could keep. It was part of the learning curve as a Dad. "David, I just want you to know how proud I am of you. You're a great son. I'm blessed to be your dad."

David said nothing. He was already standing next to Ethan. He just leaned his head over and rested it against Ethan's waist. Ethan gently stroked David's hair with his free hand. Ethan would have normally fought it, but he let a few tears escape and roll down his face. David had triggered something in Ethan. It was a sense of completion. It was the fulfillment of a purpose. He felt like there was more to David than him simply being his offspring. He tousled David's hair after a few moments of silence and said, "Come on, let's go get some breakfast."

This was the whole reason for being here. As a follower of Cultus, one did what one was ordered to do. It was spiritual, but it was also financial. Yes, there was the "religion" of Cultus, but there was always a reward. That's one thing followers of Cultus enjoyed. If you were asked by god to do something, you were rewarded handsomely. But there was also prestige. Many of Cultus's followers, though not very vocal about it, had been given high government positions, leadership of corporations, and celebrity status in the Nashville and Hollywood scenes. Some of those people who got recording contracts but couldn't sing their way out of the shower or starred in movies but couldn't act cold if you stuck them in the freezer were people who had performed favors for Cultus and its god, Gallinger. One of Gallinger's ideas. Give people what they want—fame—and the religion takes on a celebrity status. The millions they make get returned to Cultus. It was a system that was working brilliantly. But for this agent of Cultus, there would be no high-powered jobs or singing careers. It was simply devotion. Fierce allegiance to a religion that gave a person purpose.

The Cultus operative waited until Ethan left the house. He had been on the porch a few moments ago with his son. Such a touching family portrait. Ethan left, so they knew it was just Mom, Dad, and the boy. The silencer was on, and the pistol concealed. A gentle knock on the door, and Abe Zabad answered. He was about to invite the person on the porch inside, but they stepped inside first and quickly pulled out the pistol. "We're all going for a ride."

They made it past the base checkpoints easily. The driver never suspected that he had any extra "cargo" in the back. The van they had selected had been on and off base for almost a year and didn't arouse suspicion. David, Abe, and Tara were bound in the back with the Cultus operative keeping them quiet. They were gone three hours before anyone knew they were missing. Once off the base, the driver spent a few hours bound in his own van until someone found him. Another Cultus member met the threesome while the Cultus operative speedily went back to base. Abe, Tara, and David had disappeared.

"We don't even know how they left the base! What's going on? Three people just disappear, and we don't know what to do?"

Murrow had been dreading this conversation. He was sick about it and angry. Someone on his base, on his watch, had deceived everyone. There was a traitor here, perhaps several, one of whom could have been Siegers. It was unclear. He may have simply been a casualty of this secret war.

"Ethan, we have no record that they left the base."

"Then find out who did. Someone left this base in the last three or four hours and had them."

"That's a possibility," Murrow said reassuringly. "But we also have to consider that they went to one of the training areas and left the base on foot."

"You know my mother could have never done that. Her legs and hips would have never made it." Ethan angrily paced Murrow's office. "We know this is Cultus. This is Gallinger. If we find him, I'm sure we'll find them."

"I'm sure you're right. But we can't just run off looking for Gallinger. Since our last foray into the Middle East, we haven't heard anything from him. We are still trying to decode much of the information on those nanochips you brought back to us. If we find more definitive proof of what he's up to, we can take a stronger action. All we have on him right now regarding your family is a very strong hunch. If he has a reason to take them, which I'm sure he does, we'll hear from him soon enough."

"Do we know where Gallinger is right now?"

"Our sources say he's back in Frankfort. He had disappeared for a while. We can only assume he had to clean things up after Afghanistan."

"So my family is in Europe?"

"I wouldn't be so sure. He has places all over the globe. It all depends on what his end game is."

"It's me, Murrow. That has to be it. Why else—"

"That's part of it. But we know from all of our information about Gallinger that he has something else going. The virus, the credit cards, the computer systems. All of that was for his sick, twisted plan. What if we didn't stop him? If he has a backup somewhere, he could be moving forward with his plans."

"So where do I come into it?"

"You stopped him once, Ethan. He may be afraid you'll do it again. Or..." Murrow had considered it before, but he'd never shared his thoughts with Ethan.

"Or what?"

"Or Gallinger thinks he's figured out how to get what he wants from you."

It finally dawned on Ethan. "If he couldn't get the right genetics from my blood to reproduce people like me, he may be able to get the right combination from my family." Ethan felt his blood pressure spike.

"Ethan, we don't know that for sure. It's just speculation."

"I'm going to Frankfort. I'm going to find my family."

"You can't do that. You can't leave this base. You can't go on a vigilante mission."

"I can't? Are you going to stop me?"

"You're strong, Ethan, but you can't dodge a bullet."

"You'd shoot me? I lost a family and a son I didn't know I had almost ten years ago. I am not going to lose them again." Ethan turned angrily away when Murrow raised his voice.

"There's a lot more at stake. Gallinger could be up to something else. We need to wait and see his next move. We're talking about the world. Not just your family."

Ethan stepped back toward him and pointed his finger at his chest. "I will find a way. With or without your help."

"You'll never leave American soil. Just wait for the situation to change. Get more information."

"I have all the info I need." Ethan turned and slammed the door to Murrow's office. He remembered this hall from just a few months ago, walking down to the room where Murrow and the team awaited his arrival. They were so worried about whether a civilian would be able to serve with seasoned soldiers. And now here he was ready to take on Gallinger and whatever army he had all by himself.

He spent the next few hours at the empty house. He

stared at the recliner where his father had been spending his evenings watching Jeopardy and the nightly news. He looked at the couch where his mother had been cross-stitching and knitting each day. The room where his son had been creating a tentlike structure in the corner to hide out. He was going room to room when he heard a gentle knock at the door. He opened it and saw Andrea Kaplan. She stepped in the doorway, and he embraced her. She and Erik Remont and Robbie Charles had changed his life. He clung to her, knowing that she would be able to talk him through this. To help him master self-control. To contain the anger he felt. He relaxed his arms and moved back so he could look into her eyes. "I'm really glad you're here. I need someone with me right now." She reached over and touched his face with her fingertips. He leaned in and kissed her. He didn't forget for one second about his family. His son. But maybe there was someone who cared about him and would be there for him.

Andrea interrupted the moment. "Ethan. I'm so sorry. I saw Robbie on the way from the admin building. He told me what happened."

"I just talked with Murrow. He wants me to stay put. I don't know how he expects me to just sit here."

"You may not be sitting for long." She moved past him and clicked on the TV. "That's why I came over. Well, one of the reasons. To show you this."

She turned the volume up and Ethan heard the reporter. "...video message today. A professionally produced video warning people that 'unless the controlling interest of several international banks is turned over, people's greed will kill them' was released to several international media syndicates. Authorities are investigating the video and also trying to decipher the cryptic warnings contained in it.

References to an 'economic apocalypse' a 'financial plague' and 'total fiscal dominance' all have authorities wondering if this is merely the work of a sophisticated prankster or a serious threat. The video stated that the international banks have twenty-four hours to comply, or they will see the consequences played out worldwide. This is on the heels of two straight weeks of stock market decline. The banks listed in the video have headquarters on four continents. Authorities have few leads and the video is unclear about what the actual consequences of noncompliance might be. " The anchors bantered a little about the video and then moved on to the next story.

"It doesn't sound like they're taking this very seriously."

"Why would they?" Andrea responded. "They have no idea what could happen. America knows because we got lucky. We happened to be in the right place at the right time."

"Don't we have a responsibility to tell the rest of the world what could happen and who's behind it?"

"That's not our call to make."

The phone rang, which startled Ethan since he had been in silence for so long. It was Murrow. After a few brief "yes sirs" Ethan hung up the phone. "You were right about not sitting for long. Murrow wants me back at his office."

Murrow had reassembled the Afghanistan team minus Theo, who was still not 100 percent. Everyone else looked to be in good health, and Murrow had just started briefing them on what was next.

"Ethan. Have as seat."

"Thank you, sir." Ethan nodded at several of the guys as he sat down. He liked Cameron, Barton, Casey, and Pits. But Robbie was still the best.

"Mongezi, you'll be taking the lead on this one."

"Yes, sir." The young man nodded at Murrow.

"You've all seen the video. No identification. Just a corporation name for these banks to sign things over to. We can't get any info on the corporation or who set it up. Obviously we are looking at Gallinger first. This is his plan A with some slight modifications. We thought he might have a backup plan. A backup mainframe computer. The question is where in the world would he put it?"

"Excuse me, sir." It was Casey.

"Yes?"

"We've got about twenty-two hours now until doomsday. Who's warning the rest of the world about this? Don't they have a right to know what's coming?"

"They do. But—and this is from the top—we are going to try and stop this before we make any announcements. We need to avoid a cash-only scenario if possible. If we warn the world, Gallinger will probably get the financial panic he wants."

"If we wait, he gets it anyway. All due respect, sir." Casey added.

"That's why what we do after we leave this room is so important. We have four potential locations we'll be checking out. We have a team ready in Afghanistan to raid one of Gallinger's storage facilities. We have a carrier off the Asian coast that will support a team going into Thailand. He has a facility there. A team from our German installation will check out Gallinger's holdings in Frankfort. And we have a carrier group that can be to the coast of Brazil in just a few hours. That's where we're headed. Sao Paulo."

Cameron spoke up. "He must have facilities all over the world. What are the chances it will be one of these four?"

"These are the only four that meet the criteria required

to house the computer he needs. If there's one we don't know about, we're in trouble."

"And we can't just arrest him? Detain him until his deadline is past?" Ethan could not believe the foolishness of just letting the man roam free.

"If he's as smart as we believe he is, this is a plan that's been set in motion. It will continue with or without him."

"It's too bad someone hasn't taken it upon themselves to do something about him." Pits was also frustrated.

Robbie never said much during briefings, but he spoke now. "We answer to the president. To our country. We do what we're told. Not whatever we want to do. If and when we are ordered to dispatch Mr. Gallinger, I will be first in line. Not because I want to take a life, but because it means the saving of so many others. Until then we answer to a higher authority." He finished and glanced over at Ethan.

Ethan answered to a higher authority now. Not the president, not Murrow, but God himself. Now was his chance to fulfill the purpose that God had laid out for him.

The rest of the briefing was straightforward. Because the team was so small they would be flown to the carrier on a COD, the navy version of a mail plane. It was small enough to land on a carrier but large enough to bring in cargo. It was rarely used for personnel but in a pinch would perform admirably. From the carrier they would be flown in via helicopter so that they would be right next to their target. Meanwhile Murrow, the US Ambassador to Brazil, and their attaché would be flown directly to the embassy. This was a situation where it was easier for the US to ask for forgiveness than permission.

The credit card manufacturing facility was a building in the northwest part of the city of Sao Paulo. The city itself was a maze of streets with very little reason to its layout.

Streets rarely crossed at right angles and only a local would know one street or part of town from the next. Their objective was simple. Get inside the building and destroy the mainframe computer. The problem was the lack of intel. They knew the location of the building and could even get a blueprint of its construction, but they had no way of knowing what they'd find once inside.

At the end of the meeting is when Murrow dropped the bombshell. "You won't be going with the team, Ethan. This is much more difficult and risky than the last mission, and I don't want your family becoming an issue."

"My family *is* the issue."

"That's exactly the reason you can't be involved. Not to mention the fact that you had extensive training before the last mission whereas we leave for the carrier group in thirty minutes."

"Why would you let me in on the briefing if you weren't going to let me go?" Ethan was beginning to lose it. The rest of the team quietly filtered out behind him.

"You had to know you couldn't go on this one. I wanted to you to be aware of what was happening. Would you rather I just called the team together and left you out of it? Bottom line is, you're a civilian. You're staying here. You'll know how we did in twenty one hours." Murrow was whisked out of the room by several aides who had entered with more up-to-date information.

Ethan followed and was left standing in the hallway, stunned. After all he had been through, all he had learned. He thought this was his chance to do all the things his parents had always told him he would do. He simply could not stay. He would find a way. He turned with determination and almost ran into Andrea.

"Sorry, Andrea." Ethan started to make his way past her

toward the exit. In the brief second that she saw him, she must have seen the distress on his face.

"What's the matter, Ethan? What happened?" She moved toward him and reached for his arm.

"Murrow is leaving me behind. I have a chance to do something, and he wants me here."

"We don't even know where your family is, Ethan. Maybe you should stay here."

"I know it's Gallinger that has taken them, and if I can do something to stop him, I'm going to do it."

"But what good would it do for you to go and possibly be killed? Then you certainly wouldn't see you family again."

"You're really on Murrow's side on this one? I didn't expect that. I thought you'd want to help me."

"I do want to help you. But do you think I want you to be killed? I care about you, Ethan."

Ethan set his jaw. He was surprised at what he was about to say. "Prove it." As soon as he said it, he realized how stupid it sounded, but he was willing to look foolish if it meant participating in bringing down Gallinger and seeing his family again.

Andrea smiled broadly. "I think I can do that. As much as I care about you and as much as I wish you would just stay here—I will help you. After all, I *am* going with Murrow and the boys."

"You're going?"

"Murrow needs me on this one. That makes it a little less complicated."

"So where do we start?"

"Let's get you in uniform. Private First-Class Zabad, or should I say Smith?"

Time was very limited. The team would be leaving in less than thirty minutes. If Andrea and Ethan were going along, they would have to act fast.

"Can we get on the plane?" Ethan asked breathlessly as they left the administration building.

"My level of clearance will get you to the airstrip. From there we have to figure out how to get you on board."

"Andrea? What happens if you get caught helping me?"

"I'll be disciplined. Probably demoted."

"And that doesn't bother you?"

"If you do in Sao Paulo what I think you'll do, it won't really matter, will it?"

They ran to Andrea's Humvee and tore through the base to the airstrip. Along the way they planned their boarding strategy.

Andrea explained, "All you have to do is be undetected long enough to take off. Once we're off the ground they won't turn around to take you back. You'll go under guard the rest of the way."

"What about you?"

"I'm working on that."

"Because you know if they catch you helping me they'll put you under guard too, and then our trip stops. We won't be getting off the carrier unless it's in shackles."

"I know, I know! Just let me think!"

She skidded around a gravel-covered bend on her way to the airfield, narrowly missing the ditch on the side of the road.

"The best scenario would be to get on board before the

rest of the team even got there." "Doing so in one piece would be ideal."

"You're funny."

She bumped across a strip of grass that separated the incoming road from one of the small hangars and pulled around behind it. They could see a few hundred yards off, separated from all other military vehicles and aircraft, two COD planes being loaded with supplies. They would be packed lightly with the distance to travel and time constraint. They needed to travel fast. The fact that there were two was a great help to Ethan and Andrea. It doubled their chances of getting onboard. They crept around the small hangar and began looking for a way to get close to the planes without being seen. Ethan saw it first. A truck was being loaded at the entrance to the largest hanger almost one hundred yards away. They walked quickly but inconspicuously toward the hangar.

With all the other people running around, they blended well. As they entered the hangar, a PFC stepped up and challenged them but was quickly dismissed when he saw Andrea's rank. They walked toward the truck, each thinking through how to use it to their advantage. Once they arrived next to it, Ethan walked to the side that was angled away from the plane. Andrea walked up to the soldiers loading the truck and got their attention. They gathered around for a minute while she asked a series of pointless questions about what they were doing, which gave Ethan all the time he needed to find a hiding spot. Unfortunately there wasn't one to be found. Andrea finished distracting the loaders and came around the truck to see if Ethan was safely away.

"I thought you were going to get under the truck!"

"Get under an idling truck and cling to the frame?" He'd only seen it done in the movies.

"Why not? You've got to get on board that plane. It's the only way you're going to Sao Paulo. If your family is there—"

"We need something more secure. A guarantee that I can get on board."

Andrea scanned the loading area and suddenly had an idea. She drew in a sharp breath and glanced at Ethan.

"What? What is it?"

"You're going to hate it."

"Hate what? Just tell me. We don't have time to waste."

"Come here," Andrea beckoned, leading him farther back into the hangar. Ethan scanned the area trying to figure out what she was getting at. "Right there." She was pointing to a long plastic case. It was designed to hold and transport a piece of communication equipment but would snugly fit someone Ethan's size.

"You expect me to get in there and then ride in it for —for—"

"At least five, maybe six hours."

"No way. I'll suffocate."

"I know the piece of equipment that goes in there. It needs venting. You'll have air."

"What happens if I need to get out? You know, if I— freak out or something."

"You won't. Now get in so they can load you." They pulled out the instrument and several pieces of hard foam that would've held the instrument in a stable position.

"Are you sure we won't need this once we're there?"

"This is the armed forces. We're worse than the Boy Scouts. 'Always prepared' means take ten times the amount you need." Andrea pulled the last piece of foam liner from the case and turned to Ethan. "All right. In you go."

Ethan immediately broke into a sweat. "That's a really small space. It's like – it's like a coffin."

Andrea glanced back toward the plane loading area. "The truck is about to head back. It's now or never."

Ethan took a deep breath and lowered himself into the case. This had better work.

14

The truck was loaded with the instrument case carrying Ethan and driven to the plane. Another crew of soldiers went to work unloading everything into the plane. Ethan could feel as the case was picked up and slid into the rear of the plane. He could hear muffled voices for a moment, and then he heard the door slam indicating the loading was done. He was trying to control his breathing. He was also carrying on a constant internal monologue to convince himself he was not being buried alive. Once, he pushed against the lid of the case and realized that if he did freak out he could probably pop the lid off, which would blow his cover. He tried to relax. His best bet would be to simply fall asleep. But if falling asleep in his prison cell was a challenge, this would be much more difficult. There was no way for Ethan to mark time as he lay in the box. All he had were his thoughts, and they ranged from moderate fear to complete panic. He was growing accustomed to being given incredible amounts of physical strength for whatever obstacle he faced. He realized that to make this trip without going insane he would need a major boost in mental fortitude. There was only one source for such stamina. Ethan began to pray.

Things were going well so far. The announcement had triggered a small reaction in some of the larger urban centers where news seemed to travel faster. But so far no big announcements had been made by any nation's leadership. Only twenty hours to go. Now that things were wrapping up in Frankfort, Gallinger's next move was to fly to Sao Paulo to see his newest prizes, the Zabad family.

The bounce of the plane off the deck of the carrier was possibly the best thing Ethan had ever felt. He was jolted hard again as the plane was jerked to a stop by the arresting gear. While it may have been simple to get on board a plane, it would be much more difficult to get off the carrier and into the country. He wondered if Andrea had an idea for that one. He lay still, waiting to be unloaded. He was so ready to get out of his plastic prison that every moment seemed endless. For a person who had issues with small spaces, he was surprised he had managed to survive the ordeal, though if it had not been for answered prayer, it might have turned out differently. There were several moments where Ethan was tempted to just burst out of the case, but he managed to keep himself under control. After one such episode, he heard the welcome click of metal and hard plastic, meaning the latches had been popped and he would be able to get out. Just knowing he could get out was enough to settle his heart and calm his nerves.

When it had been quiet for a few minutes he cautiously lifted the lid and scanned his surroundings. He was looking at the interior and underside of the brand new aircraft carrier USS *McGavran*. After exiting the case, several sailors came in and began carrying the offloaded gear away. There was no place for Ethan to hide. When the sailors who were working glimpsed Ethan, he acted casually and waved hello. He walked past them like he was supposed to be there and hoped that his confidence would at least allow him to get someplace where he could keep an eye out for whatever mode of transportation would take them to the mainland. He was debating the merits of a plane versus a helicopter when he felt a huge hand rest on his shoulder and heard a big deep voice ask, "How was your flight?" It was Robbie.

"I can't do it, Ethan. And it doesn't matter if I disagree with Murrow. An order is an order." Robbie had been trying to defend Murrow for the last few minutes. They were in a gangway just aft of the hanger.

"What do I have to lose?" Ethan pleaded.

"It has nothing to do with what *you* might lose. There is a reason you were not even supposed to be here—on this carrier. I know your life changed while you were being held captive, but your old ways have a way of sneaking back up on you."

"This isn't 'old ways.' This is what I know is right."

Robbie glanced at his wristwatch. "The team is about to

miss me. I need to go. You need to lay low. Murrow sees you, you'll be locked up below."

"As if that would stop me."

Robbie started to walk down the gangway toward the hangar, but Ethan stopped him. "What plane are you taking?" he asked with a smile.

"Don't even think about it." Robbie turned back with a smirk.

"What plane, Robbie?"

"Find a place to hide. I'll see you in a few hours. When all this blows over, we'll have a big laugh about it."

"About my family, too?" Ethan dropped the smile and watched the big man's face soften.

"I'm not going to help you do something dangerous, illegal, and stupid. If you're being told not to go, there must be a good reason."

"It was okay for me to risk my life when my family was not even in the picture. When I didn't think I had anything to live for, and now when they're the ones on the line, I have to sit it out?" Ethan was beginning to lose patience, even with his friend.

"This is a matter of integrity."

"Integrity! It's more honest to obey the order than to do what you know is right? When you're out there, what will you do if it's a choice between your life and my son's or my father's? What will you do? Because I know what I would do. Without hesitation I would die so they could live. Or what if you have a situation like the last one? What if you can't get into the mainframe without me?"

"You should know me better than that. I do my job as a soldier, and if that means I have to die, so be it."

"My family may not even be there. They could be

anywhere in the world, but I have a chance. A chance to at least do something."

"Ethan—"

"Just tell me what plane, Robbie. You don't have to do anything else." Inside Ethan was praying that his friend would at least give him that much.

"We're not taking a plane. I'll try to get some gear ready for you." Robbie gave him a knowing look and went to meet the rest of the team.

"Thank you, Robbie." Ethan called out. He turned and began looking for a place to disappear until the time was right.

The helicopter got off the carrier without any trouble. Ethan had carefully searched the subdeck hangars until he found two helicopters. He would have had no way of knowing which was the right one except that Robbie had been true to his word and stashed a duffel bag full of the gear he would need. Included was an M-45 MEUSOC pistol, a Kevlar vest, and an identity-concealing mask that Ethan wore as they all made their way to the chopper on the deck. Robbie must have hinted at something to the rest of the team because none of them said a word about being seven in number instead of six. After they'd been in flight for twenty minutes, the time at which he was certain Murrow wouldn't turn the chopper around, Cameron Mongezi motioned to Ethan to remove his mask. Cameron shouted. "I'll brief you on our way to the Brazilian mainland."

"I'm only going for one reason. My family." Ethan shouted back.

Cameron continued as if he didn't hear him. "We'll be landing a few miles from the strike site. In case you didn't know, it's about three in the morning. So, under cover of darkness, we'll make our way to the Gallinger facility. We have a layout of part of the building, but several stories of it were unobtainable."

"Objectives?"

Cameron nodded. "Two main objectives. Destroy the computer system Gallinger is using to hold the world hostage and get your family out."

That was all Ethan needed to hear. "When do we get out of here?"

Ethan didn't know that at the same time they were preparing to land, Murrow, Kaplan, and a small attaché of American officers were on their own flight to meet with Brazilian officials at the embassy. With the possibility of a major economic catastrophe and a global pandemic, nations were willing to work together.

Dropping backwards into the pre-gray dawn sixty feet in the air, Ethan could make out the lights of Sao Paulo to the east. Their drop off point was to the northwest of the city. They would have much ground to cover in order to get into the city. At this time of night, they would be able to do so without attracting attention. Ethan had never actually rappelled before. It never occurred to him to be afraid or wonder how it worked. Something supernatural was at work in him again. He had dropped right after Robbie, and so he could just make out his form on the ground when he landed. When he touched the ground and unhooked, he saw the rest of the team on the ground already. They were staring.

"What?" Ethan asked defensively.

"You know you can use the rope to slow down, right? That's what that gear is for." Barton was pointing to the clip on his waist.

"I did come down slow, didn't I?"

"You dropped like a rock. Are your legs okay?"

"I'm fine." Ethan shrugged.

"Geez, you are nuts, you know that?" Barton walked away shaking his head.

"I guess I have to babysit you now since you missed all the briefings." Robbie gave Ethan another wry smile. "Let's go." Robbie picked up his gear and started in the slowly graying day toward the city of Sao Paulo. "Ethan," Robbie started as they jogged over the rough terrain. "You know this could be a very bad situation. Murrow warned us that Gallinger didn't respond well to being cornered. The only intel on that is from a business transaction that went bad. It was supposed to be a buyout by Gallinger's company, Qualtech. The company they were buying pulled some last-minute heroics and found a willing investor. Saved their company from Gallinger." Robbie ducked as they ran under some trees, through a hedgerow, and into a fruit tree grove. "He went nuts. People started dying. All in the most normal ways, heart attacks, car accidents, but it was just too coincidental. There was no connection in any way to Gallinger, but the company suffering the losses knew there was something going on. Gallinger won. He bought them out. But they paid."

"How can they implicate him in that?"

Robbie came to the end of the grove and turned right onto a small dirt road. "An investigation revealed that at least one of the deaths was by poisoning. That was one of the heart attacks. The only person with high access to the victim was a personal assistant. He turned out to be a follower of Cultus." Robbie stopped jogging and pulled out a small map. "This way," he said, pointing ahead and to his left. Ethan could make out the shape of more trees ahead.

"When we get to this facility, we're not going to just walk in and meet Gallinger at the door."

"That's if he's even there. Based on the number of facilities he has worldwide, the chances of him being here are one in twenty, at best." Robbie turned left sharply off the dirt road and through a small opening in some low-lying brush and scrub trees. "If anyone is there, it will be security guards, factory workers, and office personnel. People who most likely have no idea what's going on."

This concerned Ethan. His enemy was Gallinger. Not a bunch of pencil pushers or innocent factory workers. "Are we destroying the facility?"

"We're not trying to. We're supposed to go in, find the computer that's similar to the one we dealt with before, and destroy it. If by some miracle we find Gallinger, we're supposed to detain him."

"And if we're confronted by guys just doing their job?"

"We do ours." Robbie ran through a last line of trees and came into a clearing. Robbie flicked on his radio, as did the rest of the team. Ethan looked back and watched the rest of the team as they entered the clearing like faint shadows that got darker as they approached. They were all present with Casey Linz bringing up the rear.

Cameron nodded at the small circle that had gathered in the clearing. "We need to move!"

The plane landed with just ten hours before deadline. By five o'clock today it would all be over one way or the other. Time was running out. While the small plane had made the trip, Murrow and Andrea had talked about what would happen once on the ground. They would be driven immediately to the Brazilian consulate and brief their representative on the situation.

Navigating the busy streets took forty-five minutes. They approached the facility from the northwest as planned. It was a massive building. The warehouse and manufacturing portion of it looked unassuming. It was white, and at its tallest stood probably three stories. The office building built onto one end was over four times that height. It was sheathed in blue-green glass and had a silver Hyperteq logo sculpture atop its roof on the southeast corner.

"Let's hit the warehouse first," Cameron ordered.

Ethan was confident. Not at all nervous. He was feeling much the same way he'd felt in Afghanistan. He felt the same power he'd felt on the island off the Florida coast. He was ready.

The team had chosen a door that faced west and accessed an alley. Cameron turned the handle, and of course the door was locked. He nodded to Ethan, who stepped over and wrenched the handle off. The door opened easily. No sense in alerting the whole facility to their presence with a small explosive. At least not yet.

It was quiet inside. He'd expected to hear the sounds of manufacturing and machinery. But there was nothing. The door they came in led them into an area of the warehouse surrounded by pallets stacked with molded plastic units that looked to be cases for some kind of computer component. They crept around one end of the stack to survey the area. There was not much in the warehouse itself. It was cavernous, being at least one hundred fifty yards long and probably half that wide. There was no one in sight. If this mission was about destroying the mainframe computer, it seemed it would be a fruitless one. There was nothing suspicious anywhere in sight. There were a few more places in the warehouse with pallets stacked together.

Barton, Linz, and Pits went up the left side of the warehouse while Mongezi, Ethan, and Robbie made their way up the right side. About halfway through Ethan crept toward the middle of the warehouse and looked straight ahead to where it connected to the office building they'd seen outside. About thirty feet up, built into the wall of the warehouse, was a colossal window that looked from a conference room onto the factory floor. Ethan could make out the table and chairs in the room. As he watched, someone entered the room. Ethan crouched lower and pressed himself into the pallet at his back. He looked around for the rest of the team. They had continued up the right hand side of the large room.

He backed toward the outer wall. "Cameron. There's someone in that window."

Cameron spoke into his radio. "Barton, I need eyes on the northeast end of the building. Male in the window. Can you get an ID?"

"Negative. He's looking your direction. At least six foot. Light brown hair. Can't confirm without a look at his face."

Ethan crawled back toward the center of the room. He leaned around the edge of one of the pallets to get a closer look. The man in the window was staring right at him. As Ethan stared back, he felt his blood go cold. The hair on the back of his neck stood up. It was the man from his dream. The one in the gray suit. And this time he had a face. Though he had never seen him in person, he knew from the briefings that the man he was looking at now was Rolf Gallinger.

Without much thought, Ethan grabbed a pallet by the heavy duty plastic it was wrapped in and threw it at the giant window. It sailed silently through the air and then blew through the window with such force that the table in the room broke apart. Gallinger, having somehow managed to avoid the projectile, stepped through the debris and began applauding.

"Bravo, Ethan. I've been hoping to see you again. I love watching you work."

"Where's my family?"

"Mom, Dad, your son? I've already started working on them. I mean *with* them. They've been most cooperative."

"What are you doing to them?"

"It would be wonderful to have more people like you, wouldn't it? Can you imagine an army of men and women with your strength and fighting ability? All I needed was some DNA."

"You already took mine. What more did you need?"

"Yours didn't have anything unusual. That's why we decided to go to the source. And of course there's always the chance that your son has your *special* genes. We can't isolate the one that gives you your strength, but we'll find it."

"It has nothing to do with genetics. It's God."

"God? What can I do for you?"

"You think you're God?"

Gallinger laughed. "I do whatever I want. I have power over hundreds of thousands of people. I'm worshiped all over the world. I seem to bear striking similarities to others who claim to be God."

He's a lunatic, Ethan thought to himself. "Where is my family?" Ethan asked.

"No reunions today, Ethan. If it's not genetics but God who gives you strength, I have no further use for your family."

Ethan quickly grabbed another pallet and hurled it through the window again. Gallinger had already exited the room, but it smashed through the wall and into the hallway behind. When it grew quiet again, that's when Ethan heard the sound of metal clicking against metal. He didn't even bother to look around, and it was fortunate he didn't. The clatter of automatic weapons filled the room.

Ethan ducked behind another of the pallets that were grouped throughout the warehouse. He ran along the south wall back toward the door he had come in, and as he ran, he caught glimpses of what he was up against. They must have slipped into other doors on the perimeter of the building. He estimated at least fifty men but was sure there more than that waiting in reserve. He stopped behind one stack of pallets, and the gunfire stopped momentarily. Where were Cameron and the rest of the team? He leaned out to look and was greeted with more gunfire. He had to confront these men head on. With or without his allies. He began to pray a silent prayer for strength when suddenly Robbie came from behind a nearby pallet.

"Robbie, he's going to kill my family. I've got to catch up with him."

"We'll get you there. First, we have deal with this." More gunfire rang out, and they could feel bullets hitting the components on the pallet they were behind.

"I don't have time for this, Robbie. There's too many of them."

"We can take care of that," Robbie said as he hefted his gun.

"What would Samson do?"

"He would fight, Ethan. He would do what he had to."

Ethan prayed a silent prayer for strength. Then, summoning his courage, he stepped out from behind the stack of pallets.

"Ethan, wait! We can't help you if you do that!" Robbie knew they couldn't fire on the men with Ethan in the mix. Ethan ran across the warehouse floor toward the side where groups of security guards were firing their weapons. Once there he moved along the wall behind more pallets until he saw the first group of security officers. It was then that he noticed these were not just security guards. They did not have a Hyperteq logo on their uniforms but a different sort of logo. He recognized it as a symbol for Cultus.

He charged the group and grabbed the man nearest him, using the man as a shield and his gun as a club on the others nearby. More of Gallinger's security force came toward the focal point of the fighting. Bullets were flying, but most of the combat took place in such close quarters that no one had a clear shot at him.

The men tried to point their guns at Ethan at close range only to have them snatched away. Others were not so lucky as they themselves were snatched up and thrown across the room. Ethan was untouchable. As more men arrived he waded into their midst, swinging the guns he'd stolen. Men were flying in every direction. Some came so close he couldn't hit them with the gun, but he was able to grab them and fling them across the room and into each other. Several of the guns he was using broke in the middle, and he had to snatch another one. Ethan was like a man possessed. He kept swinging, grabbing, and hitting until there was no one left standing. His hand was gripping the gun so tightly he had a hard time unclenching his fist.

The rest of the team came out from their positions around the room. They had helped Ethan where they could. The only sound in the room was the groans of men who had been clubbed by Ethan. He had taken down over thirty men in the space of about five hundred square feet.

"I still don't understand how you do that. I mean I saw it, but I don't get it." Linz was still shaking his head as he walked toward Ethan.

"Samson killed a thousand men with the jawbone of a donkey." Robbie replied. Samson could do some serious damage."

"We have more to do" was Ethan's only reply. He was tired, but he knew his job was not done. He momentarily thought of the fight so many years ago in New York that had changed his life forever. That one had landed him in jail. What would be the consequences of this fight today? He pushed the concerns away. He still had a mainframe computer to destroy, which he was now sure was here in this building. Why else would Gallinger be here? He would want to be near his creation. Ethan was also now sure his family was here. Again, Gallinger would want to see them directly. He began to walk toward the office part of the building. Only steel double doors with a security key pad separated him from the rest of his mission.

Upon landing, the group of Americans was taken to meet with the Brazilian officials. The convoy was made up of black SUVs. Andrea Kaplan and Wade Murrow were shuttled into separate vehicles upon landing. As they left the airfield, Kaplan's car broke from the rest of the convoy and began speeding in the opposite direction.

"What are you doing! Turn this car around!" Kaplan shouted at the driver.

Murrow noticed the vehicle turn away from the group and immediately ordered the driver to explain. Apparently it was as much a surprise to him as to Murrow. He called Kaplan on her cell phone, but as soon as it rang in her vehicle, a hand from the rearmost seat reached forward and prevented her from answering.

"Ride quietly, or it will be very difficult for you." The voice came from the driver, who glanced in the rearview mirror at their passenger. Andrea sat back and listened as her phone finished ringing and then beeped indicating she'd missed a call.

The steel doors proved ineffective at keeping Ethan out. Once the team had made its way through, they again split up in order to cover more ground.

"First we clear floor by floor. Make sure he's not planning a rooftop escape. Then we come down and check for something underground. A basement, a bunker...anything that might resemble what we've seen before." Mongezi gave the orders, and the team broke into groups. There were four stairways in different parts of the building. First they disabled the elevators. Next, Cameron took one stairway, Barton another, while Pits and Casey paired up as did Robbie and Ethan. It was a race to the top with Gallinger as the prize.

The SUV pulled up in front of the many-storied office building. The blue-green glass reflected the now rising sun. Kaplan was roughly pulled from the SUV and led into the front entry. There was a huge Qualtech logo hanging from the three-story lobby ceiling. A large stairway dominated the view from the main doorway and led up into the rest of the building. A bank of elevators stood to the right of the grand staircase. She was led there, but the elevators were not responding to the frantic button pushing of her captors. They led her to the stairs and hurriedly thrust her up to the third floor landing that overlooked the entryway. Off to the right was a doorway leading to a glass walled stairway. As Andrea climbed the stairs, she could look out onto the surrounding buildings. This one dominated the skyline in this part of the city. There were other warehouses and small factories, but this one dwarfed them all.

Robbie heard the stairway door just two floors up open and bump shut. Someone was either coming down to meet them or trying to get away. He placed his weapon on his shoulder and began climbing, gun pointed toward the next landing. Ethan followed. He pulled out his pistol, but after his recent encounter in the warehouse, he was not concerned about using it. After the third floor, Cameron and Barton were able to pair up and take the third staircase together. So far there had been no encounters. No one in the building at all except for the men in the warehouse. They couldn't help but feel that it was a trap. It was too easy —them making their way up the stairs, with no resistance. Maybe Gallinger had hoped they would all be killed in the warehouse. Or maybe he was just toying with them.

Kaplan could hear boots on the stairs below her. Her captors moved even more quickly now. If this was the Qualtech building, then that must mean that the footsteps were her team. Cameron and the guys were here. Ethan was here.

Just before the thirteenth floor Cameron, over the radio, told everyone to stop. If after thirteen floors they had seen no one, it was possible that floor thirteen was going to be empty as well, and they would have to head back down. Of course it could also be the final trigger in a trap that had been set minutes ago in the warehouse.

"On my mark," Cameron said to the team waiting to enter the hallway of floor thirteen. Cameron had never had sole command of a team before but so far had done a great job. Tactically, his decision now was the right one though he couldn't have known what was waiting for them. As the team simultaneously kicked the three hallway doors open, gunfire exploded in each hallway.

Pits was grazed on his left shoulder by the first bullet. Marks appeared on the glass of the stairwell from the bullets striking. It didn't shatter though. In catching glimpses down the hall, they could not see where the bullets were coming from. There were no uniforms or helmeted heads looking back at them. Cameron threw a small flashlight into hallway, and before it touched the floor, it was blown into hundreds of fragments by the bullets hitting it.

"Everyone okay?" asked Cameron.

"I've got a little color on my arm, but I'm still in this." Pits was a tough one to take down.

"Where does he get these gadgets?" Cameron said in frustration. "Motion detected. Highly accurate. Any ideas?" he asked.

"Smoke?" suggested Casey.

"We'd be able to see the lasers that trigger the guns but wouldn't be able to avoid them." Mongezi was irritated. "Ethan?"

Ethan was a little surprised to hear his name. He wasn't just along for the ride after all. "I did have one idea," he ventured.

"Let's hear it." Cameron was open to anything at this point. Though he couldn't see the rest of the team in their respective stairways, he knew their set up was similar to his. Through the small window in the door, he could see a wood paneled hall with at least two side tables in sight, each with a flower arrangement on it. Farther down was a set of glass doors that looked to lead to an office suite. The guns were out of a science fiction movie. They sensed motion around and in front of the door. Mounted at the ceiling almost forty feet from the stairway, the guns only pointed one way. Once past them they would be in the clear.

Ethan spoke over the radio. "I think I can clear this hall-way. I just need some protection."

"Whatever you need" was the response from both Cameron and Casey.

"I think I can get it right here." He ran down one flight of stairs, and Robbie leaned over the railing to watch. Ethan wrenched the door leading to the twelfth floor off its hinges. He turned it ninety degrees and placed the bottom of the door in the corner of the landing walls. With a swift blow to the center of the door and steady pressure on the top, he bent the heavy steel door into a semicircle. Then grabbing the top and bottom of the door, he bent it further into a circle. Carrying his new shield to the thir-teenth floor landing, he said, "Stand clear of the door." Robbie just shook his head in amazement. Grabbing the door handle, he pulled it open to allow Ethan to run through.

He was holding his "shield" from the bottom. The moment he stepped into the doorway, his makeshift shield lit up with bullets striking it. Because it was a heavy fire door, there was no danger of the bullets piercing it, but the accumulated effect of bullets hitting him was throwing him and his shield off balance. Carrying the door and walking into a storm of gunfire was more difficult than he anticipated. He only needed forty feet. He cleared the distance in less than ten seconds.

"He's through!" Robbie reported over the radio. Ethan dropped the door and turned back to reach up and rip the guns that had just stopped firing right off the ceiling. Robbie ran through the door, and they made their way cautiously to the next hall. They needed to cross the whole floor in order to clear the other hallways for their teammates. The only way to do that was to go through the center of the top floor, which they believed to contain offices. They pushed through the glass doors that led to the center of the building. It was still. As they turned a corner to head farther into the office suite, Ethan was stunned to see Andrea Kaplan. She was sitting in a chair at the end of the hallway, which terminated in a reception area, office doors opening out behind her and to the right. Her hands were behind the chair, and her face was non-expressive.

"Andrea? What are you doing here? Are you okay?" He and Robbie began to run up to her, but suddenly Robbie stopped short.

"Ethan, that's what Gallinger wants. Just wait a sec." Robbie took a few more steps back and, crouching down, got on the radio. "Cam, we're in the center of this level. I have Staff Sergeant Kaplan here." Tactically, they needed someone on the stairs, so Cameron and Casey decided to go through the twelfth floor and meet at the stairway Ethan had cleared to provide some backup. They hated leaving their stairway open for escape, but it was better than getting blindsided.

"Ethan?" It was Andrea. "Can you get me out of here?" She didn't look hurt. Just scared. Ethan couldn't imagine how she had ended up here. Hadn't she been headed to the US consulate with Murrow?

"Are you okay? Did they hurt you?"

"No. They took me as we were leaving the airport."

"Robbie, c'mon, let's get her out. If the bullets start flying again, I don't want her sitting in the open."

"It's not a good idea, Ethan. Just wait."

"For what? So Gallinger can make more plans, set more traps? We have a time limit, you know."

Robbie nodded his head slightly. "I hear you, E. But I can't do it. I just have a bad feeling about it."

"I don't." And he got up and walked toward Kaplan. He was just a few feet away when Robbie grabbed him by the arm to hold him back. Then a sick wave of realization hit him. Andrea swung her arm up from the back of the chair, and in her hand was a pistol. It fired, and Robbie was thrown backward down the hall. Ethan was experiencing things in slow motion. He heard Robbie groan behind him and then saw the pistol turned and leveled at his head. Andrea stood, and as Ethan looked into the light behind her eyes, he saw what he should have seen all along. An emptiness that explained so much. Siegers being used, the ease with which Gallinger penetrated the military compound, his "rescue" on the beach and subsequent pickup at the hospital, his family being kidnapped, and now him being here. Why was he here?

Andrea must have guessed what he was thinking. "I needed you, Ethan. You are here to help me. I want to show my devotion to God in the only way I can."

"By capturing me?"

"By killing you." She said it plainly, with no emotion, and Ethan tried to remember what her voice sounded like before it was stripped of all feeling. They had had some moments together. Moments he thought were real. Kisses, talks. Now she was standing with a gun pointed at his head.

"I thought there was something between us."

"You're too nice, Ethan. Naïve."

"Why didn't you just kill me before now? Why bring me here? You could have done this anytime."

"I was supposed to do it before now. When I couldn't—didn't do it, Gallinger brought me here. Really, I just wanted to get out of the country first. I wanted to be with Gallinger to watch while the world falls into his hands. I wanted him to see my devotion firsthand."

"I thought you said you were doing this for God."

"I am. Gallinger is God. Or hadn't you heard?"

Ethan was stunned at the certainty of her faith. "Cultus is a lie. He's brainwashed you! You're killing people you *should* be helping."

"They don't need help. They just need to do what I tell them." The new voice came from one of the offices behind Andrea. Out of it came Gallinger. He was still in the suit Ethan had seen in his dream. In spite of having several pallets of computer equipment thrown at him, he looked no worse for the wear. He walked over to Andrea.

"I've been looking forward to this, Ethan. Knowing you're here sets my mind at ease that everything planned for today will go off without a problem." Gunshots were heard below them. "That would be your friends. I couldn't just let them wander the building unsupervised. We're only eight hours away, you know. It's too bad you won't be able to witness it. No one has ever done this before. Held the world hostage that is." He smiled at himself and then paused to stare at Ethan, looking him up and down as if to appraise him. "I was surprised the first time I saw you on Venture. That's my island. I couldn't believe how *small* you were. Where *does* that strength come from?"

"God," said Ethan.

"You've mentioned that. And where is your God now? Why aren't you tearing down the walls in here? Can you stop bullets? Do you fly?"

"I only do what God gives me to do."

Gallinger uttered a delicate laugh. "All right, Ethan." He stepped back a few paces from Andrea. "I'm bored with this. I have other things to do. Kill him."

Kaplan looked at Ethan, and something changed. She hesitated, and the gun wavered. Ethan had a split second to take advantage of the situation. He slid to the right as he brought up his arm to deflect the gun away. He grabbed the gun out of her surprised hands and threw it to the other side of the room. She flew at him with a kick, which he blocked. Angry, she unleashed a furious series of punches and kicks that Ethan was able to defend. He was trying to stop her without killing her. Had he not grown to love her he would have already thrown her the length of the room. He was finally able to apply a gear lock, a sleeper hold that can choke out an opponent almost instantly, if properly applied. Robbie had taught him that one. Gallinger was still standing there watching.

"I know she was trying to please me, but some things are just easier to do yourself." He aimed a pistol at Ethan and pulled the trigger. The bullet hit Ethan just below his rib cage on his right side. Gallinger fired again and hit Ethan in the upper chest. Ethan was stunned. He dropped to his knees. It was not supposed to happen this way. He had a mission to accomplish. There were things God wanted him to do. Maybe his parents had lied. Maybe they would all die at the hands of this lunatic.

He must have been mumbling to himself because Gallinger chuckled. "She was excellent, wasn't she? Quite an actress. She failed at the end though. I think she was in love with you. Shame." Satisfied with himself, he strode past Ethan, who had now slumped to his side, and stepped over Robbie as well on his way to the glass doors.

In the silence that remained, Ethan lay in pain, unsure about what to do. He was thankful for the Kevlar vest, but his ribcage and upper chest felt tight. Breathing was difficult. He knew he needed to keep going, not only for his family but for the millions all over the world who were in danger.

He put his hands beneath him and pushed up from the floor. He went quickly to Andrea. She was still unconscious. She was deceived and blind to the truth, but she was not beyond saving. He picked her up and put her over his shoulder. Robbie was still breathing. Barely. Ethan picked him up as well and smiled to himself as he remembered doing this months ago during training. Deep down he believed Robbie would be okay. He had to tell himself that to keep it together. Once the realization came that he was largely responsible for him being shot he struggled to focus on what he had to do. Sometimes it was easier to think only of oneself, but everyone comes to the end of that kind of life knowing they've made a grave error. Life cannot be lived without others. He had tried to do it for far too long. He had thought he was avoiding the kind of situation he was in now, but it was times like this, helping others, having purpose, that made life worth living at all.

Ethan carried his friends up to the roof, which was just one flight of stairs away. Looking around, he noted there was a helipad centered on the roof and then surrounding it were other requisite roof top items. Nothing out of the ordinary. He snatched Robbie's radio, knowing he would have to communicate with the carrier and tell them what had happened. They didn't know how Ethan became part of the team, but he hoped he knew enough protocol to convince them of what was going on. None of the other team members were responding to the radio signals, and Ethan believed the worst. He knew he had to go back into the building and find that computer. He also knew that when he found it he would find his family.

15

Gallinger had built this facility to be almost as deep underground as it was tall above ground. He knew construction, evidenced by his ingenious design in Frankfort for getting out of town unseen and his numerous projects around the world that allowed a behind-the-scenes dual purpose as this facility did. About five stories below ground was where he'd decided to plant the computer that was running everything. Originally he had been so very confident that no one would find it, let alone make an attempt to destroy it, that he had not done much in the way of securing it. But after his first encounter with Ethan Zabad, he had decided pride, at least of that sort, was a foolish reason for failure. He upgraded the security in all the ways he could think of. Of course, even if anyone got to it, they would have no place to go. There was only one way out of the room it was in. *Well*, he thought, *two actually*. But no one would ever find the second entrance. He reserved that knowledge for himself. He'd contracted to have a ladder with an access hatch built at the far end of the warehouse. Then he'd had the contractor killed. The ladder itself was contained in what looked like a support pillar. It went up past ceiling level, took a ninety-degree turn, and then went up again, opening just outside the building.

With Ethan out of the way, the American military neutralized, and only seven hours to go, Gallinger was supremely confident. He entered the third floor below ground level. The door opened into the top of a cavernous room. It was just over fifty feet deep. A set of metal stairs traced a zigzag from the door set high in the wall to the floor of the room. All of the building above sat on this room. Several mighty concrete pillars extended through the ceiling and the weight of the building rested on the floor of the room. Part of the warehouse and manufacturing building also sat on top of this room, making it the second largest area of the complex.

Gallinger walked down the steps and once on the main floor made his way to the computer. It was an exact duplicate of the system his technicians had designed in Afghanistan. This system had an even more advanced type of nanochip. The technology in that area was moving so rapidly that things changed month-to-month. The algorithms used to program the system so it would perform its function were so complex that they had to be stored on several banks of nanochips. The processors for this computer were literally kept on ice in order to keep it functioning properly. Too drastic a change in temperature and the computer would lock up, causing the whole system to fail. This is what had happened when Ethan had pulled the computer out of its protective vault. That would not happen today. After making sure everything was ready, Gallinger set the rest of his plan in place and headed back up to the surface.

Ethan left the roof after confirmation that the navy would send a helicopter. He hoped it would be in time for Robbie and any other members of the team still alive. He told them everything he knew. Hearing firsthand from the mouth of Gallinger was enough to make things happen. The carrier had made contact with Murrow, so he and the Brazilian government were now aware of the situation. Armed forces had been dispatched to the building. He went to the floor where the rest of the team had been caught in a crossfire. He couldn't find any sign of them. There was blood, but there was no way of knowing whose. He decided to continue down through the building.

He hurried back to the bank of elevators where they had first entered from the warehouse. Though it was not listed in the elevator, he knew the shaft would be his best bet for getting to the floors below if there were any. He didn't see any stairways anywhere nearby, and time demanded that he stick to what he knew. He put his fingers in the crack of the elevator door and pried it open. Next he had to get the elevator out of the way. Still disabled, the buttons brought no response. He reached inside the car and, gripping the handrail nearest to the door, began to lift. The elevator car came up a few inches. Enough for him to get his fingers under the bottom edge of the car near the door open-ing. From there it was a simple lift, and the car went up as high as Ethan could lift it. He stepped into the shaft and could see only darkness. He dropped over the ledge and gripped the edge of the floor. Reaching out for handholds, he felt a length of conduit that was promising. He tested it and then put his weight on it. He was able to lower himself, and as his eyes adjusted to the lack of light, he could make out another elevator door. He continued down with his fingertips clinging to the conduit and his feet planted on the wall. It was strength alone that allowed him to climb this way.

He continued to a third elevator door. He climbed down a little farther but didn't feel or see anything else. If there was little light near the top, then here was almost pitch blackness. The saving grace was a tiny pinprick of light at the bottom of the third elevator door. Ethan reached toward that pinprick and placed a hand on the ledge near it. He swung back from the conduit to now hang from the ledge of the floor. With one hand, he hung on and with the other he reached up and wriggled fingertips into the tight gap in the doors. Bit by bit he was able to pry it open. He hauled himself up into the hallway. A stark contrast from the floors above that were lavishly decorated with warm wood paneling and flowers, this was blank, gray, and cold. Concrete and pipe were prominent. The hallway was short and led to another door. Next to it was a door that Ethan looked through and saw stairs leading up. How had he missed that? Just knowing the stairs were there was helpful. His plan was to leave this building alive with his family. If they were down here, they would not be able to get out the way he'd just gotten in.

He looked through the other door and saw he was looking down on a huge underground warehouse. He could see people busily walking through the area. One corner of the warehouse had a steel fence around it. Above the whole room was a series of catwalks and maintenance walkways. Ethan's vision began to creep in around the edges of his conscious thought. Things were beginning to look familiar. Then it occurred to him. What if the vision on the island had shown him what his choices were? If he went to the floor of the room, he would be faced with the prospect of losing his dad, and to go over the top of the room would mean losing his son. This was the kind of decision that had a paralyzing effect on Ethan. His family was all he had. How could he make a choice like that? And then of course there was the computer. That meant lives all over the world. He decided to head to the main floor. It was from there he had the best chance of destroying the computer. He would have to trust God with his family.

Miles away, Wade Murrow was summoning a second team from the carrier. They would not arrive in time for the five o'clock deadline, but his team had missed their last check-in. Something was definitely wrong, and Ethan's info had been sketchy. Murrow knew that even if they couldn't dismantle Gallinger's plans before his deadline, they still had a responsibility to get Ethan's family out alive.

Ethan made his way, unnoticed, to the floor of the subterranean room. He was trying to form a plan in his mind. But as he planned, he realized that the times he had acted in his supernatural power he rarely knew what he was going to do. Something just took over, and he seemed to act according to a higher power. That made him nervous as he realized God may help him to act in a way that brought the most benefit to the world and served a greater purpose but allowed the death of someone he loved. Again, trying not to be sidetracked, he slid his pistol from its holster and made his way across the room boldly. He had gone about fifty feet before someone finally noticed him. It was a man carrying a clipboard. But upon seeing Ethan, the clipboard was quickly cast aside in exchange for a pistol. Ethan felt the strength of God come upon him, and he ran directly at the man. He knew the man with the pistol fired, but Ethan didn't know where the shots went. He batted the pistol aside with a left hand and knocked the man to the floor with his right. The activity drew the attention of several other men all with responsibilities in this room. They converged on Ethan with guns drawn. Ethan was considering his options when he heard his name called from above. It was Abe Zabad. He was waving to Ethan down below. The dream was coming true.

"Stay there, Dad! Stay right there. And hang on."

Abe Zabad seemed confused by the command from his son but did it anyway.

Ethan looked around at the dozen or so men that had surrounded him. "Do you know what you're doing here?" The question gave them a brief pause. Then one of them answered.

"We're serving God."

"Which God?" Ethan asked.

"There's only one," answered the same man.

Ethan slowly rotated, trying to keep all the men in his sights. "You're right. Is your God loving and kind? Has he told you anything about himself?"

"He's not a weak God. He doesn't reveal himself to us. He rewards us."

"Have you been rewarded lately? The only God I know has revealed to us who He is." Ethan knew he couldn't

convince these men of anything in the few minutes he had
to form a plan. But perhaps they would begin to think twice
about the benevolence of their "god" Gallinger.

Ethan tried another approach. "None of you are killers.
Can you really pull the trigger on me? You're factory workers, engineers, scientists. Put the guns down."

Ethan knew the only way to reach the catwalk above
him where his dad was standing was from the main door
where he had entered. If his dad had come from that direction, it stood to reason that the rest of his family was still in
that vicinity. He needed to get them out of the building.

Ethan raised his pistol and aimed it at a man in the
circle surrounding him. "What happens to you if I pull the
trigger? Hmm? Does your god let you go to heaven? Do you
get paid for that little sacrifice?"

The man backed away a few steps.

"Which one of you wants to die for Rolf Gallinger?
Anyone?" Two more men began backing away. "You can
shoot me, but I promise you this trigger finger will be the
last part of my body that stops working." Ethan stepped
closer to the nervous man and then quickly grabbed his
arm, pulling him across his body. "Drop your weapons, or
you see this man's brains on the floor. Now!" Ethan backed
toward the stairs with his hostage. Ethan was relieved to
see the men starting to put down their weapons. The last
thing he wanted to do was start shooting. In just the few
hours he had been here he had begun to understand why
these people were here. They had been deceived by
someone whose only goal was to use and abuse their allegiance. His desire to save his family was paired with a new
compassion to set these people free from a bondage they
did not understand. He didn't know how many were
enslaved in Cultus, but a familiar phrase from his child-

hood met with his consciousness: "You will restore many hearts."

When the last weapon fell to the floor he went to the man who had answered his questions just minutes ago and grabbed him by the collar and pulled him close. "Get yourself and these other men out of the building. Go now, and I will spare your life."

"Who are you?" was the man's answer.

Ethan, for just a split second, thought about that question. Just a few months ago, he would have been unable to answer that. Things had changed. "The one the true God has sent to free you. Now go and leave through the warehouse. See if there are any men in there who need help. And then get out!" Ethan released the man's collar and headed for the stairs. From the top, he could see the man talking to the others in the group. They glanced toward Ethan and started to ascend the long staircase. Then turning toward the center of the room, he saw his father standing on the catwalk. Ethan expected him to walk toward him, but he just stood as if glued to the floor.

"Dad, let's go. You need to get out of the building."

"I know, Son. But I can't leave."

"Why not?"

Abe was distressed. "You don't understand. I can't leave this spot."

"What's going on, Dad?"

Abe Zabad pointed down below, and there was David Zabad. Finally Ethan saw what he wished he had seen from the floor of the warehouse. Gallinger had given him a puzzle.

"Son, this Gallinger is a sick man. He told me to stay here or something would kill David. And he told David to stay where he is or it would kill me. And he told both of us to stay here or your mother would be hurt."

Without another word or looking any further at the situation, Ethan turned and ran toward the door leading to the surface. He burst through and ran up the stairway he had seen after traversing the elevator shaft. When he reached the main level of the building above, he had a hunch as to where his mother was. He went up three more flights of stairs to the level where he had seen Gallinger first—the same level as the conference room he had obliterated with the pallets. He reached a hallway, but he knew it was not the one that led to the conference room. That one would be hard to miss with the debris and the gaping hole in the wall. He made his way toward the corner at the end of the hallway. He thought he heard movement close by. He summoned his strength and quickly slipped around the corner, ready for anything. He was confronted with the butt of an automatic weapon. Fortunately he saw it coming and was able to dodge. He was about to disarm the attacker when he realized it was Casey Linz.

"Casey! I hadn't heard from you guys. What happened?"

Quietly Linz said, "We got shot up pretty bad. Barton, Mongezi, and Pits are all in bad shape. I got them outside, but none of our radios were working. I came back in to find you and Robbie."

Ethan briefly whispered the results of his and Robbie's encounter with Gallinger and Andrea. He also explained the situation with his family. "I know I need your help, but I'm not sure what you can do. Gallinger has made this very personal."

"I'll do whatever I can. Just say the word."

"Do you have an extra weapon?"

"Just a pistol." He lifted it from its holster on his side and hefted it once. "Same as that forty-five you've got there. Fires as fast as you can pull the trigger."

He reached out and took it from Casey. "Thanks. I hope I don't have to use it."

"You'll be glad to have it. Believe me. This place is full of surprises."

Ethan agreed and quietly tucked the extra pistol in his waistband. He asked Casey to stay at the corner and back him up while he went quietly ahead down the hall listening for any hints as to where his mother might be. He couldn't say for sure what made him believe she was here in this hallway, but something deep down gave him assurance. He stopped outside one door and could hear a TV in the background. Without hesitation, Ethan kicked the door in. His enthusiasm was unnecessary. Only two Cultus security guards were in the room. Ethan disarmed them and gave them the same chance he had given to the man downstairs. They were not as willing to abandon Cultus as the men in the basement had been. With both pistols aimed at them, Ethan ordered them to leave the room. They walked down the hall, and Ethan shouted to Casey to let them go. None of these people seemed abnormal or stupid like he had assumed when first hearing about Cultus. He couldn't believe people would be so deceived. But Evil's deception makes no apologies and has no limits.

Tara Zabad was sitting in a chair facing the TV, which was tuned to a news channel. On it were several "experts" evaluating the threats that had been made and what action the international bank should take, if any. Ethan was disturbed to think that in a post-9/11 world anyone would not take a terrorist threat seriously. Gallinger and Cultus were as dangerous as any terrorist cell. Ethan could not know that at that moment, the president, his cabinet, the heads of domestic and international security forces, the CIA, and armed forces special task teams were forming a response plan. There was much more at work in the world at the moment, but for Ethan only one thing mattered, and she was sitting right in front of him.

"Mom!" Ethan ran to her, and they embraced. "We have to get you out of this building. Dad and David are downstairs. I'll get them too."

"Ethan. You used a gun on those men." She was surprised to see her son this way.

"I had to, Mom. Sometimes you don't have a choice. At least I didn't have to pull the trigger. Now they have a chance to get out of Cultus."

"This is it, you know. This is what we were told about so long ago."

Ethan stared back at his mother for a moment, thinking about what it all meant. All the things they had taught him over the years that he had mostly rejected—until now. "I know, Mom." He paused again. "I'm ready." Tara Zabad wiped several tears from her eyes, and Ethan helped her out of the room. He handed her off to Casey.

"Casey, I'm going down to get my son and my dad. I'll be depending on you to get them out of the building safely."

"You can count on it."

"Oh, I almost forgot," Ethan said as he started back down the hall. "A chopper is coming to the roof for Andrea and Robbie. They'll be looking for me too. Tell them I'll be along." He turned once more to his mom. "I love you. I'll see you soon." And then he was down the hall and through the stairway door. He had just emerged from the stairway into the back of the lobby when gunshots ripped up the wall next to Ethan. He pulled the stairway door open and dove back through. He popped up in the door window to see where the shots had come from. Nothing. He pulled out the pistols and readied them. He had to trust his instincts now.

It was foolishness to think that he could just walk through the building and do whatever he wanted. If Gallinger had gone to the trouble to set up a little puzzle with his family, he would surely have obstacles preventing him from getting back to them.

He backed up from the door to get a running start. A few quick steps and he burst through with the pistols readied in front of him. As he came through the door, the gunfire started again, striking the floor behind him. Ethan was able to see where it originated, and he fired two shots at the source. He slid behind a reception desk in the lobby and looked around the side to see if there were any other surprises. No one. He crept back the way he came, and that's when he saw the blood. A man dressed in black was sprawled on his back with an automatic rifle in his outstretched hand. A bullet hole in his left eye.

Cautiously looking for another ambush, he made his way to the stairway leading to the underground warehouse. As he pulled open the door, another series of gunshots lit up the doorway. He stepped back quickly as bullets continued to ping off the opposite side of the door. When the firing stopped briefly, he used the opportunity to open the door and blindly fire two shots down the stairs. Whoever was on the stairs responded with a few shots of their own. Ethan was running out of time. He had fired four shots so far. That meant he only had twelve more shots total. He had to assume there were men all throughout the stairway. He was glad Casey had given him all the ammo he had. Four magazines total. He made sure he could grab them easily and opened the door again, boldly walking through firing. The first man, standing on the first landing, took two shots through the head and tumbled down the second flight of stairs. Another man, also dressed in black, jumped over the body of his comrade and began ascending the same flight of stairs. He was met with three shots from Ethan's pistol and was given a resting place atop his partner. The rest of the stairway was clear.

Ethan used the rest of his short descent to think through what he had to do to get both his dad and his son out alive. He knew Gallinger had devised this little scheme just to keep him from getting at the computer. He was using precious time, though it certainly wasn't wasted time. It was giving Cultus members a chance to get out, if Ethan could convince them, that is. It was also giving his team members a chance to get away. Though he didn't know the exact locations of each man, he hoped that they were someplace safe.

Thinking now of the task before him, Ethan knew the visions he had been given had been God's way of preparing him for his moment. What Ethan couldn't figure out was if God had wanted him to be prepared to lose one of the people he loved or be prepared to solve the problem he'd been given. And it was a problem. In the glance he'd given the setup, he had discerned that if Abe moved from his place on the catwalk, the heating unit on the ceiling would fall directly onto David. David didn't look connected to anything, so Ethan had to assume that if he moved he would trigger something that would cause the catwalk to let go of the ceiling. As he reached the final door leading to the basement, he was surprised there hadn't been more resistance. After his initial encounter in the warehouse, he had expected that kind of resistance throughout the whole building. Gallinger must be banking everything on the little game he'd created with Ethan's family and the security measures he'd developed on the computer to keep Ethan from succeeding. It made no sense to him that a man like Gallinger would go to such lengths to deal with Ethan and his family.

It seemed to Ethan that he had something Gallinger lacked. There was his family, his ability. But it had to be more than that. It had taken him a lifetime to finally acknowledge that his gifts came from something outside himself. Gallinger, equally gifted, though in other ways, would never acknowledge that his gifts came from anything other than his own determination and cunning. It was that difference that determined whether a person could truly achieve greatness or fall stunningly short.

He pushed open the basement door and again began working through a plan to get his father and his son out of that room. He surveyed the basement from the top of the stairs. The bustling activity that had characterized the room only an hour ago was now absent. Ethan had not said much to the Hyperteq employees, or Cultus followers but evidently it had been enough to make them second guess what they were doing. Or perhaps they had heard of his exploits in Afghanistan through the Cultus network and wanted nothing to do with him. Whatever the case he now had a clear path to his father and son. By the time he reached the basement floor, he could see that David was crying. "It's okay, Son. I'm going to help you. Be brave." Ethan ran close to David but not to him for fear he would trigger the trap that had been set. "Dad, when I tell you, I want you to run for the end of the catwalk."

"What about David?" Abe called down.

"I have a plan, Dad. You have to trust me. I just need you to run as fast as you can. Don't stop." David was trying to stifle his crying and was now just sniffling and taking deep, shaking, staccato breaths. "David, when I tell you, I want you to crouch down. Do you understand?" David nodded.

"Dad. Are you ready?"

"Yes." Abe Zabad looked down at his legacy and nodded once to his son.

"Go!" Ethan shouted, and Abe Zabad began to run. Within two steps something on the ceiling broke loose and the heating unit above David began to fall toward him. Ethan moved quickly to David and bent over to catch it on his back. He knew three things. One, this thing was going to be heavier than he anticipated; two, it was going to hurt; and three, the moment he stepped toward his son, the catwalk above was going to let go. He was right on all three counts. The only one that concerned him was the latter. The furnace slammed into his back with unprecedented force. As it struck him, David was crouched low under Ethan. Their eyes met for a moment, David's wide and awestruck, seeing his dad this way for the first time His legs were quivering, and he was having trouble balancing the load. He leaned to one side with the weight and said to David, "Go," as the heating unit tipped over and thudded heavily on the concrete floor. Another crash had just preceded that sound. It was the length of catwalk hitting the floor. Ethan looked for his father. He was there. Hanging from the stair landing fifty feet above the ground.

"I'm coming, Dad." With no time to stretch or complain about the beating his back had just taken, Ethan ran up the stairs with David in tow and pulled his dad to safety. He hugged them both for the first time in days. "I thought I'd lost you both. And if I don't get you out of here right now I risk that again. Mom is safe. She's with Linz." Ethan handed his dad the pistol Casey had given him.

"Son, I don't need this."

"You never know. Just carry it. It may make someone think twice."

"What are you going to do, Ethan?"

"What I was born to do." He looked down at David. "Son, you need to go with Grandpa. I'll be right behind you both. I just have one more thing to do."

David didn't say a word. He just threw his arms around Ethan and held him tightly. Ethan ran his hands through his son's hair and then gave him a kiss on the cheek. "Go."

[16]

Time was running out. He had been at this for a while now. The five o'clock deadline had to be fast approaching. There had been seven hours to go when Andrea had betrayed him. It had to have been at least two hours since she had tried to kill him, if not more. It occurred to Ethan that though she had tried to kill him, in reality she had betrayed him months ago. He thought of her for a moment. He had trusted her; grown to love her. All the steps they had taken had been contrived; part of a plot to pull him in. There was no doubt now that she had been the inside person, most likely working together with Dr. Seigers and Cultus. Gallinger had said Kaplan was in love with Ethan. She had hesitated when given the chance to pull the trigger. Perhaps that was the real reason she hadn't killed him earlier.

How could Cultus have stolen her mind? Removed her ability to see reason? He felt sadness for her and could only hope that someone would be able to turn her around. He pitied her for the conflict she must have felt, helping him to get to his family, all while plotting to kill him once he arrived.

Over two hours since he'd seen Robbie go down. Maybe more. He just couldn't get a handle on time down here. No sunlight, no watch. He simply knew he had to get the job done.

He made his way to the corner that housed the computer. Gallinger had sealed it up tight. Not only had he been able to keep hackers out, but he had also constructed a fence, an electrical current, and certainly other unseen security measures. All of these had been designed to keep just one person out. Ethan Zabad. He needed something else to get into the area that housed the processors. He made his way toward the part of the basement room that extended under the warehouse. There were a few crates and several fifty-gallon drums, but Ethan couldn't figure out what was written on them. Those words would have described their contents. He didn't want to throw something that might cause a chemical disaster. He was working through the problem of destroying the computer again when he heard the main door at the top of the stairs open behind him. It was Gallinger. He was armed. Ethan snatched a crate from nearby and threw it at Gallinger. He missed, but the crate exploded into splinters on the wall behind him.

"I thought I'd killed you. But when I saw you on my security monitors, I realized I needed to work on my aim. I should have shot you in the head."

Ethan tried to ignore his words. He grabbed another crate and began running toward the stairs. "Security monitors? What happened to your little army?" Ethan asked boldly as he ran. Gallinger stopped descending and realized what Ethan was doing. He fired twice at the crate to no effect. Ethan launched the crate up the stairs as if it were a basketball being passed to a teammate. Gallinger leaped over the rail and narrowly missed being mowed down by the projectile. He dangled by the rail almost twelve feet from the floor. Ethan stepped to the side of the stairs but had nothing else nearby to throw. Gallinger started firing wildly.

Ethan turned and ran toward the portion of the room that extended under the warehouse above. Every thirty feet or so there was a foot-and-half-thick concrete piling. Between the pillars was more of the same material he had seen earlier—crates, building materials, and fifty-gallon drums marked with a skull and crossbones and the interlocking circles indicating a biohazard. He ran back as far as he could go. He needed time.

Gallinger started toward the lower portion of the basement. "Ethan! It may be just you and me, but my men served their purpose. They kept you occupied long enough to get me to my goal. We're just a few hours away from a terror the world has never known. It will be enough to bring them all to their knees. They'll either bow down to me in worship or fear."

"They don't even know who you are!" Ethan called back from the maze of pillars.

"They will soon enough. Once the virus is unleashed, they'll know how serious this is, and they'll know that only I hold the key to it all."

"So are you down here to gloat? Tell me that you won?"

"Yes. And I came down to kill you."

Gallinger was only an average shot close up. He probably never thought he'd actually have to do this himself. He had to be angry at the abandonment by his little Cultus army but would never let on about it. Likely he had many such groups all over the world. The group here would be looked at as unfaithful if word got out of their surrender.

Ethan wasn't sure what he was looking for back here. He just knew he had to buy some time. He didn't want to kill Gallinger. He wanted him to stand trial. He wanted the world to know what he was doing.

Perhaps something to tie him up with? The only thing Ethan could find was a roll of one-inch wound wire cable. It was possible he could wrap it around one of the pillars in the great room and leave Gallinger there tied to it.

"Ethan. There's no sense in delaying the inevitable. There's no way out except the way you came in."

"I'll come out when I'm good and ready." He smashed open one of the crates and found that it contained small metal containers. To Ethan they looked like thermostat covers. He smashed open another wooden crate and saw that this one contained several colors of electrical wire wound on spools. With time ticking away in the back of his mind, he realized he needed to do something. Even an imperfect plan was better than doing nothing. He picked up a few of the metal containers, a spool of wire, and the coil of cable. He made his way from pillar to pillar until he was near the opening to the large room. Gallinger spotted him behind one of the pillars and took a wild shot.

"So you not only have great strength, but you can bounce back from gunshots? Is that it?" Gallinger couldn't see Ethan but knew he was behind the pillars.

Ethan continued to form a plan while he shouted back to Gallinger. "You think you can create anything, don't you? You can make yourself a god, create a person who will do whatever you want, genetically engineer a copy of me?

There are powers at work in me that you will never understand."

"There's a natural explanation for everything, Ethan. Your strength, my power and position."

"You have abused your power and position. You could have been someone truly great. You're just a criminal."

"You are one to speak of abuse. You're one to speak about being truly great. You, who spent almost a decade in jail. Which of us could have been truly great? I achieved greatness because of my own abilities and ambition."

"Your abilities are not your own. Neither are mine." Ethan had no hope of convincing Gallinger to do anything different than he had planned, but he thought he might be able to distract him long enough to disarm him.

"I suppose you think your abilities are supernatural. We will find the gene and isolate it. We have blood from everyone in your family. We will discover your secret."

"My secret is that I was born for a purpose. God made me the way I am. I have a destiny."

"And I too have a destiny. I suppose we have some things in common, you and I."

That just made Ethan mad. "No, we don't. You are a sick, twisted, and deranged individual. You kill for fun."

Gallinger threw his head back and laughed. He was about to spit out a comeback, but his mouth met with one of the small metal containers that Ethan had taken out of the crate. It split Gallinger's lip and blood spilled onto his once spotless gray suit. Ethan ran from behind one of the pillars and kicked the gun from his hand. He picked Rolf Gallinger up off the ground by his collar and said, "I will destroy this computer. I will bring you down."

Gallinger smiled gruesomely down at Ethan with blood all over his teeth and simply said, "No. You will not." A gun went off. Ethan slumped down to the floor and looked behind him to see where the bullet had come from. Dormand was there holding the smoking pistol.

Where had he come from? The tiny man had placed the shot just under the edge of the Kevlar vest and upward into Ethan's chest. "I remember you...from the lagoon" was all Ethan could gasp out. He coughed and blood foamed to his lips.

Gallinger leaned down. "Good-bye, Ethan. You've failed. Looks like the world is going to hell anyway." He grinned that bloody grin again. Then he stood and started toward the stairs. "Come along, Dormand. Well done." They mounted the stairs and disappeared through the doorway. Gallinger pulled out his cell phone and, with a quick call, alerted his personal helicopter pilot that they were ready to leave.

Just before Gallinger left the basement, a navy helicopter had landed on the roof and retrieved two US military personnel. Another helicopter had brought a SEAL team to help with the evacuation of Linz, Mongezi, Barton, Pits, and the Zabad family. With just a few hours to go, another team was being prepared to get inside the Qualtech facility. There was no word from Ethan and no sign of him.

Ethan lay on the basement floor. His body was completely spent. He couldn't remember the last time he'd slept. He had been shot three times, the last bullet piercing his lungs. He had been in constant tension and battle over the last six hours, and was emotionally, spiritually, and physically exhausted. He tried to raise his head from the floor. No strength. God had restored him once already today. He almost felt guilty asking God to help him again. But he realized it hadn't been any fault or decision of his own that led him to this place. He had tried to be obedient. He had tried to fulfill the destiny God had laid out before him. Since finally surrendering his will to God, he had tried to make up for years of disobedience in a few short weeks. He had tried to exercise self-control. He hadn't cut his hair since leaving prison. He had done everything God had asked. But there was one more thing. Had he learned to give generously? Had he given away what he could? Had he given of himself?

And that's when he realized what he had to do. He began to pray. He remembered that Samson had prayed a prayer that resulted in his death but also the death of his enemies. "Oh Lord God, please remember me, and please strengthen me just this time, God." Samson had prayed for vengeance. Ethan prayed for victory and a completion of his God-given task. "Remember me, God; please remember me. Strengthen me, God. Help me to do what you've asked. Have I come all this way only to die at the hands of a false god?" He immediately felt the throbbing in his back and chest subside. He could no longer feel any pain, and his breathing started returning to normal. He lay still for another minute in amazement. He was unsure whether he was dying or his prayer was being answered. Another moment answered the questions as he was suddenly filled with a new strength. He felt a surge through his body. He had strength enough to crawl to where he had seen a fifty-gallon drum just under the warehouse portion of the basement. He pulled himself up next to the drum, making sure it had the skull and crossbones on it. He had been worried before about creating a chemical disaster but that was before he had cleared the building of his family and his foes. Now, it was a last resort. He may have been given some strength to complete his task but he tried not to think about what happened to Samson after he was given the same gift. He bent and picked up the drum as prayed aloud, "God, give me your strength one last time." He turned and carried the drum to the main room and heaved it at the corner that housed the computer. He could not have known what was in the drum but when it came in contact with the electric fence surrounding the computer the explosion was extraordinary.

Gallinger was at the top floor about to run onto the roof when he felt the floor shift. He pushed Dormand out of the way and burst through the doorway onto the landing pad. The helicopter was already five feet off the tarmac. The pilot, having felt the building shift under his craft, had gotten nervous and taken off. Gallinger began to frantically wave to the pilot as he realized that the rumbling beneath him had not stopped but gotten worse. Dormand had caught up with Gallinger and was angry about being shoved out of the way to be left for dead.

Ethan was knocked backward by the blast. He was slammed into one of the shorter pillars. His back and shoulders were throbbing with pain. He lay on the floor, again unable to move, watching the initial explosion touch off a series of other explosions as chemicals, fuel, and other materials caught fire. Smoke was filling the basement, and as he watched it descend on him, he thought of his family, his son, and his parents. He remembered Sarah, her smile and her sweetness, the softness of her touch, and her love for a man to whom everyone else was afraid to be close. He thought of the people around the world, unaware of what was happening right here in this room. That a man was dying to save them. He thought of his life and if there was anything he could have done different to bring him to this place. Was it a life lived well? Flashes of his conversations with Erik Remont popped into his mind. Was this the life of greatness that he had dreamed of? What was his legacy?

A crack appeared in one of the pillars. The combination of heat and the brunt force of explosive debris striking the pillar had caused the fracture. Then suddenly there was another massive explosion, and the pillar gave way entirely.

Ethan watched through the smoke as the ceiling cracked and began to fall into the chamber around him. The section above the missing pillar began to descend. More cracks appeared in the ceiling and chunks of concrete were smacking into the floor. Ethan prayed that one of the chunks of concrete would find its way into the corner of the room and finish off the computer if it wasn't already destroyed. What Ethan got was much more effective.

Gallinger shook off Dormand and began to run toward the edge of the building in an attempt to get his pilot to come back toward him. Then the bottom fell out. The center of the building gave way and dropped almost twenty feet. Gallinger made a last attempt to leap to the helicopter but fell short. He fell one hundred fifty feet to the parking lot below. Dormand slid across the roof toward the lowest point. The building groaned, and there was a pause of just a few seconds. Then the outer parts of the building began to collapse with the redistribution of weight. Floor by floor the building fell, the first few floors going in turn and then the rest of the building on top going into a free fall.

Ethan could no longer see what was happening but felt the ground beneath him rumble as massive chunks of concrete smashed into the basement floor. The ceiling gave way entirely, and a large piece of it came to rest just a few feet above Ethan's head. In the complete darkness, Ethan heard a slight pause, and then he heard the groaning of metal and the scrape and crush of concrete. The sound of an avalanche followed, and Ethan knew that his prayer for strength had been answered. The rest of the building had come down as well. Ethan closed his eyes as the thousands of tons of building pressed in.

Gallinger and Dormand, from their respective locations, could only stare upward at the sky, the circling helicopter, the receding clouds as the building fell. All of Gallinger's work, his business, his organization, his plans for the world were now crashing down around him, literally.

From above, the pilot watched as the building dropped out beneath him. Dormand disappeared under a cloud of dust and debris while Gallinger was buried under a wave of metal and concrete. The warehouse collapsed too. It started at the point where the buildings connected and rippled out toward the far end. The ripples could be seen in the roof, and then another wave actually brought the roof down as the structure beneath completely gave way.

From a greater distance, Ethan's family and Murrow's team watched as the building collapsed. All of them knew that if Ethan was inside he would be dead. Abe held David tighter as the helicopter moved further away. Tara wiped tears from her eyes. She didn't know how the building had come down, but she felt in her heart that Ethan had been inside.

Ethan woke with a start. He felt the pain in his back and chest and remembered he had been shot. Then he remembered the explosion and the collapse of the building. Then his senses took in his surroundings. It was quiet. More quiet than he could ever remember. And it was dark. Not even a pinprick of light shone through anywhere. His back was cold, and he could feel something moist beneath him. His first thought was that maybe he was dead. But could you feel cold or warmth when you were dead? What about smells? Ethan knew he wasn't dead, but he didn't exactly feel alive. He coughed hard and felt the wetness in it, the blood. He spat to his left, trying to clear his mouth, his throat, of the thick, clotting blood. He tried to move his limbs and found he was able to shift around a little. He listened more closely for a moment and could hear the building above him settling. Little creaks here and there. He tried to remember where he had fallen. There might be a way out of here. He doubted he would survive until someone came digging through the rubble. It could be days, weeks. Chances were there wouldn't be the urgency rescue workers had when the World Trade Center towers fell. There had been no one in this building and only a handful of people in the world knew he *might* be down here. For all Murrow, his family, and his team knew, he'd been killed somewhere in the building or perhaps while trying to escape. Regardless of what they might know, he needed to get out.

He felt around and touched only concrete, feeling his terror of tight spaces come over him. He continued to feel around, every stretch of his arm sending shooting pain down his shoulder and into his back where the bullet had entered. Every breath was like a knife in his lungs and if he breathed too deeply, his breath would catch and he would cough out another spray of blood. He moved more to his right. In doing so he found a small opening. He slid his body toward it and crawled in. Every movement caused pain, and he had several coughing fits just in the first few feet.

Ethan knew there was no way to get out the way he came in. His hope was that he could crawl beneath the former warehouse. The downside there was that the only thing above the basement was thirty feet or so of earth. On the positive side, there would be less debris to crawl through or perhaps people clearing the building from above would work their way faster through the warehouse portion. In any case, Ethan knew his chances were not good.

The TV casually reported in a steady hum that was audible but not discernible from the other room. The Zabad's knew it was more of the same. "Reports from the region indicate that when the building fell, it was not preceded by an explosion of any kind. Two deaths have been confirmed so far—Rolf Gallinger, entrepreneur and billionaire, and his personal assistant, Reginald Dormand. Witnesses say the building simply collapsed. Officials are still digging through the debris trying to determine the cause of the structure's failure. In related news, a video has surfaced that names Rolf Gallinger as not just an entrepreneur in the business world but also in spiritual matters."

The screen switched to a reporter standing outside the Qualtech headquarters in Frankfurt, Germany. "I'm standing outside a building owned by Rolf Gallinger. The video that appeared online late yesterday indicates that this was not only the headquarters of a multibillion-dollar corporation but the center of new controversy regarding a world religion that has been spreading with amazing speed. A religion and organization known as 'Cultus.'"

David had walked into the living room when the report came on. He perked up when mention was made of the video that had been posted online. An excerpt began to play on the TV. It was Gallinger, pompous as ever, talking about Cultus.

"Cultus followers exist to be used by me. They have been deceived for one purpose only. To do what I want. The money, the prayers, the show of it all, is to get what I want. If you had people worshipping you, you'd understand." In the background, Dormand was there, and it appeared there were others as well, but the camera didn't focus on the faces. It was aimed mainly in one place—Gallinger. "I'm not God. I have over a million people following me who think so, but they're idiots. That was one drawback to starting my own religion. I knew I'd get money and praise. But I didn't exactly get the world's intellectual elite."

After another excerpt the reporter intoned, "Around the world, Cultus followers are angrily demanding an explanation. But without Gallinger, their questions are, so far, unanswered. Some have declared their intention to abandon Cultus while others refuse to believe what they are seeing." A clip of a young twenty-something appeared. "I don't believe the video is real. It looks like our leader, but it's not. Someone is trying to destroy this beautiful thing he created." And on it went. Fodder for news reporters enough to last a month. The debate would continue.

Ethan had made good progress but had no way of marking distance or time. He could only go by how many gaps he had crawled through, and even then he had lost count. The floor was getting wetter by the minute. The water main to the building had been disconnected, and now water under pressure was filtering down through the mess above. As he crawled farther, the debris seemed to be less concentrated. He assumed he was near the end of the warehouse. Instead of crawling through openings only fifteen to eighteen inches wide, the gaps grew to twenty-four and thirty-six inches. He crawled out of one gap and felt around for the next one, but his hands swung into open air. He crawled farther and kept feeling with his hand, but there was nothing. He tried to get his knees under him so he could stand. He got one knee up but collapsed in a heap. Loss of blood and crushing fatigue kept him from doing what had to be done.

He must have passed out because when he tried to get up again the water beneath him was a few inches deep. He lay there in the water for minute or so to summon his strength, what little there was. He abandoned his attempt to stand and decided to crawl. He crawled a few feet forward and hit solid concrete. He crawled to his right and met a corner of concrete. Continuing from the corner, he hit more debris. He was entombed. This black hole was his grave. If he was lucky, he'd be found days or weeks from now either dead in this corner or floating, drowned by the rising water. And it was rising. He could feel several inches beneath him now. Maybe he would never be found and the world would never know Ethan Zabad. He leaned his head back against the wall and, without panic or dread, prepared for death. And then he felt the faintest wisp of air on his face.

He had felt stifled all during his crawl. No air moving, all the exhaust units destroyed by the crashing building. Motivated by his excitement, he moved toward the source of the air, feeling his way in front of him with his hands. In his excitement he took a deep breath, again coughing up blood and causing pain in his back and chest. God had given him strength but had not healed the wound he bore. He again reached out for the source of air. It felt like a pillar. The air was coming from a crack in it. He followed the crack and felt it curve away around the pillar. He followed it all the way and to the best of his knowledge was feeling an oval line carved into the side of a pillar. He pushed on the section outlined by the crack, and after some pressure, he heard a metallic click. The pillar seemed to push back against him, so he released some pressure and a door in the pillar sprang open and swung away in the dark to his right. It had been spring loaded. Ethan felt his way toward the opening he had just discovered. Inside he could feel the rungs of a metal ladder. So, Gallinger had built in a little escape hatch. He slowly, pulled himself inside the tube containing the ladder. One rung at a time, he told himself.

The ladder seemed to never end. After a sharp right angle, he crawled several more feet only to find more ladder to climb. He continued until finally he reached an end. The ladder was capped somehow. He pushed against the metal and was rewarded with blinding sunlight. It looked to be midmorning of what Ethan could only assume was the day after he had brought down the building. He crawled from the hole, which was just a few feet from the door he and Robbie and the others had entered just twenty-four hours earlier. Of course the door was no longer there. It was crushed under the rubble of the building that had been there just yesterday. Ethan crawled out of the alley that backed the building and looking down the street could see fire trucks, police, and also locals standing around, some venturing atop the debris. It was the last thing Ethan saw before he passed out.

"Onde você o encontrou? Tenta feri-lo?"

Ethan heard the voices around him but couldn't seem to open his eyes.

"Por que você o trouxe aqui? Poderia significar o problema. Olha como foi tiro."

Ethan tried to make sense of the language. He finally opened his eyes a crack and saw a man talking to a boy.

Then he heard in English, "Go and get the doctor." Then the man ordered the son to do something else and Ethan watched him go out the door. The man noticed Ethan was awake and came over to him. "Who are you?" he asked. *"Você fala o português?* You speak Portuguese?" the man asked.

Ethan said weakly, "American?" The man responded by

throwing up his hands and smiling. Ethan dozed again. The voices continued. The next time he opened his eyes, there were more people in the room. Hands were on him but not to inflict pain. He felt gentle hands feeling along his limbs then his ribs. He winced as they passed over his shoulders and back where he had struck the pillar. He was also aware that he had sustained some burns to his face and hands as a result of the explosion. He could not shake the fatigue he felt. He was vaguely aware of the pain in his body but could not wake enough to try to explain to anyone who he was or what had happened to him. He continued to sleep.

Gallinger's deadline had come and gone and most of the world had no idea what had happened. There were no other deaths reported, and life went on as usual. Ethan had succeeded but no one would know who had saved them and how. Work began on the building almost immediately in an attempt to find the computer system, which had made the large scale theft possible. Getting to the bottom of the lowest room would be difficult with the entire building sandwiched inside.

Ethan's parents and David were devastated. Just a few days after their return from Brazil they were given permission to stay a few days in the house they'd been in on base. "We can only assume he is dead. I will not hold out hope for another miracle." Abe Zabad was a tired man. After his ordeal in Gallinger's custody along with his frantic escape, he seemed to have aged several years in just few short days.

"But we don't know. They're still digging. They haven't found his body."

"Tara, a building came down around him. No one could survive that." Abe hated talking to his wife this way, with no hope, but he just couldn't be optimistic only to be disappointed later.

"But did he do the things that God told us he would do? Did he finish?" Tara was looking for any shred of hope that Ethan might still be alive.

"Think about it. He told me shortly before we were kidnapped that he had been abiding by God's laws about food. If he was responsible for bringing that building down on himself, he has learned to give generously. He gave of himself as much as he could. He gave his life."

Tara knew this was true, but her love for her son was winning the battle with reason. "This was our rationale for protecting him. I knew he would give generously in this way, but I always hoped it would be different." She wiped streams of tears from her cheeks.

Abe went on. "He gave generously, and he learned self-control. He told me of times he had a chance to kill but instead he disarmed or disabled an enemy. He told me it was wrong to rob someone of a chance of redemption. I'm convinced that if he did bring that building down he did so to end the threat to the world and not just to kill Rolf Gallinger."

"You were able to talk to him in a way I never could." Tara was thankful her husband had been able to talk with Ethan but at the same time regretted the way her relationship with her son had changed over the years.

"There are some things a son needs to talk to his father about. But he loved you in a way I've never seen a son love his mother. You had something with him that I never had." Tara broke into sobs that shook her entire body. This was not the life she had anticipated and certainly not the turn she expected it to take just a few months ago.

Abe took her in his arms and comforted her. "You're forgetting the other thing that our son did. He restored many hearts. It was the one thing he did that required some help." Just then David poked his head into the bedroom where Abe and Tara were talking. Abe winked at his grandson.

Tara lifted her head from Abe's shoulder and asked, "What help? What are you talking about?"

Abe nodded toward the door as David came in. "How did you help your dad, David?"

David looked down. "I—I had my camera in my pocket when that lady made us go with her in the van. I brought it with me to Brazil. I took pictures of Mr. Gallinger."

Tara was bewildered. "You took pictures of him? I don't understand?"

Abe spoke up. "He means video. Right, David?"

David looked up and nodded. Abe continued. "He took that video of Gallinger that we saw on TV. His confession of deceiving people is what has caused Cultus to fall apart. Our son—and our grandson—have restored many hearts. Hearts that were once deceived now have the chance to find the truth."

The realization was cause to rejoice. "Abe," Tara exclaimed, "do you know what that means?" Abe was slow to pick up on the reason for his wife's sudden change in demeanor. "It means that Ethan is alive!"

"I don't understand what you're saying, Tara. I think you should go lie down. This has been stressful for you."

"Abe, listen to me. We were told before Ethan was born that *he* would accomplish those things—master self-control, learn to give generously, restore the hearts of many people. He hasn't done them all by himself. He's not done yet!"

Abe looked lovingly at his heartbroken wife. "Tara, you can't get God on a technicality. He doesn't operate that way."

"But it's not a technicality. I'm taking God at His word." Tara continued to look pleadingly up at Abe, begging him to hope with her. Abe looked back at her and slowly nodded. Then, glancing over at David, he saw a smile where just a moment ago there had been sadness. Hope would keep them going a while longer.

A long time passed, and Ethan woke again. This time he heard voices, but they were in English. Whatever he was lying on was comfortable. The room was white with occasional splashes of understated pattern or color. He slowly lifted his head and looked down the length of his body. He was covered with a white sheet. His left arm was connected to an IV, and wires from another machine ran down the edge of the bed and disappeared under the sheets. He felt better than he had the last time he was conscious. He had probably been dehydrated, in need of blood, and completely exhausted.

The door to the room was closed, and there was no TV and no windows. He adjusted his position in the bed and made an effort to sit up. He felt a slight twinge in his back and shoulders but not enough to slow him. His feet met the floor, and he slowly stood. All he could hope for was that his family was waiting somewhere on the other side of the door.

Abe, Tara, and David Zabad all sat in the hallway

waiting for Ethan to wake up. When word had come that he had been found in the apartment of a Brazilian family just blocks from the demolished Qualtech building they had been overjoyed. God still had plans for Ethan.

He opened his door a crack and poked his still nearly bald head out into the hallway. Out of habit he reached a hand up to his head to push the hair back out of his eyes but instead ran it over the stubble on his scalp. He saw his parents and son, standing now just to his right down the hall. They ran to him as Ethan threw the door open wide and stepped out to meet them. Ignoring the pole with the IV and the wires hanging from him, they embraced.

EPILOGUE

In the weeks that followed, Ethan watched as Cultus completely came apart. There were some who tried to keep it alive, but that adage about the head of the snake held true as one after another, Cultus members walked away from what had so long held them in bondage.

The computer that was pulled from the rubble at Qualtech headquarters was analyzed as evidence. Though it was analyzed over and over on every news network one question that was never addressed was how the building came down. Authorities reported it as structural failure resulting from an explosion. That suited Ethan just fine. He wasn't interested in being a hero. The world was beginning to learn how close they had come to financial ruin and death by biological weapons. They certainly wanted a hero, but it was just as easy to grab hold of someone to hate. Gallinger was on that list, but Dr. Kelso caught most of the public's hatred. As the designer of the virus, the computer, and its security measures, he was vilified and on trial for kidnapping, murder, and attempted mass murder, among other allegations. The island that had held Ethan captive was raided. Officials found evidence of genetic experiments carried out in the underground lab. Ethan and the rest of the team were never officially recognized for bringing down Cultus and Rolf Gallinger.

One year later...

Ethan was on his way to see Erik Remont. It had been a long time since he'd seen his friend. Remont had been instrumental in getting him where he was now. All of their talks about what makes a life worthwhile, what a man ought to live for, love for, were making sense and coming together. He walked the now familiar corridor to his office and went right in. Remont's office hadn't changed a whole lot. He was in uniform today, which was a change from the norm. Erik stood and greeted Ethan in front of the desk, and they embraced as only brothers do who have been through hell and back together. Ethan sat in one of the chairs by the desk and marveled at how as a teenager he could never have imagined having one true friend, let alone the half dozen or so he had now.

Erik leaned forward in his office chair. "So good to see you, Ethan. I've been hearing about you from other folks on base here. Big step you're taking."

Ethan smiled. "It's not really a big step. God is leading all the way."

"You look well. Living your calling suits you. You feel well?"

Ethan grinned again, remembering their many talks about calling. "I do. And this next step feels right."

Remont gave Ethan a knowing look. "This wasn't entirely their idea, was it?"

"Not entirely. I had to push for it. Which in one sense is pretty sad. But I'm going up against stated government policy and the interests of our military. But a man has to do—"

"What a man has to do," Erik finished. "Particularly a man who is called by God."

Ethan nodded. "So where do you go from here?"

Remont clasped his hands on the desk and looked down. "I think I'm leaving. I was here for a reason. I start my private practice in a few weeks. I understand this will be your center of operations."

"Yeah. I thought I would have to operate on my own somewhere else, but they said this would be the best way to keep an eye on me. Too bad you won't be around. I might need you around to keep my head screwed on right," Ethan laughed.

"I can help you from wherever I am." Erik changed the subject. "So where are you off to first?"

"Mozambique," replied Ethan. "The place is still a mess."

"What's your plan?"

"I don't have one yet. I just know that what's been happening there can't continue. That's about as far as it goes."

"Do you have any help?" Remont asked with concern in his voice.

"I'll occasionally have backup. Robbie Charles might come along from time to time. It depends what the job is. He's always a good one to have around."

"It's hard to believe we almost lost him last year."

Ethan shook his head in disbelief. "He's the only guy I know, besides me, who can take a bullet at close range like that and live to tell about it. Thank God for Kevlar. And I've got God protecting me! Well, God and Colonel Wade Murrow."

Remont laughed at the joke. "It sounds like things are good, Ethan. How about your family?"

"None of them like what I'm doing, but they know it's what God wants. Over the last year, they've realized the ability God gave me was not for me but for the weak and oppressed. That's why God gave Samson his ability, to lead the weak and oppressed Israelites out of captivity to the Philistines. I'm called to follow in my ancestor's footsteps."

Remont interrupted. "Did you ever think about that when you brought that building down last year? That you were going to die just like Samson?"

Ethan thought for a moment. "It did cross my mind briefly, but I knew it was what I had to do."

"Speaking of things you have to do. Did you know Sergeant Kaplan was serving her sentence near here?"

Ethan nodded.

"You ever thought about going to see her?"

"I don't think that's necessary, Erik."

"You know I worked with her, went through the deprogramming?"

"I know." Ethan was still having a hard time being reminded of Andrea. "Thanks. I wish her the best." Ethan turned to go.

"It might provide you with some closure." Ethan could tell his friend didn't want to push too hard. "I testified that she was not herself when she committed treason. Her case is being appealed."

"Erik, I appreciate all you've done. I just can't see her. Not yet."

Erik and Ethan parted. Ethan walked outside and decided to head back to the house on base that had been the site of the wonderful family reunion so long ago. He had gone just a few yards when suddenly he felt like God was preparing him to do battle. Strength surged through him, but he couldn't identify a threat anywhere. Then deep down he understood what was happening. God was giving him the courage to go see Andrea.

He was escorted through the steel door that opened into the visitation room of the prison's maximum security wing. He spotted her sitting at one of the carrels near the barred windows. He took a deep breath and sat down at the carrel opposite her.

"Hi Andrea." She looked exhausted and the once vibrant eyes were now not as bright.

She barely smiled as she replied, "I can't believe you came to see me."

"Me either."

"Are you still at Fort Bragg?"

"I'm there until God moves me on." Ethan wasn't even sure what to say. Time had passed, but he couldn't easily forget the shock he felt when he realized who Andrea really was. "Is there anything I can help you with?" The question hung there in the stillness of the room. Ethan waited patiently and then watched as tears dropped from her eyes to the tabletop.

"You can forgive me." She looked up at Ethan again,

tears in her eyes. "I'm so sorry. I hurt you, everyone I was working with, my own family. I'm sorry. Can you forgive me?"

Ethan wouldn't be so hurt and angry if he didn't care so much for her. He summoned the strength to say the words, "I forgive you, Andrea."

"Thank you, Ethan. Good-bye." Andrea abruptly turned and started to get up.

"Wait a minute, Andrea! Why are you leaving?"

"I did what I came to do. I'll leave you alone now." She turned again.

"Andrea. You're my friend. I know what Cultus did to you. I also know that under that deception there is a good person. I saw some of that. Don't go just yet."

She slowly returned to the carrel and sat down. Andrea looked at Ethan, smiled, and through tears mouthed the words, "Thank you."

Ethan watched as his mother carried in the birthday cake. It was decorated with little Lego men from David's collection. It was hard to believe David was turning nine today. The relationship he never thought he'd have was now a reality. He and David had grown close over the last year in spite of his frequent travels. But the one great thing about what he was doing was that when he was home, he was really home, and that meant David got his undivided attention. Ethan watched his son's face as the cake was brought out. He was so like his mother. He thought of Sarah again and knew that she was proud of what David had become, what Ethan had done. He thought of what might have been with Andrea Kaplan. He knew that whatever might come, he could never see himself as happy as he had been with Sarah.

When the party had ended and all but one guest had gone home, Ethan quietly crept into David's room and knelt at his bedside. He kissed his forehead and smoothed the dark hair on the top of his head. What he was doing now, he did not only for the oppressed and the poor, but for his son and his future. What kind of man would he become, and would Ethan be responsible for helping him get there? He stood and backed out of the room. As he turned into the hallway, he almost bumped into Robbie.

"What are you doing out here?" Ethan whispered.

"I came to say goodnight to the little guy. And good-bye," Robbie said.

"Sorry, he's out like a light."

"He's gonna be upset with me," Robbie said, worried. They had spent so much time together Robbie was now "Uncle" Robbie.

"He's nine. He's sleeping. He'll get over it."

"I'll call him from the plane tomorrow."

"*I'll* call him tomorrow. Now, let's talk about what we're doing."

"Just let me talk to him too, okay?" Robbie asked eagerly.

"Robbie? Have I ever *not* let you talk to him?"

"No."

Ethan gave his friend a look that said, "Then be quiet, and let's get to work!"

They walked back into the living room, sat down on the brown plaid couch, and pulled out a map of Mozambique and a smaller, more detailed map of the area they would be going to and spread them out on the coffee table.

"The village is here." Robbie pointed to an area where two small streams intersected. "They were attacked a week and half ago. Rebels in the area took their livestock and kidnapped all the boys. And you know what happened to the women. Same story over and over."

"Well," said Ethan as he sat back, "let's change the ending on this one."

ABOUT THE AUTHOR

Chris Vitarelli pastors a small multi-site church in Southeast Michigan. He and his wife Jody have four children. Along with his fiction writing he also hosts a conference for small churches and is sought after as a conference and seminar speaker.

STRONG
SURVIVAL ROAD

CHRIS VITARELLI

SMALL

CHURCH

BIG

DEAL

HOW TO RETHINK SIZE, SUCCESS AND SIGNIFICANCE
IN MINISTRY

CHRIS VITARELLI